All That Was Written

ALL
THAT WAS
Written

All That Was Written

The Inheritance Duology

Book 2

Irene Lee

STEEL THORN
PRESS

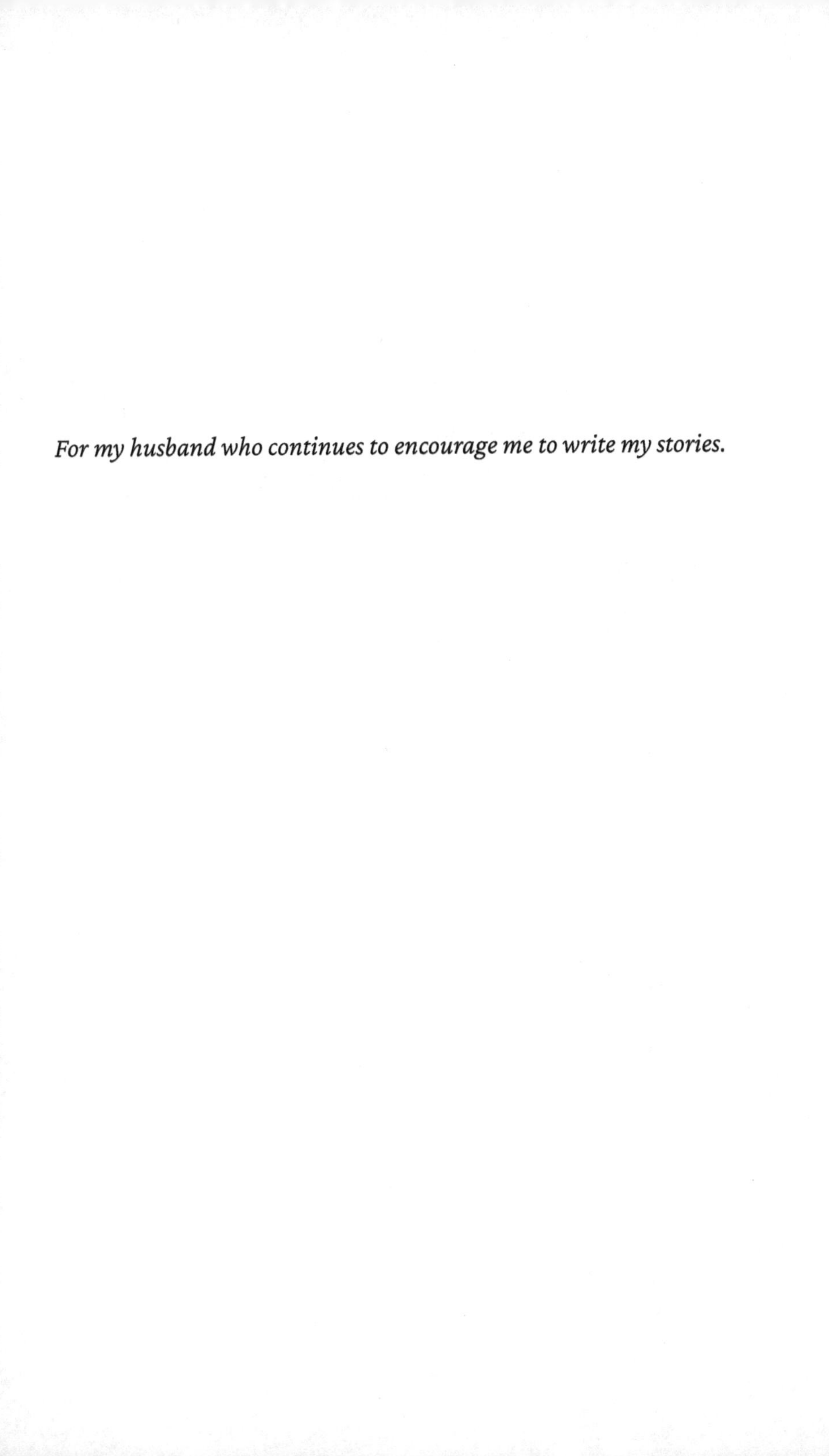

For my husband who continues to encourage me to write my stories.

Choices are the Hinges of Destiny

They're taking them all. But the Llewellyns have already hidden the Seelie Court survivors where nobody will find them. I was supposed to protect Mercy, but I can't find her. She's the only seer we have and the one who knows everything to come. And where did all the witches go?

—Alice Rhys, June 24, 1775

Alex's voice faded as he finished reading. Elias leaned over his shoulder while Abby and Emily sat across from them at the table, the old journal open between them.

"Seelie and Unseelie Courts," Abby said slowly. "Those are fae terms. From old folklore, Celtic mythology."

"Except this isn't folklore," Emily said. "This is someone's personal diary."

One Week Earlier

Alex stepped into the clearing, his eyes fixing on the shape fifty yards off the hiking trail. It lay partially covered by fallen leaves and pine needles. From the edge of the scene, the damage was clear. Deep gouges carved across the chest and abdomen, flesh torn away in ragged strips. The throat had been ripped open with enough force to nearly decapitate the victim. Blood had soaked into the ground beneath the body, turning the soil black.

He stopped near the body, broad shoulders squared, arms folding across his chest as the crime scene techs worked. The September morning was cool, the air damp with moisture that hadn't yet burned off. Birds called somewhere high in the canopy.

Elias crouched beside the body.

Green light flickered around his hands as memory magic threaded outward through the clearing, invisible to anyone without magic.

Alex stayed a few feet behind him, watching. Even from there he could see the tension in Elias' face. His green eyes were fixed on the body, focused on something only his magic could see.

Memory traces were routine for Elias, but Alex had learned over eight years as partners how easily they could overwhelm him. His thoughts drifted briefly to last December.

Elias had built a massive illusion that fooled his terrorist father, Edward Sinclair. The construct had only held because Alex's combat magic anchored him through it. Their magic worked together in ways nobody fully understood, and they'd stopped questioning it years ago.

Alex refocused on the clearing.

A local police officer stood nearby with a notebook in hand. She still looked pale since uncovering the body earlier that morning.

"Victim is a male. Identification says he's thirty-six," the lead crime scene tech called out. Her voice remained steady despite what she was documenting. "There's significant trauma to the torso."

Alex stepped closer but stopped just outside the immediate scene.

"Coyote?" the young officer asked.

"Too much damage," the tech said. "And the pattern's wrong. Coyotes mostly scavenge. This looks more like a sustained attack."

"Bear?"

"No, wrong claw pattern." She photographed the wounds from several angles. "And bears don't usually go for the throat like this."

"How do you know so much about animal behavior?" Alex asked.

The tech glanced up at him. "I grew up in Alaska. My parents hunted all the time. You learn a lot about bear attacks up there."

Elias straightened slowly and stepped away from the body.

"What are you picking up?" Alex asked in a low voice.

"Terror and pain." His gaze was still distant. "The victim was conscious when the attack started. The emotional residue is strong. He fought back, but whatever hit him was too fast."

"An animal?"

"The trace feels wrong for that." Elias glanced back toward the body, eyes narrowing slightly. "There's something else mixed in. Magic maybe. Faint, but it's there."

Alex looked down at the wounds again. The tearing. The savagery of it.

"How fast are we talking?"

"I don't know." Elias rubbed his lower lip with his index finger. "The memory fragment shows motion, but it's blurred. I don't think the victim could process what he was seeing. It almost reads like disbelief."

A second tech called from near the tree line.

"Got some tracks over here that look like paws."

The lead tech moved toward the trees. Alex and Elias followed.

"Wolf tracks," she said after crouching beside them. She photographed the prints in sequence. "Looks like only one set leading away from the body. But wolves haven't been in this area for decades."

"Could they have migrated back?" the officer asked.

"Not without someone noticing." She measured one of the prints. "These are big. Bigger than coyotes. Definitely wolf-sized."

Elias crouched near the tracks, his hand hovering over the dirt as his magic reached toward them. After a moment, he stood.

"Anything?" Alex asked.

"Same trace as the body." Elias scanned the surrounding woods. "Something magical was definitely here but whatever left these prints is long gone."

The techs continued processing the scene while he and Elias checked the surrounding woods. He noticed a second set of human footprints near the wolf tracks and studied them for a moment, wondering if they belonged to the victim or someone else.

Elias walked over to him.

"Do you want me to build a memory construct so you can see what I'm picking up? Maybe you'll catch something I missed."

Alex looked around the clearing. Several police officers stood nearby, and hikers had begun gathering along the trail behind the tape.

"No," he said. "Too many eyes on us here. They don't need to see what you can do. We can come back later."

They walked back to the access road where their car sat beside two Boston PD cruisers and the medical examiner's van.

"Second body this week," Alex said as he unlocked the car. "Same MO as the other one. Isolated location, massive trauma and no witnesses."

"Third body in two weeks if you count the one in New Hampshire," Elias said as he climbed into the passenger seat. "All within a hundred miles of Boston."

Alex slid behind the wheel, his blue eyes scanning the narrow access road before he started the engine and pulled onto the highway.

"ASAC Hayes says there are dozens of unsolved cases like this going back decades across multiple states."

"Decades of animal attacks that leave a magical signature."

"Do animals even have magic?" Alex merged onto the road. "You sense anything else at the scene?"

He glanced toward the passenger seat.

Elias was staring out the window, one elbow resting on the door.

"Just extreme fear," he said finally. "He was out here hiking and whatever killed that man terrified him. Not dread. Not even the thought of escaping. Just shock. The memory fragment was saturated with disbelief."

"And no clear image of the attacker."

"No. Just sudden motion and a blur. He knew he was going to die. That level of awareness usually means the attack lasted longer than a few seconds. I don't understand why I can't see the animal. He was attacked from the front. He must've seen it." He shook his head. "This is so weird."

Alex let out a laugh.

"Your kind of weird."

Elias leaned back in the seat and pulled out his phone.

Alex focused on the road while Elias scrolled.

Three bodies. All labeled animal attacks by local authorities. All referred to the FBI because they happened on federal land. They'd been on the case for two months and didn't have any leads.

"This should be a regular agent case," Elias said after pocketing his phone. "We're specialists," Elias said. "Not average magic users. Our skills are being wasted chasing whatever animal killed these hikers."

"Magical animal," Alex added.

"Alex, please." Elias turned toward him. "Animals don't have magic. It's just an animal. A normal everyday animal." He leaned back again. "We didn't transfer to Boston for this."

"We didn't actually choose to transfer anywhere. The Bureau moved us."

"Because ASAC Hayes wanted magic specialists for complex cases. Not wildlife management." Elias paused. "And because they wanted to get me out of Chicago and away from the media circus."

Alex changed lanes.

"We've finished our six years of mandatory service. We could leave," Elias said.

"And do what?"

"I don't know. Anything. The Department of Magical Affairs can't force us to stay in government service anymore."

"Can't they?" He glanced at Elias quickly. "I've heard stories about specialists who tried to leave. Suddenly the DMA finds reasons they're too valuable to release."

"You think they'd block us?"

"I think they know how powerful you are. Your memory magic is off the charts. And together our magic does things no one else can do. After last year they know you can create memory constructs. That makes you unique. Maybe too unique to let go."

Elias turned toward the window.

Alex already knew what he was thinking. He'd been thinking the same thing for months.

Neither of them had really chosen this life.

Alex had spent three years in the Army before transferring to the Bureau. Elias had gone straight from college to Quantico. For magic specialists, the choices were always limited.

"What would you do?" Elias asked. "If you left."

Alex had thought about that more than he liked to admit.

"The DMA tracks combat magic users early," he said. "I never really had a choice about the Army. I knew they'd move me out of combat eventually. They don't want to lose us on a standard mission when they'll need us for a real, full on war . So, I studied criminal justice because I knew I'd end up in law enforcement anyway."

"You could've been a doctor," Elias said. "With your healing magic. If you'd told them about it."

"Yeah maybe. But then I met you at Quantico," he said. "We worked well together. And my healing magic didn't show up until then anyway. Besides, I didn't want to get separated and stuck in some hospital while you went off to do fieldwork."

"You kept it secret because of me."

Alex shrugged. "No regrets. I like what we do. I just wish we'd actually chosen it."

"Yeah," Elias said. "Choices." He looked out the window again. "The FBI's all I know. I'm not even sure what else I'd be good at. A neuroscience undergrad degree isn't going to get me that far, and I have no intention of going to graduate school."

Alex glanced over at him and then back to the road ahead. "We'll figure it out," he said.

Alex parked near the federal building. They rode the elevator to the fifth floor in silence. The Major Crimes division was set up across two floors and each section had twenty cubicles. Alex heard the low sound of voices speaking across the room. Several agents were at their desks reading files and typing on computers. A few glanced their way when they entered. Conversations stopped mid-sentence as they passed three agents huddled together. One agent turned his chair slightly, putting his back to them. Another agent Alex didn't know well pretended to be very interested in his computer screen.

"Sutton. Sinclair," Assistant Special Agent in Charge Malcolm Hayes' voice shouted from his office doorway. "My office. Now."

They crossed the bullpen toward his door. More side glances. More agents who suddenly had urgent business elsewhere.

ASAC Hayes sat behind his desk adjusting a stapler a fraction of an inch to his left. His desk was the tidiest and most spotless of any ASAC he'd ever met. Hayes was in his late fifties with partially gray hair. A six-foot eight-inch, well-built man whose suits fit like a glove. Alex was certain he'd had them custom made, because there was no way suits off the rack would ever fit a man that big. He'd transferred from New York two years ago and this was his last posting before retirement. He ran the office well and kept personal relationships to a minimum.

He wasn't warm like their ASAC Corinne Lindsey had been in Chicago. He didn't ask about their personal lives or make small talk. But he was fair, and he trusted his agents to do their jobs.

After a moment of standing in his office, Hayes looked up at them.

"What's the status of the latest murder?"

"Victim is a man in his thirties," Alex said. "Significant trauma consistent with animal attack. We found a set of wolf tracks at the scene. The medical examiner is performing an autopsy, but preliminary findings suggest death occurred between six and eight hours before the body was discovered, so around 3 a.m. this morning."

"Magical involvement again?"

"Faint traces." Elias crossed his arms over his chest. "Similar to the previous two scenes. But I couldn't get anything that tells us what happened."

"So we still don't know if these are actually animal attacks or something else."

"No, sir."

Hayes leaned back in his chair. "The Director is asking questions. Three bodies in two weeks. If these are magical attacks, we need to identify the source and stop it. If they're animal attacks, we hand it off to Fish and Wildlife and move on."

"We need more information," Alex said. "Maybe the next attack might give us enough to make a determination."

"Let's hope there isn't another attack." Hayes picked up his pen and opened a file on his desk. "Keep working it. I want answers, not theories."

"We're working every lead," Alex said.

"Work them faster." Hayes looked at both of them. "You two came highly recommended from Chicago. ASAC Lindsey said you have skills that make you uniquely qualified for cases like this. So use those famous magic skills of yours and find out what's going on with these murders. If that's what they are."

"Yes, sir," they said in unison, then turned and walked out of the office.

"He's a real charmer," Elias whispered once they were in the hallway.

"He just wants results. I can't blame him. This case is making everyone look bad, and the families want answers."

As they reached the bullpen, the same agents who'd turned away earlier still avoided looking at them directly.

Alex had been dealing with this for nine months.

The whispers about Elias' father. The comments about the chaos in Chicago that he'd orchestrated. The dead FBI agents he'd left in his pursuit of a magical uprising. None of it was Elias' fault. Damn it, Elias had been the one to stop Edward and take down his entire network. His memory construct had been the only way Edward was going to be stopped. He'd risked his life that night. They both had. But it didn't matter to most of the agents here.

They looked at Elias and saw Dr. Edward Sinclair's son. A domestic terrorist with a collection of ancient and powerful artifacts that allowed him and his people to nearly mind control their way into a civil war.

They reached their adjoining cubicle space in the corner. Alex dropped into his chair and pulled up the case file on his computer. Elias sat across from him and opened his own laptop.

They spent the rest of the afternoon writing their reports and reviewing evidence from previous scenes. By five o'clock the office had mostly cleared out.

Alex closed his laptop. "Let's go home. I'm tired of looking at looking through dead end reports."

Elias stood. "Yeah, let's get out of here."

They drove back through evening traffic to Elias' house in Cambridge. It sat on a dead end street lined with old maples, a three-story Victorian house that had been in his mother's

Llewellyn family for generations. Elias had inherited it from a maternal great-aunt he'd barely known as a child.

Inside, they kicked off their shoes and dropped keys on the hall table. Alex grabbed the mail while Elias headed for the kitchen.

"Do you want to read the journals?" Alex called after him.

"Yeah. Let me grab a beer first."

They'd received the journals from his mother back in April. A large wooden chest full of leather-bound books, some so old the bindings had cracked and darkened to black. Others looked newer, their spines still intact and the leather supple. They'd been trying to read them for months, but work kept getting in the way.

Alex walked into the library, knelt beside the chest and ran his fingers along the spine of the topmost journal. He could smell the slight mustiness of old paper and aged leather, and something slightly metallic.

"When my mother told us that our families go back generations and she had the journals in a safe place, I didn't expect there to be this many or that they'd be this old."

Elias stood behind him, beer in hand, staring down at the collection. He set the bottle on the side table and knelt beside Alex. "In a million years I never would have imagined my mother's family was related to your dad." He touched one of the journals. The leather was smooth under his palm, worn by centuries of handling. "Your mother didn't want our connection to each other to influence our decisions."

Alex rolled his eyes at him. "She still won't tell us everything. She wants us to read and discover the story for ourselves."

Elias set the journal back in the chest with care. "I can't believe she kept it secret from us all these years. Colleen is a patient woman."

Alex reached for another journal, bound in dark brown leather with brass corners dulled and greened with age. "We should start with the ones that look like they've been handled the longest and work forward."

"Which one is that?" Elias leaned closer.

"This one, I think." Alex drew a bundle from near the bottom of the stack. The wood cover was worn smooth. Inside, the leaves sat uneven and loose. Each page varied slightly in thickness, some stiffer than others, their edges rounded from handling. The surface showed shallow scrape marks and faint discolorations where it had been worked thin. A coarse thread ran through the fold, but its fibers were intact.

Alex opened the journal carefully. "I can't read this, it's not English."

"Maybe Abby can translate these. She's a linguist and understands old Welsh. Which I assume some of these are, given our family history." Elias touched the corner of the journal.

The moment both their hands touched the wooden cover, the air around them shifted. A faint whistle rose, barely audible, as if it came from the journal itself. Then a strong wave of energy rippled through them and outward toward the house.

Elias met his eyes. "Did you feel that?"

"Yeah." Alex tightened his grip on the journal as he tried to read it.

The pages were covered in a script he almost recognized but couldn't read. The ink had thinned and faded, breaking in places, but some strokes were still legible. He stared at the first page.

Then the text moved.

The letters shimmered and reshaped themselves before their eyes. Each word shifted and settled until the ancient language transformed into English.

"What the hell?" Alex breathed.

Elias leaned into the book, watching the transformation complete itself. "I think it's responding to us."

The text now read clearly in English:

Set down by Rhiannon Llewellyn in The Year of the Forgotten Season.

I have never lived without the echoes, yet they are not memories, not in truth. They are a knowing once held by another mind.

A loud thump upstairs startled Alex and he jerked his hand away from the journal.

"Damn it, this house is going to give me a heart attack."

The moment he broke contact, the text shimmered again and reverted to the odd script.

Alex stared at the page. "It's gone. What the hell is this, Elias?"

"I have no idea. I can sense that it's very old but it's obviously warded. Here, touch it again."

Alex held the other end of the journal and again the writing shimmered and changed to English. The whistling sound was louder this time and again they felt the tremble in the air. More of the entry became visible to them.

This gift is a curse. I do not wish to know the memories of the dead. Or the living. What purpose the Dawn of the Otherworld had for entrusting us with this power I know not. The priests tell me not to write my words for others to see but I am compelled to warn those that come after me. This gift is a curse.

Elias let go of the journal. "They're talking about memory magic." He looked at Alex. "It's my ancestor, and she's writing about memory magic in your family's journal."

Alex took a deep sigh as he held the journal with both hands staring at the unreadable letters. "Why are they saying it's a curse?"

When Elias didn't answer, Alex looked up at him and found him staring back.

"Because it is a curse. You don't know what it's like to see the memories of someone on the verge of death, or to feel the thoughts of a murderer just before they set off a bomb that kills people. Reliving the most intense memories of people isn't a gift. It's a burden. And yes, maybe it is a curse."

Alex set the journal down and turned to Elias. "You've never described it like that before. I assumed you saw it as a divine gift."

"Even a gift can carry a cost. I don't reject it, or the good that it does in solving or preventing crimes, but it's one I sometimes wish I didn't have."

Alex didn't know what to say. He loved his own combat magic, and his healing magic was definitely a gift. One that he felt guilty for not using. Elias had looked away from him.

"I know that your memory magic is hard on you. I wish I could make it easier."

Elias turned his head, and his bright green eyes sparkled with magic as he met his eyes as he said, "You do make it easier. What do you think you do every time you help ground me?

Without your help, my magic is sometimes a runaway train. You're like the emergency brake."

After a beat, they both started to laugh. "That's the dumbest thing I've probably ever said."

Alex was still laughing when he replied, "I'm finally rubbing off on you."

"Okay, look. I'm hungry and it's getting late. Let's make dinner and eat. These can wait."

They stood and walked toward the kitchen.

"Abby's translation magic might help her date the manuscripts. She deals with old books every day as the curator at the Athenaeum. I wonder if she'd mind taking a look at the journals," Elias said.

Dr. Abigail Morgan was Elias' girlfriend. They'd met during their first case after arriving in Boston. The Athenaeum had a theft of old invaluable documents from the American Revolution, and they'd been tasked with investigating it. Abby and Elias had made a connection from the moment they shook hands. Elias asked her out almost immediately. Alex was happy for him. Especially since she'd introduced him to her best friend Emily Cabrera, who was now his girlfriend. Emily joked that fate had brought them all together.

"Abby won't mind helping us. I'm pretty sure she'd do anything you ask just to get you to smile and stop brooding." Alex glanced at him. "And it's your turn to cook."

"I know." Elias looked at the kitchen with an expression Alex recognized all too well. Elias hated cooking.

Alex pulled out his phone. "I'm texting Abby and Emily now."

He typed out a quick message in the group chat.

Alex: Hey, can Abby help us translate the journals? we finally got around to looking at them and of course the first one we grabbed we can't read. prob in old welsh.

Abby: Of course! I can't wait to get my hands on Elias!

Alex: what?

Abby: I meant on the journals. Stupid autocorrect.

Emily: That wasn't autocorrect hun 😄

Abby: Stop texting me Em, I'm in the same room with you

Alex: right. so dinner tomorrow? our place?

Emily: Is Elias cooking 😉

Alex: maybe. he's supposed to cook tonight but judging by the look on his face right now I think we're ordering pizza

Emily: The last time he tried to cook for us he set off the smoke detector 🔥

Abby: He got distracted.

Emily: The pasta was on fire. How does that even happen? Okay. We'll come for dinner but we're bringing the food

Alex: sounds great. thanks. love you Em.

Emily: Love you more and I'll prove it tomorrow night 💋

Alex: yeah? promise?

Abby: guys. group text here remember.

He put his phone on the counter. "She says absolutely," he said. "And they're bringing the food because Emily doesn't trust your cooking."

Elias laughed. "My cooking isn't that bad. Besides, Abby quickly stopped the fire with her elemental magic."

Alex picked up his phone again. "Right. We're ordering pizza tonight."

2
The Call

The dried coffee stain on the granite countertop refused to budge. She scrubbed harder and the smell of ammonia burned her nose, but she kept working until the brown ring finally disappeared. Mrs. Patterson would check her work later and find something to complain about. She always did.

The house was too big for one person. Four bedrooms, three bathrooms, a dining room that could sit a family of ten. Mrs. Patterson lived here alone with her two cats and her collection of porcelain figurines that had to be dusted every Tuesday.

She wrung out the sponge and moved to the stovetop. Grease had built up around the burners. She scraped at it with her fingernail, feeling the grime collect under the nail.

This was what her life had become. Scrubbing other people's messes. Invisible labor for people who barely looked at her when they handed over cash at the end of the week. No records. Just cash in hand and the understanding that she wouldn't complain about anything.

Being an unregistered magic user meant no legal work. No

official job and no paper trail. She cleaned houses, babysat when someone was desperate enough not to ask questions, and sometimes helped at a flower shop in the North End where the owner paid under the table.

She finished the stovetop and rinsed the sponge in the sink. The kitchen window looked out onto a manicured lawn. September sun filtered through the trees. People outside went about their ordinary lives, unaware that the woman scrubbing their countertops had once belonged to a world far older than theirs.

She dried her hands on a towel and checked her phone. Three o'clock. She had two more hours here and then another house across town at six. The Rodriguez family paid better but their three kids left toys everywhere and the baby had started throwing food.

She walked to the hallway bathroom to refill her cleaning supplies.

The mirror above the sink reflected her face back at her. Red hair braided over one shoulder. Green eyes stared back at her from the mirror, far older than the face they belonged to.

She looked tired. The kind of tired sleep didn't fix. The kind that came from waiting too long for the world to change.

Her mother used to tell her she was beautiful. That her hair was the color of autumn leaves, her eyes like the forests of the old world. Her mother had told her a lot of things. Stories about courts and magic, about their people scattered and in hiding.

Stories that were true. Her magic had proven it. So had the fact that she didn't age like humans.

She turned away from the mirror and grabbed the bottle of glass cleaner from under the sink. The Pattersons had too many mirrors. Every room had at least one. She started with the one in the hallway, spraying it down and wiping in circular motions.

The hairs on the back of her neck stood.

A pulse rippled through the air. Not sound exactly, but something that moved through her chest and settled behind her ribs. She stopped mid-wipe and looked around. The house was silent. No one else was home.

The pulse came again. Stronger this time. Like a whistle cutting through distance, calling to something old inside her.

She set down the cleaning supplies and pressed her hand to her chest. Her heart beat faster. The pulse thrummed again and her magic responded, flickering purple around her hands.

She knew this feeling. Her grandmother had described it once. The Call. The pull of old magic waking after a long sleep. Magic that predated registration and government oversight. Magic from when their people walked openly and their Courts held power.

The Defenders' Call.

Her mother's voice echoed in her memory. "When you feel the Defenders' Call, child, you must find the source. No matter what. It means the Defenders' bloodline has been reunited."

She stood in the Pattersons' hallway with glass cleaner dripping onto the hardwood floor and felt the pull settle into her bones. It came from the north. Somewhere across the Charles River, maybe Cambridge.

She should ignore it. She'd spent years keeping her head down, staying invisible, surviving on the margins. Following this would mean exposure and questions she couldn't answer.

But the pulse thrummed again and her magic rose to meet it, sparking again around her before she could suppress it.

Her people had been waiting for two hundred and fifty years. Hiding and surviving. Passing down stories and warnings through generations. Now something had woken. Something powerful enough to send out the Call.

She cleaned up the spilled glass cleaner and finished the mirrors mechanically. Her mind was already elsewhere. She needed to finish here, get through the evening job at the Rodriguez house, and then tomorrow she would follow the pull and find the source.

Whatever had called out to her, it was old magic. The kind that didn't exist anymore. The kind that had been buried with the courts.

She finished cleaning at five o'clock. Mrs. Patterson came home and walked through the house with her usual critical eye.

"Aisling, you missed a spot. Do it again."

She redid it while Mrs. Patterson watched. Then the woman counted out the cash. Sixty dollars for five hours of work. She took the money and left without speaking.

The evening job went faster. The Rodriguez kids were at soccer practice, and the baby was with his grandmother. She cleaned in silence while Mr. Rodriguez worked in his home office. He left her cash on the kitchen counter and barely looked up when she called goodbye.

By nine o'clock she was back in her own apartment. A studio in Somerville with water stains on the ceiling and a radiator that clanged all winter. She dropped her bag on the floor and sat on the edge of her bed.

The Call had dissipated as quickly as it came, but her magic had locked in.

I'll go tomorrow, she thought. After her morning cleaning job she'd follow the pull and see what had woken after all these centuries.

Her mother's stories might not have been stories after all. If the Defenders were real, and their magic still existed somewhere, then maybe everything else was real too.

The courts. The old ways. The possibility that her people didn't have to hide forever.

Aisling lay back on her bed, exhausted, and stared at the water-stained ceiling. Tomorrow she would find the source of the Call. Tomorrow, everything might change.

3

A Legacy of Love

Elias opened the front door and found both women standing on the porch. Abigail held a large covered dish, auburn curls loose around her shoulders, blue eyes bright in the porch light. Emily stood beside her, dark hair falling over one shoulder, hazel eyes full of amusement.

"We brought actual food," Abby said as she stepped inside. "Because Alex said you were going to order pizza again."

"I wasn't going to order pizza," Elias protested.

Emily raised an eyebrow. "What were you going to make?"

He cleared his voice. "Pizza."

Both women laughed. Alex appeared from the kitchen and took the dish from Abby.

"Chicken marsala, it just needs to be reheated." Abby handed him the dish and turned to kiss Elias. Her lips were cold from the September evening but warmed quickly against his. When she pulled back, her blue eyes were bright. "Hi."

"Hi." He helped her out of her coat.

Alex kissed Emily, tucked her auburn hair behind one ear, and took the bottle of wine she was holding.

They moved to the kitchen where Alex was already heating the oven. Emily poured wine and handed glasses around. "To real food."

They clinked glasses.

When the food was ready, they carried everything to the dining room. Abby's chicken marsala was perfect. Tender meat, rich sauce, mushrooms that melted on the tongue. Elias made a mental note to ask her to teach him how to cook something other than pasta.

"This is amazing," Alex said around a mouthful. "You should cook for us more often. I'm starving here with Elias cooking half the time."

"I will if you keep letting me use your kitchen." Abby smiled at Elias. "Your stove is better than mine."

"My stove is yours," Elias said.

Emily laughed. "Smooth."

The conversation flowed easily between the four of them. Emily told a story about a patient who'd tried to convince her that he'd seen an angel walking through Franklin Park. He was thoroughly convinced and now wanted to quit his job and join a religious order. "Belief can change someone's entire life overnight," she said with a small shrug.

Abby had cataloged a collection of Revolutionary War documents that had been donated to the Athenaeum. Elias avoided talking about the case. Animal attacks weren't dinner conversation. Alex mentioned that his mother kept asking to meet Abigail and Emily.

"Elias," Emily said, "you mentioned a while back that you inherited this place."

"Yeah. From my aunt on my mother's side." He didn't say that he'd barely known his aunt, that the inheritance had been a surprise. Another piece of family history he didn't understand. "Apparently it's been in the family for generations."

"A Cambridge property isn't something a person leaves to someone they barely know." Emily raised her eyebrows.

"I know." Elias shifted in his seat. The house itself was just another piece of real estate, no different from his Chicago apartment in practical terms. But it was a part of his mother's family and felt more meaningful than the small fortune he'd received after her death when he was ten years old. He barely had any memories of her anymore.

Alex looked at him and something passed between them. Alex knew what the house meant to him. He knew everything about him.

"It's a good house, Elias," Alex said simply. "It doesn't matter who owned it before you, just that it's yours now."

"And big enough for both of you," Emily added. "Which is convenient since Alex is apparently incapable of finding an apartment."

Alex laughed. "I'm looking."

"You've looked at sixteen places," Emily said laughing. "None of them are right."

"Because I'm already where I need to be." Alex looked at Elias. "This works for now. Why change it?"

Elias felt something settle in his chest. "Yeah. It does work."

Abby reached over and squeezed his hand.

Elias broke the silence by saying, "This house actually gives me the creeps. It makes weird noises. I think it's haunted."

Everyone stared at him. Emily's hazel eyes went wide and Abby started to look around the room as she asked, "Have you tried to read it and see what the memory trace tells you?"

Elias turned his head quickly toward her and replied, "I just said I think it's haunted. So no, I haven't used my magic to uncover whatever horrific murder happened here."

Alex started to choke on the wine he'd just swallowed. "Murder? Someone was murdered in this house?"

"I don't know. I mean, why else would a house be haunted?"

Emily and Abby looked at each other and started to laugh. The laughter turned into giggles.

Alex finally stopped coughing and started laughing. "Elias, you need to chill, brother. You're taking this whole "Boston is haunted" thing too literally."

Elias leaned toward Alex. "Alexander, you didn't go on the ghost tour me and Abby went on. You have no idea all the deaths this city has seen."

Everyone except Elias broke out into laughter again, until he finally gave in and started laughing too.

Elias felt happy. This was what he'd never had growing up. People who wanted to be with him. People who laughed at him out of love.

After dinner they cleared the table together. Alex loaded the dishwasher while Abby put away leftovers. Elias liked the way it felt natural and comfortable. Like they'd been doing this for years instead of only eight months.

When the kitchen was clean, Emily picked up her wine glass. "So, can we finally see the mysterious journals?"

"Come on," Alex said.

They moved to the library down the hall. The large wooden chest sat on the floor near the couch where Elias and Alex had left it. Abby set down her wine glass and knelt beside it. Her fingers traced the edge of the wood and her magic flickered faintly. Earth-toned and steady.

"May I?" she asked.

"Of course." Elias sat on the floor next to her. Alex and Emily settled on the couch behind them.

Abby lifted the lid. The scent of old paper and aged leather filled the room. She reached in and pulled out the top journal, supporting the spine as she opened it. Her expression shifted as she examined the pages.

"This is old. Really old." She turned a page with delicate fingers. "The preservation spells are incredible. I've seen similar work on manuscripts from the medieval period, but this is more sophisticated."

"Can you read it?" Emily asked from the couch.

"Not without the activation magic. This isn't old Welsh, I'm certain of it. I can't read this script." Abby looked at both of them. "You two need to trigger it. Let me see how it works."

Elias glanced at Alex, who moved from the couch to kneel on the other side of the chest. They both placed their hands on the journal's cover. For a moment nothing happened. Then Elias felt the faint whistle of magic responding. The air around them shifted slightly.

The text on the page shimmered and transformed, the strange language changing to English before their eyes.

Abby leaned closer. "That's remarkable. The spell recognizes your bloodlines and translates specifically for you."

Emily pulled her legs up on the couch and leaned in behind Abby, propping herself up on her elbows to look over her shoulder. "What does it say?"

Alex read aloud.

Set down by Mael Rhys in the Year of The Great Plague.

When the Llewellyn fall too deep into memory's well, when the past pulls them beneath the surface and they cannot rise, the Rhys answer. Our silver magic rises unbidden. Combat magic shaped for war but used for rescue. We are the shield that stands between them and the drowning. We are the anchor that holds when memory would sweep them away.

I have stood guard while my cousin walked through the memories of the dying. I have shielded him when the weight of what he saw threatened to break him. My magic reached for his without thought or command. Silver wrapping around green, pulling him back to the living world.

This is our duty. This is our gift. The Llewellyn bear the burden of memory. The Rhys bear the burden of protection. We catch them when they fall.

The bond is as old as the Romans. Older than the roads they built across our lands. It was formed in combat and magic and choice. A Rhys warrior chose to stand beside a Llewellyn seer when others turned away. That choice became legacy. That legacy became us.

I do not know what the future holds. But as long as there are Llewellyn who carry memory's weight, there will be Rhys who stand ready to bear them up. We are bound together. We are stronger together. And we will endure.

Alex's voice faded. No one spoke for a long moment. Elias' mother was a Llewellyn. Alex's mother was a Rhys descendant. It made sense. His memory magic flared green where it touched the book, and Alex's silver magic answered across the pages, a thin thread of silver light reaching toward the green.

They made eye contact, and he could see the recognition in Alex's blue eyes.

The way Alex had always been able to ground him when memory traces pulled too hard. The way their magic reached for each other without conscious thought. It wasn't just training or friendship.

It was a bloodline inheritance.

"Your families protected each other," Emily said quietly. "For hundreds of years. That kind of bond doesn't survive that long unless people choose it again and again."

Elias looked at Alex. "The emergency brake."

Alex laughed. "Yeah. The emergency brake."

"Try another one," Abby said. "See what it says."

Alex pulled a different journal from deeper in the chest. Older, more fragile. The writing was almost invisible to the naked eye. They both touched it and the transformation happened again.

This entry was from a Llewellyn woman, written nearly two thousand years ago. She described the first time a Rhys warrior chose to stand beside her family. To protect them from the Roman legions when others turned away. The simplicity of her speech was remarkably potent.

Bran stood with us when we had nothing to offer but danger. He chose us. And I chose him.

"They weren't born into the bond." Abby moved her hand toward the journal and then stopped before touching it. "They were bound together by choice during war. The way your magic works together now, that's nothing new. It's ancient."

"It was more than an alliance of protection. She fell in love with him. People don't risk everything for someone unless there's something deeper driving it," Emily said.

Elias read the next passage that spoke of children. "Then

they married into each other's families and had children who carried both gifts."

Abby smiled. "My God, these are love stories that span generations."

"You're a hopeless romantic," Emily replied.

"I read it as a tactical alliance between families during a time of occupation," Alex said casually.

Elias chuckled when Abby looked at Alex with furrowed brows and a look that said she was judging him.

"Okay, yeah. I mean, I see the love story too. Of course I do," Alex said, trying to recover. He looked at Elias. "Elias, a little help here, please."

Elias shook his head. Alex had a way of saying what he was thinking.

"The two facts are not mutually exclusive," he said looking between Alex and Abby. "It was obviously an allegiance based on mutual defense. But it makes sense that there would be some marriages between them. That's how allegiances were maintained back then," he said confidently.

Abby just stared at Elias.

"But yeah, it's a love story. Of course it's a love story," Elias quickly added.

They worked through more of the journal. Each time the text transformed, Elias felt the pull of recognition on the edges of his mind. Battles their ancestors had fought and lives they'd saved. The Rhys and Llewellyn names appeared together across centuries, always protecting each other.

Roman Britain. Tribal conflicts. Magic that answered to instinct rather than training. He traced the words with his finger and felt the weight of what he and Alex had inherited.

"This explains a lot," Alex said. He sat back against the couch. "Why we've always worked together so seamlessly. Why our magic seems to blend together."

"Your mother knew," Elias said. And then he remembered another conversation nine months ago in Chicago. "DMA Deputy Director Catrin Rowan knew too. Remember, she's the one who told us to go talk to your mother. She knows about this."

Alex nodded in agreement. "That's why she protected us. Protected you after your elemental magic was discovered as being unregistered. She said she was friends with your mother. How do she and the Rowan family fit into this?"

"I have no idea." Elias had more questions, and for a moment thought maybe they should call Rowan. But one didn't just pick up the phone and call the deputy director of the Department of Magical Affairs. They weren't the most accessible of government agencies even though their headquarters stood large and prominent in D.C. "Maybe we could email Rowan and ask for an appointment?"

Alex just stared at him with wide eyes. "No. We are not going to call the DMA. We don't know what we're dealing with here. If we ever want to leave the FBI, calling the DMA and telling them that we have a trove of magical books that detail our centuries long connection to a powerful ancient bloodline isn't the way to get out."

Elias put his hands up in surrender. "Okay, no. Of course, you're right."

Abby examined the binding on one journal. "These need to be preserved properly. Climate-controlled storage, careful handling. They're priceless. You shouldn't rely on the magic alone."

"We'll be gentle," Elias promised. "But we need to read them first. Understand what we inherited."

They glanced through several more journals and found that the rest were in English. The chronology jumped around. Some entries were brief, others ran for pages. All of them painted a picture of two families so entwined they functioned as one. The newest journal started in the 1700s and was the most well preserved. It was a larger leather-bound book dyed red with a strange symbol on the cover that was too faded to make out.

Abby finally sat back, rubbing her hands together as her magic sparkled around her hands the way it always did when she got excited about something.

"I can help you organize these. We need to date them, identify the writers, figure out a chronological order. But it's going to take time. Oh, we need to try to create a genealogy chart. This is going to be fun." She was buzzing with excitement, and it electrified the air around them. Elias felt the touch of her magic as the skin on his arms tingled. It excited him. He wanted to grab her and take her to his bedroom.

"We have time," Alex said, laughing.

Elias wondered if Alex had read his mind or if he was replying to Abby.

Emily checked her watch and groaned. "It's past eleven. We have work tomorrow."

"Stay," Elias said. "It's late. You've both been drinking."

Abby looked at him, and something warm passed between them. "You sure? We don't normally stay during the week."

"Of course I'm sure. And I speak for Alex on this as well," he said, smiling and throwing Alex a knowing wink.

Emily looked at Alex, who nodded while adjusting his jeans. Alex wasn't reading his mind. He had his own thoughts on the matter.

"Okay," Emily said with a smile. "But I'm stealing one of Alex's shirts to sleep in."

"Help yourself." Alex grinned. "You two go on up. Me and Elias will put the journals away and lock up."

Abby and Emily nodded in agreement and made their way to the stairs, talking to each other about what time they needed to set the alarm for in the morning.

As they put the journals away, Alex asked, "What do you think?"

"About the journals?"

"About all of it. The journals, Abby and Emily." Alex gestured toward the stairs as he shut the light off in the library.

Elias sat on the couch. "I think they're going to change everything. I think they already have."

Alex walked back and sat beside him. The full moon had been the night before, but its light still shone bright enough through the window that they weren't sitting in total darkness.

Elias looked at his best friend. "I never thought I'd have this, you know. This house. Abby. You." He probably shouldn't have had that fourth glass of wine. Too much always made him say what was on his mind.

"I know."

"I don't want to lose it."

"You won't." Alex's voice was firm. "We've been working together since Quantico. Our magic has been reaching for each other the whole time. Now we know why. And knowing doesn't change anything except making it make sense. We'll figure it out together, like we always have."

Elias heard the truth in his words.

"Emily's the one," Alex said suddenly. "I know it's only been eight months, but I know."

Elias looked at him. "Yeah?"

"Yeah." Alex smiled. "Is Abby?"

Elias waited a beat and then answered, "Yeah."

"I want to ask Emily to move in with me," Alex said so quietly Elias had barely heard him.

"Then do it," he replied.

"Are you okay with that? With her living here with us?"

Elias thought about it. The house was huge and he loved the idea of not having to live in it alone. And he never wanted Alex to feel like it wasn't his home too. "Of course I'm sure. Alex, for as long as you want, this is your home. If you want Emily here with you, then ask her. You guys could have the whole second floor to yourselves. Well, you and the ghost that favors that floor," he said with a smirk.

He saw Alex inhale deeply. "Thanks."

"No thanks needed. We're family." Even as he said it, he felt the truth of it in his heart. Alex was the only family he had. He was the family he'd chosen, and who had chosen him back. There was nothing Alex could ask of him that he wouldn't give.

They sat in silence for a while, the house quiet around them. Outside, he could hear cars passing, and the distant sound of a police siren.

"We should get some rest," Alex said finally. "Early start tomorrow."

Elias nodded but didn't move. He was thinking about the strange animal attacks, the enchanted journals in the chest in front of them, and what life would be like if he left the FBI.

"Something's different here," he said. "In Boston. I can feel it."

"Different how? And don't say ghosts."

"I don't know yet." Elias stood. "But I'll let you know when I do."

Alex stood with him and headed toward the stairs. "You do that."

Elias paused before reaching the bottom of the staircase. As he turned to look toward the dining room, he saw a candle on the table flare to life.

"This house is definitely haunted," he whispered to himself, and made a mental note to look into the history of the house.

Alex had disappeared into his room on the second floor as Elias continued to the third floor where his bedroom was. He could hear Abby moving around in the bathroom as he took his clothes off and got under the sheet. When Abby came back out, she was naked and her hair was loose around her shoulders. She slowly walked to the bed and he reached out for her hand. She climbed in beside him and he pulled her close. She fit against him perfectly.

"I love this," she said quietly. Her head rested on his chest and her hand spread over his heart. "Being here with you. Reading the journals. All of it."

"Me too." He kissed the top of her head. "I'm glad you stayed."

"I'm always glad to stay." She tilted her head up to look at him. "Eight months and I still can't believe I get to do this."

"Do what?"

"Be with you. Sleep next to you. Wake up with you." She smiled. "You're kind of amazing, you know that?"

He kissed her. Slow and deep. Her hand slid up his chest to his neck, fingers threading into his hair. He rolled them so she was beneath him and she made a soft sound against his mouth.

"Elias," she whispered.

"I love you," he said.

"I love you too," she replied as he kissed down her neck. Her hands gripped his shoulders as she pulled him closer, and he reached down to cup her breast, his mouth closing over her nipple. She gasped and shifted beneath him, spreading her legs to pull him closer.

They took their time.

He'd memorized her body over the past eight months but was still discovering new ways to please her. The sounds she made as he sucked and bit gently on her breast made him harder. The way she pulled him closer like she couldn't get enough.

"Suck harder, mark me," she gasped. "I want to look in the mirror tomorrow and have a reminder of you."

Elias was happy to follow her orders. He sucked and bit until he saw a purple mark form near her nipple. She'd be remembering him for more than a day and that made him smile.

When he finally slid inside her, she wrapped her legs around his hips and pressed him tighter against her. She was a demanding lover, and he loved it when she took charge. He moved slowly, watching her face as she closed her eyes and her lips parted. She shifted her head to the side and her blond hair spread across his pillow, pulling a groan from him at the sight of her finding pleasure.

"God, you're beautiful," he said as she grabbed the back of his head and pulled him down for a kiss. Her tongue in his mouth was deep and demanding. They found their rhythm when her hips rose to meet his, and he raised her slightly, grabbing her ass and changing the angle. He knew she liked it deep and slow. He rotated his hips in tight circles, pulling back and pressing in again just enough to find the place she liked most.

"Oh yeah, right there, don't stop," she breathed, and squeezed him tighter.

Elias groaned. Her words nearly pushed him over the edge, but he forced himself to wait. He wanted to make this last for Abby.

A few minutes later Abby cried out and tightened around him. He buried his face in her neck and shouted as he thrust repeatedly and emptied into her. Her heavy breathing tickled his ear as they both caught their breath.

They lay tangled together afterward. Her head on his chest, his arms around her. "God, that felt good. I don't ever want to leave this bed," she said.

"Then don't."

She laughed softly. "We have work tomorrow."

"Call in sick."

"Tempting." She kissed his chest. "But I have a meeting with a donor at ten."

"Fine." He tightened his arms around her.

"But you're staying tomorrow night too."

"Obviously." She settled against him.

"You could keep clothes here."

She looked at him. "Are you asking me to move in?"

He hadn't been. Not consciously. But now that she'd said it, the idea settled in his mind and felt right.

"Would you want to?"

"Ask me properly and find out."

He pulled her back down and kissed her. "Move in with me."

"Let me think about it."

"How long do you need to think?"

She pretended to consider. "Another eight months should do it."

He tickled her side and she shrieked, laughing. They wrestled on the bed until she was beneath him again, both of them breathless and grinning. "Move in with me," he said again.

"Ask me again after you learn to cook something other than pasta."

"I'll take cooking lessons."

"Then maybe." She kissed him. "Probably. Ask me again later this week when I'm not half asleep."

"Deal."

He slowly rolled off her and she rested her head on his shoulder.

Abby's breathing evened out. Her body relaxed completely against his. He kissed her hair and closed his eyes. Coming home to her every night. Holding her. Waking up with her. This was what he'd been missing his whole life. And he knew he wanted this with her forever.

4

The Language of Sisters

Emily woke wrapped around Alex in his bed, sunlight streaming through the windows. His arm was heavy across her waist, and his breathing was slow and even against her neck.

She didn't want to move. Didn't want to face the day, or her ten o'clock patient, or the paperwork waiting at her office. She wanted to stay there in bed with her man and pretend the rest of the world didn't exist.

Alex stirred behind her. His hand slid up her ribs, and she felt him smile against her shoulder.

"Morning," he mumbled.

"Morning." She turned in his arms to face him. His hair was a mess, and his eyes were still half-closed. "We should get up."

"Or we could stay here."

"Tempting." She kissed him. "I have patients today and you have a crime scene to visit."

He groaned and buried his face in her neck. "Don't remind me."

They lay there for a few more minutes. Finally, Emily sat up and looked around for the shirt she'd borrowed. It was on the floor beside the bed. She pulled it on and stood.

"I'm going to steal your shower," she said.

"Steal whatever you want."

She showered quickly, letting the hot water wake her up. When she came back to the bedroom, Alex was still in bed watching her with an expression that made her want to climb back in with him.

"Stop looking at me like that," she said.

"Like what?"

"Like you're thinking about keeping me here all day."

"I am thinking about keeping you here all day."

She laughed and pulled on her jeans. "We'll both be back tonight. You can think about me then."

"I'm always thinking about you."

She walked over and kissed him. "Good."

"Are you and Abby still thinking about moving out of your apartment?"

"Yeah, the neighborhood has gotten worse. Boston PD made an arrest down the street yesterday."

"Move in here, with me."

Emily wasn't expecting that, and for a moment she didn't know what to say. "Alex, this isn't your house. Don't you think you should talk to Elias first before you make an offer like that?"

"He's fine with it. He adores you. He grew up without siblings and in foster care with family friends after his parents were killed. He loves to have friends around him. I can't tell you how many times I stayed over at his apartment back in Chicago."

Emily didn't think he'd actually asked Elias. "Why don't you ask Elias, if he's okay with it, I'll think about it. I want to talk with Abby first. It's not right to leave her looking for an apartment alone after we agreed to share a place. Even on our salaries, it's expensive for one person to rent an apartment in this city."

"I talked to him about it last night and he said we could have this entire floor. Even gave us his ghost."

"You did? Oh, well if he's comfortable with it."

"That sounds like a yes." Alex was smiling.

"It's a strong maybe," she said, smiling back as she left the room.

By the time she made it downstairs, Abby was already in the kitchen. She wore one of Elias' shirts and her hair was still damp from the shower. She stood at the counter looking around the room.

"So," Abby said. Her eyes were bright with mischief. "How was your night?"

Emily felt heat rise to her cheeks. "Good. Really good."

"Just good?"

"Amazing. Incredible. The man is very talented with his hands." Emily grinned. "What about you? How was Elias?"

Abby's smile went soft. "Perfect. He's always perfect."

"Even after eight months?"

"Especially after eight months." Abby set down her coffee mug. "I know this sounds ridiculous, but every time with him feels like the first time. Like I'm discovering him all over again."

Emily understood. She felt the same way about Alex. "It's not ridiculous. It's what happens when you're in love with someone."

"I am in love with him." Abby looked toward the stairs. "He asked me to move in last night."

"Are you serious? Alex asked me this morning."

They looked at each other and started laughing.

"Both of them," Emily said. "At the same time."

"What did you say?"

"I said I'd think about it. What about you?"

"I told him to ask me again later this week." Abby picked up her coffee. "But I'm going to say yes. I want to wake up with him every morning."

"Same." Emily thought about it. About living here with Alex and Elias and Abby. "It would be fun. The four of us here together."

"You don't think it would be weird? Living with your boyfriend and his partner?"

"No weirder than the fact that we're dating men who are basically brothers." Emily smiled. "Besides, we're basically sisters. We've been living together on and off since our college sorority days."

"True." Abby smiled. "Can I say something without you judging me?"

"Always."

"I think it's kind of sexy. The way they are with each other. How close they are."

Emily laughed. "Oh, thank God. I thought I was the only one who felt that way."

"You think it's hot too?"

"Absolutely. The way they trust each other completely. The way their magic is so connected. Alex would do anything to protect Elias." Emily took a sip of coffee. "It's incredibly attractive."

"Right?" Abby leaned closer. "And the way Elias looks at Alex sometimes. Like he hung the moon. It makes me want to kiss him."

"I know exactly what you mean." Emily set down her mug. "Alex treats Elias like he's the most important person in the world. It's sweet and protective and somehow also really hot."

Abby whispered, "You know their magical bond is very intimate. Elias has told me how Alex has entered his mind a few times to pull him out when his memory trace pulled him too deeply."

"Do you think they've ever... you know." Emily wiggled her brows. "Been together?"

They dissolved into giggles. Abby covered her mouth to muffle the sound.

"You're terrible, Em. No, they don't think of each other like that. Stop it," Abby said.

"I am terrible." Emily grinned. "And I'm glad we can talk about this. I was worried you'd think it was weird."

"Not weird at all. I'm pretty sure it's part of why I fell for Elias in the first place." Abby picked up her coffee again. "The way he talks about Alex. The way he trusts him. I knew anyone who had that kind of loyalty in them was someone special."

Emily understood. She'd fallen for Alex partly because of how he was with Elias. The protectiveness and unwavering support. The fact that he'd moved into this house just to make sure his partner was okay after everything that happened in Chicago. She knew his story that he couldn't find the right apartment was just an excuse to keep an eye on his friend. Alex was going to make a great dad someday.

"I'll tell you a secret," Abby said. "Elias comes across as reserved in public. But in bed he's completely different."

Emily felt her face heat. "Let me guess. All that control just disappears?"

"Exactly." Abby's smile was wicked. "Elias gets this intensity. Like I'm the only thing in the world that matters. And the things he does with his mouth."

"Stop." Emily was laughing. "I don't need details about my basically-brother-in-law's bedroom skills."

"You started it by asking about my night."

"Fair point." Emily took another sip of coffee. "But seriously, I'm happy for you. You two are perfect together."

"You and Alex too." Abby looked around the kitchen. "This house is perfect for all of us."

"You think the bedrooms are far enough apart?" Emily raised an eyebrow. "Because if these walls are thin, things could get awkward."

Abby laughed. "Our bedrooms are on separate floors. I think we're safe."

"Thank God. Because Alex can be loud."

"Emily!"

"What? You brought it up."

They were still giggling when footsteps sounded on the stairs. Elias appeared first, looking rumpled and sleepy. He went straight to Abby and kissed her.

"Morning," he said.

"Morning." Abby's smile softened. "Coffee?"

"Please."

Alex came down a minute later. He walked over to Emily and pulled her close, kissing her thoroughly despite the fact that Elias and Abby were right there.

When he pulled back, Emily was breathless.

"Morning," he said to Abby as he reached past her for the coffee pot. "You two plotting something?"

"Just girl talk," Emily said innocently.

"It's never just girl talk." Alex poured coffee for himself and Elias. "What were you talking about?"

"How hot our boyfriends are in bed," Abby said. She didn't even try to hide her grin.

Elias choked on his coffee and started to cough.

Alex laughed and pulled Emily closer.

"Good to know," Alex said.

After breakfast, Emily and Abby went upstairs so Abby could change back into yesterday's clothes. Emily braided her long dark hair while Abby twisted hers into a ponytail.

"We coming back tonight?" Abby asked her as they came back downstairs.

"Definitely," Emily said.

The guys walked them to the door. Elias helped Abby with her sweater while Alex got her tote bag.

Emily turned to Alex. "I'll text you later. Be careful." She squeezed Alex's hand. "Both of you."

"Always," Alex said.

She kissed him. Long and slow and deep. His hands framed her face and she melted into him. When they finally broke apart, she had to remember how to breathe.

Beside them, Elias and Abby were similarly occupied. Elias had backed Abby against the doorframe and was kissing her like he might never see her again. Her hands were tangled in his hair, and she was making soft sounds that made Emily look away.

"Come on, Abby," Emily said. "We have to go or we're never going to leave."

Abby pulled back slowly. Her lips were red and her cheeks were blushed. "I love you," she said to Elias.

"I love you too."

They finally made it out the door and down the porch steps toward Abby's car. As they drove away, Emily glanced back and saw both guys standing in the doorway watching them.

"They're still standing there aren't they?" Abby asked without looking.

"Yeah," Emily replied as the house disappeared from view. She worried about them. Her grandmother back in Asturias told her to always pray for the ones she loved.

Emily whispered the prayer under her breath, something her grandmother had said all her life.

"Reza, hija. Cuando una mujer de esta familia pide con fe, el Cielo responde."

When a woman of this family asks in faith, Heaven responds.

She felt her magic respond as her hands warmed and her memory magic surfaced.

She knew Abby had felt it when she said, "You're praying for them." Abby's magic responded with a golden spiral that lightly touched her own.

Emily was thinking of the stories her grandmother told her when she went to visit. She turned to Abby. "My grandmother said there was a time when using our magic to pray made people call us bruxas."

Abby didn't speak Spanish, but after years of friendship she understood certain words.

"Witches," Abby said. "My father's family, the Morgans, were called witches once too. My dad said they were healers but they had to hide their magic."

Emily nodded in agreement. "What nonsense. Magic just exists, and people calling themselves witches are just non-magic users pretending they have it. They dress up in costumes and go chant in the woods."

They were still laughing when they pulled up to their apartment twenty minutes later.

5

Wild Things

Elias was going to die of boredom. He was certain of that now. They'd spent the day looking over old files of animal attacks that had been reported in other states. Some on the same day, which definitely meant they were dealing with different animals, unless they had a serial killer on their hands and these were copycats.

"This is a colossal waste of our time," he groaned to Alex. When he looked up, Alex was stringing paperclips together. He wasn't the only one dying a slow death.

He checked the time and it was just before four o'clock.

"Hey, let's go back out to the crime scene and see if I can pick up anything. Then we can head home from there."

Alex stood up quickly. "Let's go."

Elias was glad no one was around when they arrived at the crime scene. The news had reported that the area was off limits due to an animal attack, and it looked like people were taking it seriously. The ground crunched under their shoes as they made their

49

way to where the attack had happened. Elias crouched near the site and let his magic spread outward, and this time, the memory trace came up immediately.

What he read stopped him cold. A school corridor, lockers, two friends talking over each other about something trivial. The memory had the texture of someone young, in high school, maybe.

Then it fractured.

Not in the way a memory fractured under violence, which Elias knew well. This was different. The thoughts were still there, but something else had torn through them. It felt like a second set of memories fighting with the first. The trace went wild and circular and dissolved into something that made no sense.

Elias pulled back and stood.

"What did you get?" Alex asked from behind him.

"I don't know how to explain it." Elias pressed two fingers against his temple. "The traces the attacker left. I got a clear read at first, and it was human. A teenager at school with friends. And then it broke apart in a way I've never encountered. There was still human thought in it, but something else was running through it at the same time, and they couldn't coexist." He shook his head. "I have no idea what I just read. None."

Alex looked at the ground. "The tracks are bigger than the last scene."

The lead tech crouched near a set of prints in the soft earth at the tree line. "Same paw shape as the other scenes. Whatever left these was heavy and moving fast."

Elias let his magic reach toward the tracks. The same fractured signature as the body. He pulled back.

He saw Alex pull out his phone. It was ringing and he guessed it was ASAC Washington calling and asking for an update. Elias walked away from the scene, down the path toward the water, and tried to clear the pressure building behind his eyes.

"Excuse me."

He turned. A woman stood at the edge of the tree line. He hadn't seen or felt her presence. Red hair loose around her shoulders, green eyes calmly moving between him and Alex. She stepped forward onto the trail.

Elias felt it immediately. Fae. Unregistered magic user. He'd encountered a handful of them over the years and recognized the strange signature that always struck him as old and wispy. Alex had laughed at him the first time he had described it that way.

"This area is restricted," he said. Alex had ended his call and was moving quickly toward him.

"I need to speak with you both," she said.

"You need to leave," Alex said. "This is an active crime scene."

"I know what this is." She looked at the trail behind them. "I know what killed that man. And I know who you are."

"And I know you're an unregistered magic user," Elias said. "If you know who killed this man, tell us."

She looked at him without any change in expression. "My name is Aisling. I felt a pulse two days ago from somewhere across the Charles River. Old magic, the kind that doesn't exist anymore. I tracked it here." She paused. "You two are of the Llewellyn and Rhys bloodlines."

Elias didn't look at Alex. He kept his eyes on her.

"Look, I don't know what you're talking about, but being unregistered is a federal crime. If you have information about what happened here, just tell us."

"There is a new werewolf hunting in Boston," she said. "It's killed four people and it will kill again. Not until next month since the full moon has passed. But it will kill again."

"We're going to need you to come with us," Alex said.

Something pushed at the edge of Elias' awareness. Soft pressure that tried to enter his mind. He recognized it for what it was and pushed back hard until it stopped.

Beside him he felt Alex go still.

Aisling studied both of them. Something shifted in her expression, not surprise exactly, more like confirmation.

"That's compulsion magic," Elias said. "Another federal crime. Don't do it again."

Aisling's eyes widened slightly. "You resisted me. Both of you." She looked genuinely surprised. "Interesting," she said quietly. Purple light flickered around her hands.

"I came here to help you. To explain what you are. What your families were. What we could accomplish together if you just listen."

"We don't need your help," Alex said. His combat magic sparked in response to her display. "And we're done listening."

The undergrowth across the trail rustled.

Something large moved through the brush.

Then it burst out of the trees.

Elias barely processed what he was seeing before it charged them.

Alex's silver shield flared to life. The creature slammed into it with enough force to crack the barrier. Magic radiated off the wolf in waves that made Elias' skin crawl.

"What the fuck is that?" Alex's voice was tight.

The wolf was huge. Its shoulder reached Elias' chest. Muscles rippled under gray fur as it circled, looking for an opening.

A violent swirl of shimmering magic lashed out. Aisling's magic wrapped around the wolf's legs like chains. "Told you. Werewolf."

The creature snarled and broke through her magic with a violent twist. It rounded on her and lunged.

Elias' memory magic reached out instinctively but there was

nothing to read. The wolf had no past he could access. Just present moment fury and hunger.

Alex threw up another shield between Aisling and the wolf. It shook as the creature hit the barrier and bounced back, then immediately turned and went for Alex.

It was too fast and strong. Alex's shield shattered under its weight.

Elias could see Alex drawing on his magic, trying to form a new shield, but the creature was too fast even for him. Its claws extended and its jaws opened as it lunged closer.

Elias acted without thought. His memory magic was useless here. The wolf was pure instinct and violence.

He reached for the magic he never used. The elemental power that terrified him because he didn't understand it and couldn't control it. Fire and wind and earth waited just beneath his conscious awareness.

It answered immediately.

Air whipped around him, violent and chaotic. Fire sparked in his hands. The ground beneath his feet trembled.

The wolf was lunging for Alex when Elias released the raw power.

Fire exploded from his hands and tore across the clearing. It slammed into the wolf and the creature yelped. The smell of burning fur filled the air. The wolf hit the ground and scrambled backward.

The wolf growled and veered away from Alex. It shook itself and looked for a way out.

Elias advanced. He couldn't stop. The elemental magic poured out of him, wild and uncontrolled. The wind was howling and debris lifted from the ground.

"Elias." Alex's voice cut through the roar in his ears. "Elias, it's running. Let it go."

The wolf turned and crashed back through the undergrowth. Gone as suddenly as it had appeared.

Elias stood with his hands raised and the elemental magic still churning, pulling against him the way it always did when he'd let it out, resisting the attempt to withdraw. He pulled harder and it held its ground. The air churned around them and threatened to bring down the nearby trees.

He felt Alex's hand come down on his shoulders from behind. His combat magic threaded into Elias' awareness, steady and cool, and wrapped itself around the edge of his magic. He didn't force it, just held it. Elias exhaled and the elemental magic subsided slowly until he had it under control again.

He lowered his hands.

"Breathe," Alex said quietly. "Just breathe."

"You really are what I thought," Aisling whispered. She looked at both of them. "Memory and combat together. And elemental magic that powerful. You're the bloodlines from the old stories. The ones who stood with us."

When he looked over he saw Aisling standing at the edge of the trail watching him.

"Will you listen to me now?" Aisling asked. Her composure had returned. "Will you let me explain what you are? What we could do together?"

"Leave now and we won't arrest you," Alex said.

He could hear the shouts of the Boston PD officers at the scene running toward them. When he looked up again, she was gone.

Alex looked at Elias. "You okay?"

"Getting there." Elias' hands still trembled, but the fire was under control.

They stayed another hour. Alex handled the report—animal attack, large wolf, engaged and driven off. Elias answered questions when asked and photographed the disturbed earth where the animal had been and tried not to think about the memory trace he couldn't explain. By the time they got back to the car the sun was low.

They drove in silence for several minutes.

"What was that thing?" Alex asked finally.

"I don't know."

"It was too big. Too fast. And it had a magic signature."

"I know."

"She called it a werewolf."

"Werewolves aren't real, Alex," Elias said. But the words felt hollow.

"She knew about our families," Alex said. "About the Rhys and Llewellyn bloodlines."

"And that thing we just fought was real."

Elias looked at his hands. They looked normal now. No flames. No magic visible on the surface. But he could feel it underneath. Ready to burst free again if he let his guard down.

"Your elemental magic," Alex said quietly. "That was the strongest I've ever seen it."

"I couldn't control it."

"But you did. And we're both okay. Nobody was hurt."

Elias wanted to believe that. But the memory of flames pouring from his hands, wild and uncontrolled, made him sick to his stomach. He'd spent months learning to suppress the elemental magic after Chicago. And in one moment of panic, it erupted without his control.

"One of these days you may not be around and I'm going to get someone killed."

"That's not going to happen, Elias. I will always be here."

"You can't be sure of that. I have a bad feeling about this. Something is triggering my elemental magic, and I don't know why or what." He didn't want to admit that he was scared.

"I know you're afraid," Alex sighed deeply. "We'll go talk to the trainer at the DMA that you worked with last Spring. She said you might have some control issues as your magic manifested. And she seemed like someone we can trust.”

“Yeah, maybe. But right now we have other problems. What was that woman talking about?”

“She said we activated something a couple days ago,” Alex said. “Some kind of old magic that sent out a pulse.”

“The journals.” Elias rubbed his face. “When we touched them together and the text transformed. There was that whistle, remember? And a small shockwave.”

“You think that’s what she felt?”

“I don’t know. Maybe.” Elias looked out the window at the city passing by. “But how would she know what it meant?”

Elias thought about the character of her magic. The strangeness of it. The way she’d held her ground when the animal appeared when she could have run.

“I don’t know what I believe yet.”

They pulled up to the house and Elias saw Abby’s car and the lights on inside.

Abby was at the stove when they came through the door, stirring something that smelled like garlic and white wine. Emily was at the island with her laptop and a glass of wine beside her. Abby looked over her shoulder at both of them, took in whatever she saw in their faces, and turned the burner down.

“Sit down,” she said. “I’ll get you something.”

He crossed the kitchen and kissed her. “Hi,” she said against his mouth.

“Hi.” She pulled back and looked at his hands but didn’t say anything. She just took one of them in both of hers and held it for a moment before she let go and poured him a glass of wine.

They sat at the table and told them everything. The memory trace he couldn't explain. The woman who had appeared at the scene knowing their bloodline names. The animal. The elemental magic coming up without permission and Alex pulling it back down. They didn't leave anything out.

Emily closed her laptop before they were halfway through and didn't open it again. She placed her hands on the lid.

"The memory trace," she said. "Human thought with something else running through it at the same time. Something that didn't coexist with it?"

"That's the best I can describe it," Elias said.

"It could be someone with a dissociative disorder. And the woman mentioned your ancestral family names?" Emily glances at Abby.

"Your Llewellyn and Rhys ancestors aren't in any public registry that I could find," Abby said. "The DMA catalogs magic ability type and registration status, not bloodlines." She sat down at the table.

"Oh, the hell they don't," Elias almost shouted. "I have it on good authority that they most certainly do keep track of bloodlines." He realized he sounded angry.

"But she wouldn't have access to those records. If she knows those names, she got them from somewhere else," Abby said.

After a few minutes of silence, Emily spoke again. "We should read more of the journals tonight."

"But first, dinner. I'm starving," Alex declared as he made his way to set the table. They ate dinner without bringing up the events of the day again. When they were done, they moved to the library. Elias lifted the lid of the chest and they settled into the arrangement that had become familiar over the past days, Abby on the floor beside him, Alex and Emily on the couch behind them.

Abby worked through the Latin sections first, her translation magic surfacing as she held each journal, her hands steady on the covers. She summarized as she went rather than reading word for word. Accounts of the two families moving through time alongside each other. The nature of the bond. The way it had been renewed across generations not by obligation but by the same instinct that had started it. References to something beyond the family connection, other alliances, a short mention of a dragon.

"A dragon?" Alex shifted forward to look at the text he couldn't understand. "Are there any drawings?" he asked.

Elias found himself laughing for the first time that day. Alex and his absurd question.

"Alex," Elias said slowly. "There's no such thing as dragons." Alex gave him a look that made Elias feel like the grinch that stole Christmas.

A couple hours later, they reached for the large red leather journal from the bottom of the chest, the newest, and most intact. Elias had held it before, but they hadn't read it. Unlike the other newer journals, this one had the same unknown writing in it that the ancient ones did. He set it on the table between them, and he and Alex both placed their hands on the cover.

The entire book seemed to unlock, not just the passage they were looking at.

"Well, that was interesting," Abby said when Elias let go of the book and the text remained English. "The warding is different on this one."

Alex read sections as Emily asked precise questions and tracked the answers in the small notebook she'd started to use.

He turned to the first entry and began to read the dates. The journal opened in early 1774 and ran forward in entries that were sometimes weeks apart, sometimes days. A woman named Alice Rhys. Her writing was direct and descriptive. She wrote the way people do when they're recording history. She'd started detailing events related to a growing dissent against the British. Some mentions of traitors to the colony.

And then he turned to a solitary entry on a blank page.

June 24, 1775.

Elias leaned into Alex as he checked the pages after it. Blank. He turned back and checked the dates again, running his thumb through the final section of the journal. The entries lead up to June 1775, and then nothing.

"That's it," he said.

"What do you mean?" Emily leaned forward.

"The entries stop on June 1775. There's nothing after it." He fanned the remaining pages so they could all see. "And there's no newer journal after this one in the chest. The previous one ends in the 1760s. This covers 1774 to 1775 and then the record just stops."

Abby leaned in. "She stopped writing."

"Or something happened to her," Alex said

"We don't know that," Elias said. "But even so, there should be more. If the pattern held across every previous generation, someone should have continued after Alice."

None of them had an answer for that.

"Read what's there," he said to Alex.

Alex turned back through the journal and kept reading. Alice wrote about people by name as though she assumed her reader knew them. A woman called Mercy appeared several times in the entries. Alice wrote about her with admiration and warmth. He turned to the last entry Alice had written in June of 1775 and read it.

They're taking them all. But the Llewellyns have already hidden the Seelie Court survivors where nobody will find them. I was supposed to protect Mercy, but I can't find her. She's the only seer we have and the one who knows everything to come. And where did all the witches go?

—Alice Rhys, June 24, 1775

Alex's voice faded as he finished reading. Elias leaned over his shoulder while Abby and Emily sat across from them at the table, the old journal open between them.

"Seelie and Unseelie Courts," Abby said slowly. "Those are fae terms. From old folklore, Celtic mythology."

"Except this isn't folklore," Emily said. "This is someone's personal diary."

No one spoke for several seconds.

"She was there," Abby said after a moment. "Wherever this was happening, Alice was in the middle of it."

"And she's looking for someone." Emily had her eyes on the journal. "Mercy. The seer." She looked up. "Alice doesn't find her. She writes it like she already knows she won't."

"We don't know who Mercy even was. And what is a seer? Magic can't see the future," Elias said.

"She did seem vague about who she was," Emily said. "By the tone in the earlier entries I'd guess either a close friend or relative, though."

Elias looked at the entry again. The handwriting was beautiful and steady, even in the urgency of it. Alice Rhys had been someone who had taken the time to ensure that her record was legible. No matter what horrible thing was unfolding.

Abby looked at him and asked, "Can you create a construct

from this journal, or from the others so we can see what is happening?"

Elias had been waiting for one of them to ask. "Yes, I'm pretty sure I can. But not tonight. My magic is drained, and honestly, I'm just exhausted."

With that declaration, Alex stood up and decided it was time to stop and let him get some sleep. Emily put her notebook away, and she and Abby walked toward the stairs together.

Elias smiled to himself. He wished, as he had so many times before, that he'd known Alex when he was ten years old. He could have used a protective big brother to defend him from the nightmares that plagued him the years after the train explosion that had taken his parents. Alex would have made an insufferable, but loving big brother.

He closed the journal carefully and set it on top of the chest.

The house had gone quiet around him. It was past ten. Alex went around checking the alarm system and shutting off lights.

"You going to bed?"

"In a minute."

"Good night. Text me if you need me, okay?"

"I'm fine, Alex. Go to bed." Alex looked at him a moment longer as if deciding how true his statement was before turning and heading upstairs.

Elias stood in the hallway thinking about the future. About Abby and Emily and the four of them building something that felt oddly like a family. He thought about the journals that proved Alex's family had been protecting his for hundreds of years. This felt right.

In that moment he knew he would do whatever it took to hold onto it. If anyone ever tried to take this from him, they would learn exactly what he was capable of.

Revelations

Abby was leaning against the counter with her coffee, watching Elias at the stove when Alex and Emily came downstairs.

"How's it going?" Alex asked.

"I'm teaching him how to make the scrambled eggs with cheese that you guys like so much," Abby said.

"It's not that hard," Elias said without turning around.

She pointed at the pan. "You forgot to add the bacon bits."

"I didn't forget."

"You were about to."

Alex looked at the stove over Elias' shoulder. Scrambled eggs with manchego cheese and bacon folded in to make it firm but creamy. He looked at Abby. She nodded once, confirming the situation was under control.

Emily went straight for the coffee. "Did he start the eggs or did Abby start them and hand him the spatula?"

Elias turned toward Emily. "I started them—"

"—He started them," Abby said at the same time. She paused. "I just guided the process."

"So Abby made the eggs," Emily said, laughing.

"I made the eggs." He knew Emily enjoyed teasing him and he secretly liked it. She was the little sister he never had.

Emily looked at Alex, who looked down at his coffee cup smiling.

"I'm writing down the recipe," Abby said. She had a notepad on the counter beside her. "Exact steps. So he can do it again without me here."

"There are five steps to scrambled eggs," Elias said. He wasn't sure, but it sounded right.

"There are nine steps." She tapped the notepad. "I've written all nine, and instructions."

Elias laughed. He loved having her teach him to cook. His mother died when he was too young to learn and his foster parents ordered out a lot. It was another thing he missed about having a mother. He decided at that moment that his children would be involved in the cooking and learn from Abby. She told him she wanted children someday. He wasn't sure if he'd be a good father. He'd never had a role model that was worthy of the title until he met Alex's father. His own father was a psychopath who nearly started a civil war back in Chicago. He thought society should be governed by magic users with him a their leader. What if that mental illness was genetic?

"Elias, stop thinking and turn off the heat. They're done." Abby's words broke through his thoughts.

Emily pulled out a stool at the island. "I'll eat them if Abby supervised. That's my only condition."

"Everyone is eating them," Elias said. He slid the eggs onto plates, set them on the island, and looked around at all three of them. "They're fine."

They were fine. Better than fine. Abby took a bite and made a small sound of approval, which satisfied Elias more than he let on. Emily ate without further comment, which from her was its own form of praise. Alex finished his in four minutes and reached for the toast. He could eat anything without complaining.

They ate without hurrying. It was Saturday, and they didn't have work to think about. Nothing needed to happen before they were ready.

When the plates were cleared, Emily opened her notebook on the island. "I've been thinking about the construct you could make."

She turned to a page she'd marked. "The Rhiannon entry. The ford at Com—" She looked at Abby. "That's Coom-dee?"

"Close. Cwm is the difficult part. It sits further back in the throat. Coom-dee. Cwmdu."

"I'm never going to say that correctly," Emily said.

"Neither am I," Elias said.

"That's Rhiannon Llewellyn's account about Rhys Maredudd protecting Owain Llewellyn at the ford of Cwmdu. When raiders came seeking the memory stones."

"The first time a Rhys chose to protect a Llewellyn," Alex said.

"The love story that started it all," said Abby.

She looked at Elias with a hopeful look. "Can you build a construct from that entry?"

Elias had been thinking about it since he woke. He knew she would pick that one. Abby clearly wanted to prove she was right about the love story. "Yes. For you, anything."

"When?"

"Now if you want," he said, chuckling.

Abby put her hand on his arm briefly. "How are you feeling?"

"Fine."

"You were up at two," she said.

"I went back to sleep."

She held his gaze for a moment, then nodded and picked up her coffee.

They moved to the library. Emily took her spot on the couch with her notebook. Abby settled in next to her.

He sat on the floor with Alex in front of the chest. Alex took the journal from Emily and opened it to the Rhiannon entry. They held the book together. The magic responded immediately. Silver and green light rose from the text, winding around each other. Elias felt Alex's combat magic arrive at the edge of his awareness. Steady and comforting.

He let his memory magic reach into the journal and concentrated.

Green light filled the room as it appeared to dissolve.

He felt a cool breeze.

Then the sound of a river moving nearby.

Abby drew a sharp breath behind him.

They stood on the bank of a shallow ford. The river ran narrow and quick between low wooded hills, the water clear over smooth rounded stones. In a clearing behind them was a circle of standing stones rising from the earth. Tall and imposing.

The sky was gray and night was approaching. Wind moved through the tops of the trees causing leaves to fall to the ground.

Figures came through the trees on the far bank. Roman soldiers, their armor catching what little light the gray sky offered, shields and short swords at their sides. They spread along the bank and started into the water.

A young man stepped out from beside the circle. Dark-haired, sleeves pushed back despite the cold. He raised his hands and green light rose at his fingers, the same shade as Elias' own magic. He planted himself in front of the stones and held his ground.

The soldiers kept advancing through the water.

Then the second figure appeared from the same bank, moving fast through the trees. Taller, broader across the shoulders, red-haired. He went straight past Owain and stepped down into the ford, placing himself between the soldiers and the circle.

Silver-blue light blazed from his hands.

Combat magic. The same brilliant silver-blue as Alex's. Elias realized he must be Bran Rhys.

Beside Elias, Alex went very still.

Shields formed above the water. The first soldier slammed into the shield and staggered back, water splashing around his legs. Another pushed forward beside him, striking the barrier with the rim of his shield. The shields shuddered when the soldiers struck them, but Bran held them steady. The impact rang across the water. One of the soldiers forced his way deeper into the ford before Bran shifted the shield and drove him sideways into the current. Bran moved forward into the ford and the shields moved with him, layering as he went. He was holding a line. Every placement planned. There was no aggression in it, just defense.

Owain added his magic behind him, feeding power into the shields. The standing stones responded, green light brightening along their bases, the old power in the circle pulling tight at the edges.

Silver and green magic wove together.

On the far bank a centurion barked an order. The soldiers pulled back into formation. The centurion studied the shields a moment longer, then gave a sharp command, and the soldiers withdrew across the ford in disciplined steps.

Bran stood in the shallows and watched until they were gone. Then he lowered his hands. The shields dissolved as he turned away.

Owain stood at the edge of the circle. He said something. The words didn't come through clearly but the meaning behind them did.

Bran looked at him for a moment then walked out of the

water and up the bank to stand beside him. They smiled at each other and clasped forearms, then faced the empty far bank.

The two of them stood together in front of the circle, in front of the stones that still held whatever had been stored inside them. A woman with long dark hair—who looked unmistakably like Owain—came running through the trees, dressed in a white dress and green cloak, and threw her arms around Bran.

Elias held the construct a moment longer before letting it go.

The river faded. The library came back into focus around him.

Elias released the book as Alex put one hand on his forearm, and his healing magic threaded in at the edges, turning the exhaustion into something more manageable.

"Thank you," Elias said.

Alex squeezed his arm once and lifted his hand.

Emily was on the couch with her pen hovering above the open notebook. She was looking at the center of the room. Abby sat with one hand on her mouth and her eyes teary. "They were in love. That had to have been Rhiannon. And their magic, it looked exactly like yours. Both of them."

"I know," Elias said.

"Those shields," Emily said. She looked at Alex. "The way he built them and moved them through the water. Can you do that?"

Alex stood with his hands in his pockets and nodded. "I have, when I was in the Army."

Elias looked at his own hands. He thought about Owain's green light brightening along the base of each standing stone. Memory woven into rock. He thought about Rowan that day back in Chicago, the lead-lined case opening on the table, and the way his memory magic had reached for the ancient artifacts inside it before he could stop it. The way it had felt like something recognizing him.

Rowan's words came back to him clearly. *The Llewellyn line descends from the original Druids who forged them. That's why your memory magic responds to them with such precision. It recognizes you.*

"The stones," he said. "The Llewellyn line could weave memory into objects. Preserve it in stone or metal objects. That's what Owain was doing. That's what the circle held."

Alex looked at him. "And the artifacts they created."

"The artifacts came later I think, shaped into weapons to use against the Romans." Elias looked at the space where the ford had been. "Rowan told me in Chicago that my ancestors forged them. I didn't fully understand what that meant." He looked at Alex. "Now I do. We just watched where it started."

The room was quiet.

"And the Romans knew what was in those stones," Alex said.

"That's why they kept coming." Elias looked at the journal still open on the floor. "Three times. They weren't after the land."

"And Bran stood with Owain and wouldn't let them have it," Emily said. She looked at Alex. "Two thousand years ago. The same way you stand between Elias and anything that comes for him."

Alex looked at Elias and nodded.

Abby got up and went to the kitchen. She came back with a glass of water and set it beside Elias without comment, sitting back down next to him on the floor. He drank it. Emily began writing again.

Emily checked the time on her phone. "It's almost noon."

"I'll order lunch," Alex said, reaching for his phone.

The journals passed through Abby's hands one by one, her translation magic surfacing in warm amber flickers as she worked through the Latin and Welsh entries that weren't warded. Emily sat beside her with her notebook and recorded the main points. Who chose whom. Who stayed. Who left.

Which marriages looked strategic and which ones were something else entirely.

By midafternoon they had confirmed what the construct had already shown them. The alliance between the Rhys and Llewellyn families had started in protection, but it had survived because generation after generation someone kept choosing it. Marriage and friendship. Duty and love. Sometimes one, sometimes all four.

Abby was midway through explaining why the ink marks on one entry suggested a date change when Elias' phone buzzed on the floor beside him.

"Hello."

"Good morning, Mr. Sinclair. This is Donna at Brightside Cleaning. I'm sorry to contact you at the last minute. I wanted to let you know that Cindy is unwell and won't be able to come in today."

"Is she all right?"

"She'll be fine, just needs a few days. I do have someone available this afternoon if you don't mind someone different. She's new to our roster but comes well recommended."

Elias looked at the journals spread across the room and the mugs on the side table. "That's fine. I just need basic cleaning done. Cindy did a thorough cleaning last week. What time is your new cleaner coming?"

"Around two. Same time Cindy was scheduled for."

"Great. Thanks, Donna." He ended the call.

Alex looked at him.

"Cindy's sick," Elias said. "They're sending someone new this afternoon."

Emily looked up from her notebook. "Cindy, the one who comes every week? Sweet old lady who cleans while listening to hard rock?"

"That's her."

"Hope she feels better. That woman is a hoot. You know she used to be roadie for a band when she was young. She tells some crazy stories." Emily looked back down at her notes. "Who are they sending?"

"Someone new. That's all I know."

They worked through more journals. Abby made notes about dates and writers. Emily formed theories about the family dynamics and tested them against the entries aloud, adjusting when the evidence didn't fit. Elias and Alex activated the translation magic over and over, Alex reading sections to them, both of them learning more about the people whose blood ran in their veins than they had ever expected to know.

As the afternoon light shifted through the windows, Abby pulled Elias aside while Alex and Emily were debating a particular entry across the room.

"Elias, your elemental magic," she said quietly. "What happened at the crime scene. I think Em is right that it's tied to your emotions. To your fear of losing Alex."

"I know."

"That doesn't make it wrong or dangerous. It just means you need to understand it." She touched his face briefly. "You're not broken. You're scared. And that's allowed."

He looked at her for a moment. "Thank you."

She kissed him once and let him go.

The doorbell rang just before two.

All four of them looked up.

Elias felt it before anyone moved. Old magic, wispy and faint, but unmistakable. The same strange signature that had brushed his awareness at the crime scene.

Alex set down his beer. "That must be the new housekeeper."

"No," Elias said, already rising. "That's someone who shouldn't be here."

Abby's eyes sharpened. Emily closed her notebook.

"Who is it?" Alex said, standing quickly.

"That woman from the crime scene. The unregistered user."

They crossed the hall together. Alex reached the door first but Elias touched his arm before he could open it. "Let me do the talking."

Alex gave him a look that said he had no intention of promising that and opened the door.

Aisling stood on the porch in jeans, boots, and a dark green sweater, her red hair loose over her shoulders and catching the afternoon light. She was grinning, and it made her look more dangerous than it should have.

"I was hoping you'd answer," she said.

"How did you find us?" Alex asked.

Abby and Emily came to the doorway behind them. Aisling's eyes moved to them, registered them and held their gaze.

"Invite her in," Abby said quietly.

"Absolutely not," Alex said without taking his eyes off Aisling.

"She already knows we're here," Emily said. "Standing on the porch arguing about it isn't going to solve anything."

Aisling widened her grin and Elias looked at Alex. "Just into the entryway."

Alex's jaw tightened. Then he stepped back.

Aisling crossed the threshold slowly, her hand brushing the doorframe lightly as she passed through. The temperature in the hall seemed to drop suddenly.

She stopped and looked around once, taking in the journals visible in the library.

Alex stood with his arms loose at his side, well out of reach and ready to respond. "Start talking."

Aisling looked at the journals again, then at Elias. "The Call I felt came from this house. The Defenders' lines had been separated for generations, diminished and scattered. Then you activated a magic that has not been felt in two hundred and fifty years."

Abby frowned. "Defenders?"

"That's one of the names they were once called."

"By who?" Emily asked.

"By those who needed them. By those they protected." Her gaze settled. "By my people, and the others."

"Us meaning who?" Alex asked.

Aisling smiled faintly and slid a hand gently down her hair. "I think you may already know the answer to that." She glanced toward the library again where the journals lay open. "Those books are sending out a signal. I won't be the only one who felt it. But I'm probably the only one in this city who knows what it means."

"Who are you?" Abby said.

Aisling looked at her for a moment, amused. "You already know."

"You're an unregistered magic user," Alex said flatly.

Aisling's smile widened slightly. "That's what your government calls us."

Abby frowned. "Us?"

Aisling tilted her head. "The Fae."

Elias studied her. The confidence she presented. The age of her magic. The way she spoke without drama or shame about her unregistered status. And she was staring at Abby too long.

He shifted to block her view. "You tracked us because of the books," he said.

"I tracked the call. I found you because of them." She looked again toward the library as she took a couple of steps toward the room and stopped.

"And the wolf," Alex said. "You know what that is."

Aisling's attention shifted to him. "Yes."

"Then explain it."

She moved around the entryway slowly, looking up the stairs and around the house, running her fingertips along the wall. "There are creatures in this city that your government files will never explain. Some are remnants. Some are cursed. Some are the result of old pacts that should have stayed buried. "The wolf you encountered isn't simply an animal, nor a man. Sometimes it is one. Sometimes the other."

Elias thought of the memory trace in the woods. Human thought breaking apart beneath something wilder. That part, at least, fit.

"And why is it here?" he asked.

"It lives here. As do the rest of us."

"There's that 'us' again," Elias said.

"The Fae. The real ones, not what your government refers to as unregistered magic users. That name has become corrupted. It's used now to describe any magic user who dares to defy registration. But it started with us. The real Fae Courts who refused to be regulated. The Courts stood at the edge of history and chose sides. One chose wrong, and we were all punished for it. We survived because of the Defenders."

Alex was the first to break the silence. "You keep saying Defenders. What exactly do you think that means?"

Aisling studied the two of them for a moment. "You're what remains of an old alliance that has diminished over time. Memory and combat. Bearer and shield. The lines still choose each other even with the long passage of time." Her eyes shifted to Elias. "And sometimes they produce something unexpected."

Elias felt his heart beat faster and his hands shake slightly. Something in her words unsettled him.

He heard Alex move closer to him.

"What do you want?" Alex asked.

Aisling's smile vanished completely. "I want to see your books. And I want to help you understand what you're capable of. I'm not a threat to you."

No one answered.

The house shook suddenly. Everyone startled, even Aisling. Windows rattled and the floors creaked loudly. Elias felt a breeze, though no window was open. He heard the trees outside shaking as if a storm approached. He thought he heard a voice in the wind say his name. This wasn't his magic doing this.

Aisling looked around at the house. Her smile was gone. "What the hell was that?"

"This house is haunted," he said with a grin.

He glanced toward the journals in the library. For the first time since Aisling had appeared in the woods, he believed she might actually be telling the truth.

7

What History Forgot

The house settled back into silence.

Abby was gripping Emily's hand.

Emily replied, *"Maldita casa."* Damn house.

Alex tapped Elias on the arm. "Kitchen. Now. You two mind keeping an eye on our guest?"

"Gladly," Emily said.

Abby stepped closer to the library door and stood with her arms crossed, staring at Aisling.

Elias walked into the kitchen and pulled the door most of the way closed.

"No," Alex said.

"No, what? I haven't asked anything."

"You want to let her stay. The answer is no."

Elias leaned against the counter. "She knows something about our families, and she felt that pulse from the journals. And the wolf that attacked us."

"Tell me you're not actually considering this. She's an unregistered magic user and in violation of multiple federal laws. And we don't even know if she's involved with those dead bodies. We're obligated to detain her for questioning at the very least."

"I'm aware."

"No, I don't think you are." Alex kept his voice low. "She tracked us to our house, Elias." Alex looked up toward the entryway with a look. "Wait a minute. Is she the person the cleaning service sent? Damn it. We should be calling this in, not inviting her inside."

Elias leaned one hand on the back of a chair and lowered his voice to match. "You felt her magic. She's not lying."

"That isn't the point."

Alex looked at him. "You've already decided."

"No. You want to arrest her and end this, then we will. You know I trust your judgment, and I will always take your side. But we need to know what she knows. The case isn't going away, and she seems to have information. And frankly, I'm disturbed by the fact that she knows about our ancestors and felt whatever that pulse was that the journal sent out." He took a deep breath and stared down at the counter.

"She scares you. I can feel it." Alex's tone had softened.

He met Alex's eyes. "You really can read my mind."

"Of course I can't read your mind. You know our magic is connected. The bond between us lets us sense each other's presence and feel strong emotions. But I don't know what you're thinking. I just know you."

Elias was quiet. He could feel the concern coming from Alex.

"She's not going to tell us anything useful standing in the hallway," Elias said.

"And when we're done talking to her?" he asked.

Elias didn't answer right away.

"We decide if we're going to arrest her, or look the other way," Elias said finally.

Alex ran a hand across the back of his neck.

"I think this is insane. Nothing good can come of this."

"Probably."

A small laugh escaped Alex before he could stop it.

"You know this is exactly the kind of thing that gets people kicked out of the FBI."

Elias grinned. "Well, we were looking for a way out."

Alex shook his head. "A way out of the Bureau. Not a way into prison."

Alex looked at him another second, then nodded once.

"Okay, we'll do it your way for now. But we control the conversation and how much we share. If she does or says anything that I think is even remotely dangerous, or we catch her in a lie, I'm arresting her. I won't place you or the girls in harm's way just to appease our curiosity."

"I agree. You're supposed to protect me according to the journals. So protect away," Elias said with a big smile.

"Shut up." Alex gave him a gentle one-handed shove as he walked past him and out of the kitchen.

When they reached the entryway, he saw Abby and Emily standing in front of the library door where he'd left them. Abby's arms still crossed and Emily with her hands on her hips. Aisling was leaning against the front door. Elias thought they looked like lions circling their prey. He just didn't know who was going to pounce first.

"Okay. Aisling, come into the library. But don't touch anything," Elias said.

Aisling walked into the room ahead of them. She looked at the bookshelves, the chest, the journals on the table. She chose the chair near the window and sat without waiting to be asked.

Alex took a position near the doorway.

Aisling spoke first as she looked at the chest and the journals. "How long have you had them?"

Alex answered. "That doesn't matter. What do you want from us?"

"To help you understand what you have accessed." She looked back at Elias. "The magical signature your journals sent out when you activated them is quite unique. There are others in this city, in this country, with old magic who will have felt it even if they don't know where it came from. They won't allow you to uncover what is likely in those journals. It's just a matter of time."

"Why?" Elias asked.

"Because I'm guessing that one of those journals tells of a story long forgotten to time. One that was intentionally unwritten. One that the Others want left hidden."

Elias felt the goosebumps on his arm and suddenly felt cold. He crossed his arms trying to get warm, and caught movement toward the bookshelf.

"Elias." He barely heard Alex

For a moment he thought he saw an old woman standing beside the bookshelf. She was crying. Her clothing looked strangely old-fashioned, the sleeves long and narrow like something from another century. Her mouth moved as if she were speaking, but he couldn't hear anything.

"Elias." Alex was shouting his name.

He turned back toward Alex and realized everyone was staring at him.

"What's wrong?" Alex asked with concern.

"I don't know. It feels like someone just walked on my grave." He glanced back at the bookshelf and then looked at Alex again. "It's nothing."

Alex kept looking at him, and Elias knew he didn't believe him. But this wasn't a conversation to be had now.

"What exactly do you think is in the journals someone would want? And who are these people you say will stop us from reading them?" he asked Aisling.

"There is too much to tell, and I'm afraid that you won't believe me. Would you tell me what you found in the journals first? It'll help me know where to start. They're written by your Llewellyn and Rhys ancestors, correct?" Aisling asked.

Alex looked at Elias.

"Yes," Alex said. "How do you know those names? You mentioned them in the park."

"My mother spoke of them. They are names my people haven't forgotten, even if yours have."

Abby picked up Alice's journal. "Elias, the entry here from the 1770s. Could that be a place to start?"

Aisling's eyes moved to Abby and the red journal. She stood and walked over to the couch but didn't reach for it.

"What does it describe?" she asked.

"It would be easier to show you," Emily said. She looked at Elias. "Can you make a construct from Alice's entry?"

"Make a what?" Aisling asked.

Alex walked over toward him and quickly answered, "No."

Elias hesitated. His memory magic wasn't a secret, but the construct ability was something he used sparingly. It was powerful, revealing, and it left him vulnerable in ways he didn't like. He'd only recently started using it more openly after the events in Chicago had shown the DMA and the Bureau what he could do.

"Elias, I don't think this is a good time."

"She already knows your names," Emily said to Alex. "She knows about the journals. A construct just shows her what we're talking about."

Elias looked at the journal in Abby's hands. "All right." He saw the disapproval in Alex's eyes.

"Okay, fine. But Aisling, I want you standing on the other side of the room." Alex pulled him toward the couch. "Would you two mind sitting in the arm chairs?" he asked Abby and Emily.

Elias recognized this for what it was. Alex positioning himself in a way that he could quickly deal with Aisling without having to stand up from the floor. Elias was sure Alex already had a plan formulated in case she tried something while he was deep in the memory trace.

Abby opened the journal to the entry and placed it in Elias' hands. Alex gripped his forearm as silver and green magic wound together.

"Don't move from that spot or I will put you down before you know what hit you," Alex told Aisling, who just smiled at him and nodded.

Abby never sat in the armchair and remained standing near Aisling. Elias suspected that if it came to it, she'd stop her before Alex even noticed. She never used her elemental magic for offense, but he knew she was powerful even if her friendly demeanor never gave it away.

Elias let his magic touch the journal.

Green magic moved through the library, threading between the shelves and across the open journals on the floor. The books and walls fell away. The floor beneath them shifted from hardwood to packed earth, and the darkness of a forest night closed in around them. Large oak trees surrounded them. A group of people stood close together near the center, their voices low and urgent.

A woman with red hair stood slightly apart from the others. Her clothing was fine despite the dirt on her cloak. She was speaking to a dark-haired woman who faced her, hands glowing faintly with silver combat magic.

"We should never have made ourselves known to them," the

red-haired woman said. "This is my fault. I believed they would accept us if they understood us. I was wrong."

"There is no use in that now," the dark-haired woman said. "We need to move quickly. I have a plan to hide your people, but I need time to put it all in place."

"How much time?"

"A few days." She looked toward the edge of the clearing. "I have men here who came to help."

At the edge of the lantern light, two figures stood back in the shadows. Elias couldn't make out their faces.

A small girl pushed through the group and stopped beside the red-haired woman. She was perhaps ten, red-haired, clutching the woman's cloak in both hands and looking at the dark trees around her.

The red-haired woman put her hand on the girl's head without looking down. "It's alright, princess. We're safe."

"What about the Unseelie?" the red-haired woman asked. "Will you hide them as well?"

The dark-haired woman shook her head. "No."

"They're still fae. Whatever they have done—"

"I know what they have done." Her voice was quiet and final. "I will not help them. Not after this. Your people, I will protect with everything I have. Our alliance is old, and you have always been true to it. The Unseelie made their choice."

The red-haired woman looked at her for a long moment. Then she nodded once.

A shout came from beyond the trees. Everyone in the clearing went still. The dark-haired woman turned toward the two figures at the edge of the light and said something Elias couldn't hear. Both men moved immediately, positioning themselves between the group and the direction of the sound.

The construct faded suddenly.

"What happened?" Alex asked.

"I don't know. It was a strong memory. Something pulled me out."

"It wasn't me. I didn't pull you out. That felt like a switch being flipped." Alex was still gripping his arm. "Are you okay?"

"Yeah, I'm fine, but that was weird." He didn't even feel drained. He set the journal on the coffee table, still open to Alice's entry.

He looked at Aisling.

She stood with both hands in fists beside her, eyes fixed on the space where the forest had been. Her face had gone pale.

"Aisling," Elias said. "Are you alright?"

She didn't answer right away. When she did her voice came out just above a whisper. "That's what happened. That's exactly what they did to us."

"To who?" Alex asked.

She looked up at him. "My people. I remember... I mean the stories my mother told me about what happened."

"What did she tell you?" Abby asked.

"We lost everything the day the clocks stopped."

Elias asked, "What does that mean?"

Abby frowned slightly. "It's an old expression," she said. "A moment in time when everything changes."

The room remained quiet for a moment until a loud whistle broke the silence.

Emily made a startled sound. She was staring at the journal on the table where Elias had set it. "The page," Emily said. "Look at the page."

They all turned. The journal was glowing. Not the entry they had been reading. The next page, the one that had been blank when Elias had mentioned it that morning.

Light spread across the blank parchment.

Letters began appearing one by one, written by an unseen hand.

The handwriting wasn't the same as Alice's.

"What's happening?" Abby breathed.

The writing continued, spreading across the page in dark ink. Elias leaned closer, trying to make out what was forming.

From the years yet to flow
Came the strangers unbidden.
To rewrite what was written
And unmake what we know.

They all stared at the page in shock. Elias' hands suddenly sparkled with his green magic, and Alex's silver magic reached for his, intertwining without their control before it faded. Their magic had reacted to whatever was happening, but he didn't understand it.

"I don't understand," Alex said. "How is this possible?"

Elias replied slowly, "The journal shouldn't be able to do this. The journal's magic is preservation, it reveals existing text. It can't create new writing."

Emily knelt in front of it. "Uhm. It just did."

Abby said, "It's a poem. A quatrain to be exact."

Aisling moved closer to the journal, her eyes fixed on the page that had stopped glowing.

When she spoke, her voice was steady and confident.

"I might be able to help," she said. "I think I know what this is."

8

The Prophecy

Aisling knew what the words meant the moment the ink finished forming on the page.

She stood with her hands loose at her sides and kept her face composed as she read it twice. An old memory surfaced, from a time older than the four people in the room.

Her mother had told her about this. Not about the journal, but about men who would come. Men from a time not yet written. Men who carried the old magic in their blood and could change what had been done to her people, if they could be made to understand.

Her mother had told her she would know them when she found them.

And she was certain she had.

Elias' construct magic was something she had never seen before. As far as she knew, it had never existed.

But the poem—that wasn't a surprise.

It wasn't even a poem.

It was a message from the past.

A prophecy.

The journal itself, the red leather one Alice Rhys had owned, held magic that went beyond preservation. She could feel it from across the room.

Portal magic.

Someone had put powerful fae magic into this book deliberately, power woven through the binding itself. The prophecy had been waiting inside it all along for the right moment to surface.

She knew portal magic once existed, but she had never seen it used. And Alice Rhys' journal had it woven into its pages.

She didn't know who had done it or why.

It didn't matter now.

She had found the defenders of old.

And the means to change the fate of her people.

She didn't tell them any of this.

They wouldn't believe her.

Or worse.

They would refuse to fulfill the prophecy.

"The journal writing itself isn't ordinary preservation magic," she said. "Whatever is in those pages goes deeper than text. You have the ability to reach it."

She looked at Elias.

"But you need more magic than your own. There are places near this city where old workings are still present in the ground. Where the earth holds memory of the time in that book. A site like that would anchor and amplify what you can already do."

"What site? I've never heard of a memory specialist needing a location to enhance their magic," Abby said.

"Middlesex Fells Reservation. There is an earthwork there, pre-colonial. My people used places like that for their most important workings. If the journals are trying to show you something, that is where you will be able to see it clearly."

"You want us to walk into the woods with you," Alex said.

"Yes."

"Based on a poem that appeared five minutes ago."

"Based on everything I have told you today. And based on what you saw in that memory."

She held his gaze.

"You know I haven't lied to you."

He said nothing.

"Whatever pulled Elias out of that construct didn't want you to see the end of that memory," she said. "The Others who felt that journal activate will not wait as long as I did before they come to find you. I came to help. If they come those books will disappear. And perhaps you with them."

She caught Alex's glance toward Elias; a second later, Elias looked at the journal.

"Tomorrow evening," she said. "Around 7 p.m. I have work before that. And the earthwork will be easier to open on the new moon."

She was halfway to the door when Elias spoke.

"Stay for dinner."

She stopped.

It wasn't what she had expected. She turned around. "I don't think that's necessary."

"You know things about our families that we're only beginning to understand. We know nothing about you." He looked at her steadily. "Stay."

She glanced at Alex.

He stared at Elias and started to say something but stopped.

Abby was already moving toward the back door.

"Very well, if you insist."

Alex grilled burgers in the back garden. The September evening was warm enough to eat outside, but they brought the food in and sat at the dining room table with the windows open and a pleasant breeze.

Aisling took the empty chair and watched them move around one another. She hadn't eaten at a table with other people in a long time. She also noticed what they didn't know about themselves.

Emily's magic brushed constantly against the people around her, subtle and searching, as if the world itself left impressions she couldn't help but feel.

Abby's was different. Earth-rooted. Steady in a way that felt older than the city around them.

And the two of them had the shape of something else entirely. Not the bond Alex and Elias shared. Something older. The beginning of a circle.

Neither Emily nor Abby gave any indication that they were aware of their heritage. Aisling had always assumed the Others knew one another when they crossed paths.

Apparently, that wasn't the case.

Aisling kept that to herself.

"What do you actually do?" Emily asked after a few minutes. "For work."

"I'm a housekeeper," Aisling said. "Sometimes I work part time at a flower shop on Newbury Street when they need extra help. Cash work. Nothing that requires documentation."

"Because you're unregistered," Abby said.

"Because I'm unregistered."

She set her burger down. "The government requires magic users to register with the DMA. Name, address, magic type, strength assessment. Once you're registered, you're tracked. Every significant use of magic gets flagged. Your employment options are determined by your classification. Of course, you know this. You're all registered."

"We know the system," Elias said. "We work inside it."

"Then you don't know what it feels like from the outside." She picked up her food again. "If you're unregistered and you're caught using magic, you're cited. Fined. The fines compound. If you can't pay them you're placed on a watch list. After that, any magic use is treated as a criminal act."

"Have you been cited?" Emily asked.

"Three times," she said without feeling. "The last one was two years ago. A man followed me from a market in Roxbury. I used compulsion to make him stop. The DMA monitor in the area flagged the signature. I moved apartments the next day."

Elias looked at his plate.

Alex said nothing.

"How do you eat?" Abby asked. "If the fines compound and the cash work isn't consistent."

"Sometimes I steal. From markets. Never from people."

Abby and Emily exchanged side glances.

"I'm telling you because you asked," she said before any of them could respond. "Not because I want your sympathy. I've managed for a very long time."

"Why don't you just register? It's not the worst thing in the world, and you would legally be allowed to work." Emily said.

"It's complicated. My people aren't exactly allowed to register. If I walked into the registration office tomorrow, there are people there that would identify me as fae. I know you don't believe that I'm different, but I am. My people don't register. There are reasons for it. I've been able to live under their radar, and the enforcement division hasn't flagged me."

Elias picked up a french fry. "You have very strong magic. I can sense it's different," Elias said. "Strong enough that the DMA would classify it as Specialist level. You really should register."

"I am fae. I'm not a Specialist," Aisling stated firmly. She saw Elias' glance at Alex.

"So, how long have you been in Boston?" Elias asked.

"Longer than Boston has been Boston." She said it simply and watched them decide whether to take it seriously.

Emily's eyes met Abby's and she shifted in her chair.

"The fae," Abby said. "You said earlier the term was corrupted. That your people are different."

"Yes."

"How different?"

"We're older," Aisling said. "The fae predate your registration systems by centuries. We predate this country and the old world. We were here when the first settlers arrived and long before that. We have our own structure, our own laws, our own history." She glanced around the table. "None of which your government recognizes, because as far as the DMA is concerned, we are simply unregistered magic users who refuse to comply."

Alex sighed deeply and mumbled something under his breath as he stood and went to get something in the kitchen. He obviously didn't believe a word she said.

"The Courts," Abby said. "Seelie and Unseelie. Those are real?"

"Yes."

"And you're a Seelie?"

"Yes."

"What happened to them?" Abby asked. "After what we saw happening in the construct."

Aisling thought about the clearing. Her mother's hand on her head. The dark pressing in from the trees on all sides. "We survived," she said. "Scattered and hidden, the way you saw. The Court diminished over generations. The old magic faded. The fae who remain now are mostly half-blooded, their abilities weakened to the point where the DMA classifies them as low-level unregistered users and doesn't look closely enough to care what they actually are."

"But not you?," Emily said.

"No," Aisling said. "I'm different."

Emily chimed in. "How long have you believed that?"

Of course. The psychologist thought she was delusional already. She didn't elaborate and ignored her question, asking for the tray of burgers instead. The distance between who she appeared to be, and who she was, remained too large to cross tonight. "The fae who have real power quickly learn to hide it," she said instead.

"The DMA doesn't like what it cannot control." She turned to Elias. "I suspect you know what I mean."

He held her gaze. "I do."

They talked for another two hours. She answered what she could and deflected what she could not. Their skepticism softened without disappearing entirely.

They didn't believe her. She hadn't expected them to.

"I have to work tomorrow morning," she said as she stood. "I should go. Seven, tomorrow evening?"

Alex walked her to the door. "Tomorrow at seven," he said.

"Goodnight," she said.

She walked out into the night. She was the Queen of the Seelie Court. Even if her Court was diminished and in exile. And she had spent two hundred and fifty years waiting for tomorrow evening.

The following evening Aisling arrived at the house and they left promptly at seven P.M..

Aisling caught the sharp edge of Emily's whisper to Alex and Elias as they were getting in the car. "don't trust that woman. She's hiding something."

The sky was darkening when Alex pulled into the lot at

Middlesex Fells. She watched Alex drop his keys in the gravel. Emily found them first and slipped them into her pocket.

Elias and Alex had brought flashlights, but Aisling had them on the trail before they lost the light.

The path was narrow and rocky, the forest close on either side.

Elias carried the journal wrapped in a velvet cloth. She could feel it from several feet away. The green shimmer at his fingertips had started at the trailhead without him noticing.

Alex walked half a step behind and to his left.

She had been observing them move around each other for two days now and still found it remarkable. The instinctive positioning, the way their magic reached for each other without either of them calling it.

They reached the mound as the last of the daylight went amber through the canopy. The trees around it were older than those on the trail.

Elias slowed.

"There are layers here," he said. "Centuries of workings. Some of it feels like the journals."

"Yes," she said.

He climbed to the top and knelt, pressing both palms flat to the earth. Green light spread from his hands and sank in.

After a moment he pulled back. "I can't read it clearly. There's too much layered over itself."

"That's why you need the journal," she said. "The earthwork and the journal together will open what neither can alone."

Alex stepped beside his partner as Elias took the journal out from its covering.

"You should both hold it," she instructed them.

Elias and Alex placed their hands on the book. The familiar whistle rose, louder than it had before.

Elias was the first to notice. "Why is it whistling? This book isn't warded anymore. It never responded the way the other journals do. Why is it doing that now?"

Aisling placed her hands over theirs. She felt the power in the earthwork rise through the soles of her feet the moment she made contact. Over two hundred and fifty years of stored intention. Workings laid down in the years before everything was lost. She felt it recognize the journal. Felt it recognize the two men. She opened herself to it completely and a white light erupted from the point where her hands met theirs and spread outward across the mound.

She felt Alex's combat magic surge first, instinctive and violent, pushing against the hold she had placed on them. He was trying to break them free.

She tightened her grip on the working and forced the power down.

"Aisling," Alex said quietly. "Stop this now."

"I will not," she said.

"Alex, something is very wrong here. Pull us out now," Elias shouted. "What are you doing?" he asked her.

She looked at Elias. "Sending you back to where this started. To the only place where what was lost can be made right."

"Sending us back where?" Alex asked while still trying to force his way out of her hold.

"To the beginning." Aisling's eyes were bright now, something desperate breaking through the calm she had held all evening. "Find Mercy Bishop, the seer. She will guide you."

"Mercy Bishop?" Elias tried harder to pull his hand away. "Aisling, what are you talking about?"

"You're the ones the poem describes," she said quietly. "I knew the moment the journal called across the river."

"You knew?," Alex said.

"Yes."

The wind rose around them.

Emily and Abby shouted at her to stop and tried to reach them, but the power around the mound held them off. She felt the tear beginning beneath the mound, the seam between now and then opening.

Elias looked at her, fear in his eyes. "Aisling."

"I know," she said softly. "I am sorry for the manner of it."

The tear opened completely. The white light collapsed inward. She was almost pulled through with them but broke the contact in time.

Alex and Elias vanished in a swirl of blue, green, and purple light that lingered.

Silence returned to the mound. Aisling fell to her knees exhausted. Hold on, she thought. they're on their way.

Emily reached her first. She looked at the empty space where Alex and Elias had been standing, and the book lying on the ground open. Then she looked at Aisling and lunged. She grabbed her by her shoulders and pulled her up with a force she wasn't expecting. "Where are Alex and Elias?" she screamed.

Abby was picking up the book and crying.

Aisling raised her head. I sent them back," she said.

"Back where?" Emily shouted.

"June 1775."

9

Across The Fractured Tide

Alex hit the ground hard. The impact drove the air from his lungs and sent pain shooting through his shoulder. He rolled onto his side, gasping, his hands scraping against rough stone.

"Fuck. What the hell?"

He pushed himself up to his hands and knees, blinking hard to clear his vision. The last thing he remembered was a bright blinding light and a feeling of falling. He heard Elias shouting at him to break them free. He'd tried to reach for his combat magic to pull them away from the book and Aisling's hold, but it wouldn't come. Then the world disappeared.

He looked around, trying to orient himself. Where was the forest? Why was it daylight?

A groan came from a few feet away. Elias was on his side trying to sit up, blood dripped from his nose onto the stone beneath him.

"Elias!" Alex stumbled over and knelt beside his partner. "Are you okay?"

"No." Elias' voice was rough. He lifted his head and Alex saw

97

that his eyes were unfocused, the pupils blown wide. "Something's wrong. My head hurts."

"You're bleeding."

"Not that." Elias touched his temple with a shaking hand. "I don't feel right."

"What the hell happened to us?" Alex got to his feet unsteadily, his legs shaking.

"Where are we?" Elias asked.

"I don't know." Alex helped his partner to his feet. Elias swayed and Alex steadied him. "Can you stand?"

"Yeah." Elias pressed both hands to his temples. "But my magic feels weird. I can't explain it. Everything feels muffled."

Alex looked around again, his training kicking in despite the confusion. Assess the situation. Figure out where they were and what had happened.

Buildings rose on either side of him. Wooden structures, their upper stories jutting out over a narrow street. The air smelled different. Smoke and something rancid.

The street was narrow, maybe twelve feet wide. Cobblestones covered the ground.

No power lines. No streetlights. No pavement. No cars.

Alex pulled out his phone. The screen lit up immediately. 11:02 a.m., September 15.

But in the corner where the signal bars should be it said SOS. Not searching for a signal.

"No signal," he said.

"Mine either." Elias was holding his own phone, staring at the screen.

"Yeah." Alex tried his maps app but it couldn't find their location. "Cell towers must be down."

Elias pocketed his phone with fumbling fingers. "We're out of range."

"Yeah." Alex looked around again. The street curved ahead of them, disappearing around a corner. Behind them, it opened onto what looked like a wider area.

Elias looked around but nothing seemed familiar. "I don't recognize anything."

The sound of hoofbeats echoed off the buildings. Alex turned and saw a horse coming down the street toward them, pulling a wooden cart. The wheels creaked as they rolled over the cobblestones.

Alex stared at the horse-drawn cart.

The cart was rough wood, unpainted and weathered. The wheels were iron-rimmed, clattering loud on the stone. The cart bed was loaded with barrels and sacks tied down with rope.

The driver sat on a simple bench seat at the front. He wore a loose linen shirt with the sleeves rolled up. Pants that ended below the knee, showing thick stockings underneath.

The man stared at him and Elias as he approached. His eyes widened and his mouth opened slightly as he took them in.

"Hello," Alex said, raising a hand in greeting.

The man didn't answer. He snapped the reins hard and the horse broke into a trot. The cart picked up speed, rattling past them faster than necessary. Alex watched him disappear around the curve in the street.

"That must be one of the re-enactors they used for this year's Revolutionary War parades," Elias said quietly.

"Maybe." Alex looked in the direction the man had gone.

"Or maybe we're in Dorchester Heights? They've been doing activities all summer."

"Something doesn't add up. Look at the buildings. This isn't Dorchester." Alex shook his head.

The sound of drums reached them from somewhere ahead. Rhythmic and military. Alex recognized the sound immediately. The marching cadence from the Revolutionary War band that had played earlier in the month during the July fourth celebrations.

"Come on." He moved toward the sound, Elias following.

They reached the end of the street and stepped out into a wider thoroughfare. The drumming was louder here. Alex looked left and saw them coming.

Soldiers. A full column of them, marching in tight formation.

They wore red coats with white cross-belts and white breeches. Black boots that came to the knee. Each man carried a musket with a bayonet fixed to the end.

An officer walked alongside the column. His coat had gold braids on the shoulders and cuffs. A gorget hung at his throat, the brass plate catching the light. A sword in a leather scabbard swung at his hip.

A young drummer boy led the column, beating out the march rhythm on a drum almost as big as his torso.

The soldiers marched in step, their boots striking the cobblestones in unison. As they got closer, it became clear their uniforms were British colonial style.

The officer's face was serious and alert. His eyes scanned the street.

They marched past only twenty feet away. Close enough that Alex could smell them. Sweat and powder smoke. Unwashed bodies and damp cloth.

One of the soldiers glanced at Alex and Elias. His eyes widened slightly but he didn't break step. The column marched on, the drumbeat fading as they turned a corner and disappeared.

Elias was staring after them. "It's a reenactment, it has to be."

But Alex wasn't sure. Reenactors didn't usually march through city streets in full gear with no crowd of onlookers. And those soldiers hadn't looked like hobbyists. They'd moved like actual military, their formation tight and disciplined. Not the ragged, old looking volunteers he'd seen during the parades this year.

"We need to find someone," he said. "Find out where we are."

They walked down the wider street. More people were visible now. A woman came out of a building ahead of them carrying a basket over her arm. She wore a dress that brushed the ground, the fabric a dark blue covered by a white apron. A white cap covered her hair, tied under her chin with ribbon.

When she saw Alex and Elias, she stopped walking and her eyes widened. Her gaze traveled from their faces down to their feet and back up again.

Alex realized how they must look in jeans and running shoes. They stood out on the street.

"Excuse me," Alex said, keeping his voice calm and non-threatening. "Can you tell us where we are?"

The woman took a step back, clutching her basket closer. "Boston." Her voice had an accent Alex had never heard before. It sounded English but not, with a hint of something else. The vowels were rounder, the consonants harder. "King Street," she said.

"Boston?" Elias repeated.

"Yes." The woman was still backing away. "I don't know who you are, but you should go. Before the regulars come back through."

She turned and hurried away, glancing back twice before she disappeared into a building.

"King Street," Alex said slowly. "That's the old name for State Street."

"So, we're somewhere near downtown." Elias looked around. "But I don't recognize any of this."

The buildings were wrong. The street was wrong.

They kept walking. The street opened onto a square with a brick building at one end. Alex recognized it immediately.

The Old State House.

But this building looked different. The brick was a darker red, less weathered. The wooden trim around the windows was painted white and looked newer. The balcony where the Declaration of Independence had been read to the people of Boston jutted out from the second floor, its railing solid and unworn.

Except there were no skyscrapers around it.

Alex felt his heartbeat speed up. This couldn't be real.

People moved through the square around them. Men wearing breeches and long coats walked with purpose. Some had tricorn hats. Others wore simpler caps. Their stockings showed beneath the breeches, and their shoes had buckles instead of laces. Women in long dresses moved between the buildings, some with baskets, others with children holding their hands. The children wore simple shifts and breeches. Some of the younger ones were barefoot despite the cool morning.

Every single person was dressed like they'd walked out of a history book.

And every single person who passed Alex and Elias stared.

"Yeah." Alex's training was screaming at him. "Elias, can we be inside a memory construct? Did Aisling create this? Can you tell if this is an illusion?"

He could see Elias reach out with his memory magic and immediately withdraw. "This isn't a construct. Alex, something's really wrong here," Elias said. His voice was shaking. "The memory trace...it's...No, this can't be right."

Alex saw the growing panic in Elias' face. Something was very wrong and he wasn't able to verbalize what he was seeing. That wasn't like Elias at all. Something had unsettled him. He needed to figure out what was going on and adapt quickly.

A man in a leather apron came out of a building near them.

He was middle-aged with graying hair pulled back in a queue at the nape of his neck. When he saw them, he stopped and crossed his arms over his chest.

"You boys lost?" he asked.

"Yes, sir," Alex said. "We're trying to get our bearings. Where are we?"

The man's eyes moved down over their clothing.

"What kind of question is that? You're in Boston. King Street square."

"We know we're in Boston," Alex said. "I'm sorry, we just need to know what the date is."

The man's expression shifted. "You hit your heads or something?"

"Something like that. Please. Just tell us what day it is."

The man studied them for a long moment. His eyes were sharp and assessing. "May seventeenth."

"What year?"

The man's jaw tightened. "What year? 1775, of course."

The words hung in the air between them.

1775.

Alex heard the words but they didn't make sense. His brain refused to process them.

"What did you say?" Elias asked. His voice was barely audible.

"May seventeenth, 1775." The man took a step closer. "Now you tell me. What kind of men don't know what year it is? What kind of clothes are those? Where are you really from?"

"We need to go," Alex said to Elias. "Now."

They walked away quickly, leaving the man staring after them. Alex could feel eyes on them from every direction. People were watching. Some openly. Some pretending not to. All of them registering that something was wrong.

They turned down a narrower street away from the square. Alex's heart was pounding. His hands felt numb.

"Alex, I can feel these people believe it's 1775. They aren't lying."

"I know."

"That's not possible. That doesn't make sense."

Alex didn't answer. He was trying to force his brain to accept what his eyes were seeing.

Every building was wood or brick. Every sign was hand-painted. Every window had thick, imperfect glass. The streets were cobblestone, uneven and worn. Water pumps stood at intervals along the streets. Horses were tied to posts. Carts and wagons moved through the streets carrying goods.

And the smell. Sewage running in channels along the edges of the street. Animal waste. Woodsmoke from dozens of chimneys.

"Alex." Elias had stopped walking. He was leaning against a building wall, his face white. "My magic. It's getting worse. I can feel traces everywhere but they're not present day. They're old. I feel like I'm standing inside a giant memory of the past. It's trying to overwhelm me."

"Can you control it?"

"Barely." Elias pressed his hands to his temples. "When I try to use my magic, my head feels like it's going to explode."

That was a problem. A serious problem. Elias' magic was one of their best defensive tools. If he couldn't use it, they were vulnerable. He reached out to Elias and placed his hand on his shoulder, letting his combat magic ground him. It seemed to work. Elias took a breath and nodded.

Alex forced himself to think tactically. Assess the situation. Accept the reality, no matter how impossible.

They were in what appeared to be colonial Boston. Every detail suggested they were actually in 1775. The man had said

May 17. He vaguely remembered the tour he'd gone on a few months ago. The British attack on Lexington and Concord had happened sometime in the spring of that year. Boston had come under British occupation with a rebel army surrounding it.

If this was real, if they were actually in the past, they had immediate priorities.

"We need shelter," Alex said. "Somewhere we can think without drawing attention."

"Everyone's staring at us."

"Because of our clothes." They marked them as outsiders, as potentially dangerous. "We need period clothing. We need money to buy food and pay for a place to stay. And we need information."

"How do we get any of that?"

Good question. They had no colonial currency. Their modern money was worthless here. Their phones were useless. Their credit cards were plastic rectangles that wouldn't exist for over two hundred years.

They had nothing.

Except their training and each other.

"First we find somewhere quiet to talk," Alex said. "Then we figure out our next move."

A tavern stood on a corner ahead of them. A wooden sign hung from an iron bracket, painted with the image of a green dragon.

The Green Dragon.

Alex stopped.

"What?" Elias asked.

"That's the Green Dragon Tavern." Alex stared at the building. "In our time, it's a historical site. This is where the Sons of Liberty met. Where they planned the Boston Tea Party."

Elias looked at the ordinary building. "So this is real?"

"Yeah."

A man came out of the tavern. He was around fifty with graying hair tied back. He wore a leather apron stained with soot and ash. A blacksmith, probably. He stopped when he saw them, and his eyes narrowed.

"You two look lost," he said.

"We are," Alex admitted. "We're trying to figure out where we are and what's happening."

The man didn't answer right away. He studied them instead, his gaze moving slowly from Alex's shoes to Elias' jacket and back again.

"Where are you from?" he asked.

"Far away."

"Must be." The man's voice was cautious rather than friendly. "I've never seen clothes like that. And your accent's different. Not British. Not French. Not Spanish."

He let the silence stretch a moment.

"So where?"

"It's complicated," Alex said.

"I bet it is." The man glanced up and down the street before looking back at them. "You're drawing attention standing here. That's dangerous." He jerked his chin toward the tavern behind him. "Come inside. We can talk without half the street listening."

He didn't wait for an answer before he turned and walked back through the door.

Alex and Elias exchanged a look.

"Do we trust him?" Elias asked quietly.

"We need help," Alex said. "Information and somewhere private."

"And if he can't help?"

"Let's take this one step at a time."

They followed the man into the Green Dragon.

The interior was dim after the morning light outside. Rough wooden tables filled the room. A few men sat drinking from pewter mugs. Every one of them looked up when Alex and Elias entered. Conversations stalled. Eyes lingered.

The blacksmith led them to a corner table and sat down. He gestured for them to take the bench across from him.

Alex and Elias sat.

"I'm John Freeman," the man said. "My forge is two streets over."

He leaned back in his chair, still watching them.

"Now, tell me why two strangers dressed like that are walking King Street."

Alex weighed his words carefully. They needed help, but the truth would sound insane. "We're travelers," he said. "We got separated from our group. We're trying to find out how to get back."

"Back where?"

"Home."

Freeman waited but Alex didn't elaborate.

"You're in trouble," Freeman said, exhaling slowly. "That much is plain enough. Question is what kind."

"We don't want to cause you any problems," Elias said.

Freeman gave a short, humorless laugh. "Too late for that. The moment you walked in here dressed like that, everyone in this room marked you as strange." He lowered his voice slightly. "And strange men asking questions draw attention. Especially these days."

"We're not spies," Alex said.

Freeman shrugged. "Maybe not. But if the regulars think you are, that won't help you much."

Alex knew he was right. Boston in 1775 would be crawling with suspicion.

"We need help," Alex said. "Information about the city. And we're looking for someone."

Freeman's eyes sharpened. "Who?"

"A woman named Mercy Bishop."

The reaction was immediate, though Freeman tried to hide it. His jaw tightened slightly. "Why?"

"We were told she might be able to help us."

"Help you do what?"

"Understand what's happening to us."

Freeman watched them for a long moment. "Mercy's not in the city," he said at last. "She lives outside Boston, in Cambridge. She moved across the river to Cambridge when the British attacked Lexington and Concord. Getting there means crossing the Charles River. The British control the crossings from this side and they're watching everyone who tries. What makes you think Mercy can help you?"

"We don't know if she can," Elias said. "But we have to try."

"Why?"

Because she was the only lead they had. Because Aisling had said she would guide them. But they couldn't explain that.

"We have a family connection to her," Alex said.

Freeman leaned forward slightly. "You've got bigger problems than finding Mercy." He nodded toward their clothes. "You need something to wear that doesn't make you look like escaped lunatics. You have any of that?"

"No," Alex said.

Freeman grunted. "Then finding Mercy can wait." He glanced around the tavern again. Several men were still watching them. "You're lucky I came out when I did," he said quietly. "Another ten minutes and someone would've gone looking for a patrol."

Alex believed him. "Can you help us?" he asked.

Freeman hesitated. "Maybe." He rubbed a hand across his beard, thinking. "I can lend you clothes. Plain work clothes. That'll stop half the staring. I can point you toward lodging. But money's another matter."

"What do you need us to do?" Alex asked.

Freeman looked at him. "What can you do?"

"I can work," Alex said. "Physical labor, whatever's needed."

Freeman nodded. "You look strong enough. You have any magic in you?"

"Some combat magic. Nothing out of the ordinary," Alex lied.

Freeman turned to Elias. "And you?"

"I can read and write," Elias said. "I'm very good with math." He chose not to mention his memory magic.

Freeman considered that. "Educated, then. That might be useful." He sat back again. "All right. I'll take you to my forge. Get you cleaned up. Find you clothes that won't get you arrested." He pointed a finger at them. "But you keep your heads down. Don't talk about where you're from. Don't ask too many questions. And don't mention Mercy to anyone."

"Why not?" Elias asked.

Freeman's expression hardened. "Because people who ask about her get noticed." He stood. "And being noticed right now is the last thing you want."

Alex rose from the bench. "Thank you."

Freeman snorted. "Don't thank me yet. You might not survive long enough to make it worth the trouble." He headed for the door. "Come on. Let's get you off the street."

They followed Freeman outside. Alex fell into step beside him without a word. Elias kept his eyes down. Neither of them spoke. There was nothing to say that would help.

10

The Shape of Things to Come

"Did you say 1775? That's not possible." Emily still had her hands on Aisling's shoulders. She released her and stepped back, staring at the spot where Alex and Elias had been. Abby was on her knees clutching the journal to her chest.

Aisling got to her feet. She brushed the dirt from her knees and took a step toward the trail.

"Don't you even think about it." Emily's voice cut through the clearing.

Aisling took another step away from them.

Emily grabbed her arm. Purple light flared at Aisling's fingers and Emily thought with absolute certainty that she should let go, that everything was fine, that there was no reason to hold on.

Abby rose from her knees. The ground beneath Aisling's feet rumbled and the wind around them began to blow hard. Emily felt Abby's elemental magic and realized that Aisling had done something to get her to back off. Emily reached for her own elemental magic. She rarely used it for more than small things around the house, but now her power wove together with Abby's, the wind tightening into a spiral through the trees.

Their combined magic created a whirlwind in the forest where they stood, barely visible in the darkness that had now fallen.

Aisling went still. She looked at Abby. Then at Emily.

Emily remembered what Alex and Elias had told them about Aisling's magic, and she knew Aisling could have fought them. But she didn't fight back, and the odd feeling Emily had felt that made her release Aisling was gone.

Emily saw Aisling look over to where Alex and Elias had disappeared. "I owe you an explanation," she said.

"Yes, you do," Emily said. "And it better be the truth or so help me, it will be the last thing you say."

Aisling lowered her hands. The purple light faded. Abby pulled her magic away and the wind stopped as quickly as it had started.

"Let's get back to the house," Emily said.

She pulled Alex's keys from her pocket and walked ahead of them down the trail without looking back.

The drive back took thirty minutes. Abby had tried to call Alex and Elias, but the calls went to voicemail. She tried to ping Elias' location but her phone wasn't able to locate him.

Emily parked in the driveway, got out and unlocked the front door with Alex's key. She held it open as Aisling walked through with Abby following close by.

Abby set the journal on the table in the library and sat on the couch.

"Where are they?" Emily's voice was ice.

"1775. Hopefully here in Boston."

The words didn't make sense. Emily heard her say it in the forest but it couldn't be true. "You're lying."

"I'm not. The portal worked. I saw them go through."

"Bullshit. Time travel isn't real."

Emily pulled her toward the armchair near the window. "Sit down," Emily ordered.

"It is for the fae." Aisling straightened, rubbing her throat. Her voice was barely audible. "My magic works differently."

Emily stood in the middle of the room with her arms crossed. "Time travel," she said. "That's what you're saying happened in the forest."

"Yes."

"And somehow, you can do that?"

"Not normally. Just with the right conditions."

"And the right conditions were Alex and Elias." Emily's voice was very controlled. "Two people who put their careers on the line to hear you out. Who allowed you into this house, fed you and treated you like a guest in their home. When they should have arrested you and instead wanted to help you." She looked at Aisling steadily. "And this is how you repay that trust?"

Aisling met her eyes. "Yes."

"Why?"

"Because of the prophecy," Aisling said. "When the journal wrote itself last night, I recognized it for what it was. My mother told me before she died that portal magic had been woven into the binding of Alice's journals. That they would recognize the Rhys and Llewellyn bloodlines when the time came again."

Abby stared at her. "You're saying the journal was waiting for them?"

"Yes." Aisling paused. "The words appearing the way they did, I knew it was the journal recognizing them. The pulse the journals sent out was a beacon. I have been waiting for that call for a very long time."

"So you decided it was what? Fate?" Abby said.

"It is fate. It was written in that journal hundreds of years ago and it showed itself now."

Abby looked at her. "I still can't accept that any of this is real. Fae, time travel, a portal inside a journal." She shook her head slightly.

"And yet Alex and Elias are gone."

"What are they supposed to do in 1775?" Emily asked.

"Stop the events that led to the destruction of my people," Aisling said. "What happened in 1775 cost the fae everything. If they can change it, my people survive and my Court returns."

"Your Court?" Emily said.

"Yes."

"How do we bring them back?"

"They need a fae with enough power to open the portal from the 1775 side," Aisling said. "Alice's journal is the anchor between both times. Another portal has to be opened on a new moon."

"A fae in 1775," Abby said. "How do they find one?"

"Fae lived openly in society back then. It can't be just any fae, only the fae queen has the knowledge. There was a woman outside Boston at that time. A woman named Mercy. She would know where to find who they need."

"Mercy," Emily repeated. "That's the name from Alice's journal," she said to Abby. The one Alice was looking for, remember?"

"Yes, the one she couldn't find. She called her a seer."

"And on this side," Emily said. "What needs to happen here?"

Aisling pursed her lips. "The same conditions. The journal, a new moon. And a fae queen with the right magic."

"A fae queen? Let me guess, that's you?"

"Yes. My mother was queen of the Seelie Court and I'm her only child—."

Aisling looked at her hands.

"But," Emily said. She had caught something in the pause.

"The conditions on this side need to align with what happens on their end. Both portals need to open at the exact same moment. I know what my mother told me and I know what I felt on that mound." She looked up. "I don't actually know what we need to do."

"So you don't know for certain that they can come back? You're not even sure they're in Boston" Emily said. "Even if they find the fae queen, your mother, in 1775. Even if they convince her that they're from the future and get her to help. You don't actually know what to do from this end."

"No," Aisling said. "I don't know for certain. My mother died during the American Civil War, and my memories of what she told me... may have faded."

Emily crossed the room in four strides. She grabbed Aisling by the front of her shirt and pulled her up out of the chair, walking her back into the library wall hard enough to shake it. She grabbed Aisling's throat with one hand and squeezed just enough to hold her against the wall.

"Emily." Abby was on her feet.

Aisling met Emily's eyes without flinching.

"They trusted you," Emily whispered. "Alex doesn't trust easily and he followed you into that forest. You have any idea how rare that is? Elias looked at you and decided you were worth the risk. You convinced him to trust you, and you used that." Her voice dropped lower. "You used that and now you don't know if they're coming back."

Abby's hand was on Emily's arm. "Let her go."

Emily held Aisling against the wall for another moment before she released her and stepped back.

Aisling straightened her shirt. She didn't return to the chair. "I'm the Queen of the Seelie Court," she said. "The last one. I've spent two hundred and fifty years watching my people scatter and diminish and disappear because of what happened in 1775. I have a Court in exile and a throne to reclaim, and nothing left to reclaim it with."

She looked at Emily. "You want Alex back. I want my people back. I want my birthright. I did what I believed I had to do."

The room was quiet.

"Twenty-eight days to the next new moon," Abby said as she looked at her phone.

"Yes."

"Then we have time." Abby looked at the journal on the table. "You need to tell us everything that happened in 1775. The things that aren't in the history books. Anything that might help us find a way to get them home."

"I can do that. But before I tell you, you need to understand something." She looked between them. "You will learn things about your own families that the Others clearly haven't told you. Information that could place you both in danger. The truth was meant to stay hidden forever."

"My family was still in Spain in 1775," Emily said. "Whatever happened in Boston has nothing to do with my family."

Aisling looked at her but said nothing.

"Mine were here in Boston," Abby said. "But they weren't a notable family. I have a Morgan ancestor who enlisted in the Revolutionary War after the Battle of Bunker Hill. I told Elias about him when we went to the lecture at the museum this year. His name is listed on the roster of the patriots who were part of the siege. But he didn't even fight in that battle."

"You're a daughter of the American Revolution," Aisling said.

"Yes," Abby said. "So what?"

"It connects," Aisling said. "Everything connects."

Emily heard that word again. Others. "Who the hell are these Others you keep referring to?"

"It's a long story," Aisling replied with a wide smile.

11

Two Bloodlines Bound
by More Than Vow

Freeman's forge was a single-story stone building with a roof of wooden shingles darkened by years of smoke. The front was open to the street, showing the fire pit and anvil. Heat poured from the doorway even though the fire had burned down to coals. The smell of hot metal and ash was thick in the air.

"Wait here," Freeman said. He disappeared inside and returned a moment later with folded clothes. "These belonged to my brother. He went to sea two years back and hasn't returned." He thrust the bundle at Alex. "You're about his size."

The fabric was rough homespun linen and wool. Alex took it without comment.

Freeman pulled out another bundle and handed it to Elias. "You're smaller. These were mine before I put on weight." He gestured toward a door at the back of the forge. "There's a room back there. Change and leave your things. I'll see what I can do about getting you somewhere to sleep tonight."

The back room was cramped and dark, lit only by a small window set high in the wall. Alex and Elias changed quickly. The clothes were strange against their skin. The linen shirt had no buttons, just ties at the neck. The breeches fastened below the knee with buckles. Thick stockings went up to meet them. The shoes were leather with brass buckles, stiff and uncomfortable.

Alex pulled the waistcoat on over the shirt. It fit well enough. He glanced at Elias who was struggling with the stock that wrapped around his throat.

"Here." Alex took it from him and tied it properly. The white linen covered Elias' neck and fastened with a small buckle at the back.

Elias touched it and grimaced. "This is awful."

"It's what they wear." Alex finished with his own and stepped back. "How do I look?"

"Like you stepped out of a painting." Elias turned in a slow circle, looking down at himself. "We really are here. This is real."

"Yeah." Alex bent to gather their own clothes. Jeans, shirts, shoes. Evidence of a world that didn't exist yet. "We need to hide these."

They stuffed the bundle behind a stack of wood in the corner and covered it with scraps of leather. It wasn't perfect but it would do for now.

When they came back out, Freeman was banking the fire. He turned to them and nodded. "Better. You'll still draw eyes, but at least you don't look like escaped madmen." He wiped his hands on his apron. "The print shop isn't far. John Llewellyn runs it. He's always looking for help, especially someone who can read and do figures."

Elias went still. "Llewellyn?"

"You know the name?"

"It's familiar," Elias said. "Common name, I suppose."

Freeman gave him an odd look but didn't press. "Come on. He'll be working through midday. Printers keep long hours."

They followed him out into the street. The sun was higher now, warming the cobblestones. More people were out. Women with baskets over their arms, their long skirts brushing the ground. Men in work clothes moving with purpose. A few better-dressed men in proper coats and tricorn hats walked past, deep in conversation.

Alex kept his head down and watched his footing on the uneven stones.

The printing shop was on a corner two streets over. The sign hanging above the door showed a printing press in faded paint. Through the open door, Alex could hear the rhythmic thump of something heavy.

Freeman led them inside.

The shop was larger than Alex expected. The ceiling was high, supported by heavy beams. Sunlight came through tall windows on two sides. The air smelled of ink and paper and something sharper, lye, or some kind of chemical. A massive wooden press dominated the center of the room. A man stood at it, pulling down on the long lever. The press descended with a heavy thump, pressing paper against the type bed below. The man lifted the lever, inspected the sheet, and set it aside to dry.

He was in his thirties, dark-haired and lean, sleeves rolled up and forearms stained with ink. His hands moved without hesitation, each step of the work done in the same order every time.

"John," Freeman called.

The printer's gaze moved quickly across the three of them, settling on Alex and Elias. "Freeman. What brings you by?"

"Brought you a couple of men looking for work. The taller one's strong and can handle labor. The other one can read and write, do accounts."

John Llewellyn set down the lever and wiped his hands on a rag. He crossed the room and stopped in front of them. "Where are you from?"

"We've been traveling," Alex said. "Came up from New York."

"Odd time to be traveling. With the troubles."

"We didn't know how bad it had gotten until we arrived."

"Most people are leaving Boston, not coming to it." John turned to Freeman. "You vouch for them?"

"I vouch that they need help. What they are beyond that, I can't say."

John turned back to Alex and Elias. "I could use someone to help pull sheets and move paper. The work's hard and the pay's not much. Couple of shillings a day if you're good at it."

"We'll take it," Elias said.

John nodded. "Tomorrow morning then. Be here at dawn." He paused. "What are your names?"

"Alexander." Alex held his gaze.

"Elias."

John's eyes moved to Elias and stayed there a moment. "Elias. That's not a common name around here."

"My mother liked it."

"Your mother." John said it slowly. "Where is she now?"

"She passed when I was a child."

John stared at him a moment longer, then turned back to Freeman. "Thanks for bringing them. I'll see they're paid fairly if they work hard."

Freeman clapped Alex on the shoulder. "Good luck to you both. Keep your heads down and you'll do fine." He paused at the door. "John. They're looking for Mercy Bishop. Thought you should know." He nodded once and left, the door closing behind him.

John didn't move. He stood with the rag in his hands, shifting his attention from the door to Alex and Elias. His jaw had tightened but nothing else in his face changed.

"Who are you?" he asked. "Really."

"We told you—"

"You told me what you thought I wanted to hear." He set the rag down on the press. "Nobody asks about Mercy unless they want something." He moved closer. "I'm going to find out who you are."

His magic reached out.

Alex felt it happen. A thread of power extending from John toward Elias. This wasn't something people did in their time. It was considered a violation of privacy and against the law.

The magic touched Elias.

Both men staggered.

John grabbed the edge of the printing press, his face going white. Elias stumbled backward, his hands flying to his temples.

Green light flickered around Elias' fingers.

Silver flared around Alex's hands. He stepped between them without thinking. The silver and green rose together the way they always did, intertwining before he could stop it.

John was breathing hard, staring at the light between them. "What the hell was that?"

"I don't know." Elias' voice was rough. He was still holding his head.

"Your magic—" John stopped and pressed his palm to his forehead. "My head feels like it's splitting."

"Mine too."

John straightened slowly. His eyes settled on Elias. "You're a memory worker."

"Yes."

"Strong. But when I tried to read you something pushed back. Memory magic doesn't do that." He looked at the silver and green light still fading between Alex and Elias. His eyes moved from one to the other and back. "The two of you together." His brow pulled tightly and his gaze shifted between them. "I've only ever seen that combination work that way in one other pairing."

Alex looked at him. "Who?"

John's mouth pressed flat. He picked up the rag from the press and dropped it on the worktable. "You're coming with me."

They followed him through smaller lanes and alleys, climbing uphill. John didn't speak and didn't look back. Alex watched the set of his shoulders the whole way.

John stopped in front of a modest two-story house with a stone foundation and a small garden in front.

"Inside," he said.

The interior was dim. A table, chairs, a fireplace. Dried herbs hanging from the ceiling beams. The smell of lavender and rosemary.

A woman stood at the table kneading dough. She looked up when they entered.

Young, late twenties. Dark hair under a cap. Flour on her forearms. Her attention went to John first, then to Alex and Elias, and her hands went still on the dough.

"This is my wife Alice."

"John?" She wiped her hands on her apron. "Who are these men?"

John closed the door. "Strangers. Looking for work. And for Mercy." He looked at her and pointed at Alex. "Reach out to him. Tell me what you sense."

Alice stared at her husband. Something passed between them without words. Then she moved closer to him and extended her hand, not touching him, just reaching out.

Alex felt her magic brush against his.

Alice's eyes widened. She pulled back. "He's a Rhys."

"I know."

"Strong. How—"

"I don't know." John looked at Elias. "And that one is Llewellyn. Strong memory magic. But when I tried to read him the magic pushed back. Hurt us both."

Alice turned to Elias. She studied his face for a moment. "May I?"

Elias hesitated. Then nodded.

Alice's magic reached out, gentler than John's had been. It touched Elias.

She didn't flinch and Alex saw Elias' magic start to touch hers before he pulled away.

"Interesting," Alice said. Her voice had gone quiet. "He isn't just any memory worker." She turned to her husband. "But did you feel what was underneath before it did?"

John was pressing two fingers to his temple. "Yes."

"The same as ours." Alice looked between Alex and Elias. Her expression wasn't the same as John's. Where John's face had closed, hers had opened. "When our magic touches, it does exactly that. The two lines working together." She looked at them steadily. "You are Rhys and Llewellyn. Both of you."

"That's impossible," John said. "I know every Llewellyn still living."

"Not all of them," Elias said quietly.

The room went quiet.

"What?" John's voice was flat.

"Your magic recognized it. Both of you felt it." Elias met his eyes. "I believe that we're related to you. To both of you."

Alice had gone very still by the table.

"I know my family lines," John said.

"I can't prove it in a way you'd accept right now," Elias said. "But your magic felt it when it touched ours.

John glance toward Alice.

Her eyes turned back toward Alex. "I felt your combat magic. I recognize my Rhys line in you." She looked at Elias. "Same with you, Llewellyn magic. But changed somehow."

John walked to the window and stood with his back to them, looking out at the street. His hands were loose at his sides.

"If you're family," he said without turning, "then you're in trouble. And you need more than work at a printing press."

"We need to find Mercy," Alex said.

"Why?"

"We can't explain that."

John turned back. "You're asking me to trust you. To help you. To risk my family for strangers who won't tell me the truth."

"Yes," Alex said.

John and Alice exchanged looks.

"All right," Alice said. She moved away from the table. "You'll stay here tonight. Tomorrow we'll go to Mercy." She looked at them both. "She's not in the city. She lives across the river in Cambridge, at our farmhouse there. Away from the British and anyone else who might try to use her." Her voice was even.

"We can't ask you to—"

"You're not asking. I'm offering." She looked at them steadily. "If you're family, even distant family, then you're under our protection. That's how it works." She turned to the fire. "You'll eat with us and spend the night here."

Alex let out a breath. "Thank you."

Alice nodded once. "John, show them upstairs."

John gestured for them to follow. They climbed narrow stairs to the second floor, and he pointed to a room on the left.

"I'll bring you some water to wash up." He paused in the doorway. "We'll talk more after you've rested."

The room was small and clean. A narrow bed, a washstand, a window that looked out over the darkened street. Elias sat on the bed and put his head in his hands.

"Still hurting?" Alex asked.

"Yeah." His voice was muffled. "What the hell was that? Why did the magic react that way?"

"I don't know."

"It felt like it recognized John's magic. Like it knew what it was. But when it touched—" He winced. "It just bounced."

"But why?"

Alex sat beside him. "Maybe because we're separated by time. The magic knows we're family but can't connect properly across two hundred and fifty years."

"That doesn't make sense."

"None of this makes sense."

Elias lowered his hands. His eyes were red at the edges. "They believed us."

"They felt it."

"Yeah. They're like us, Alex."

"I know."

They sat in silence, listening to the sounds from below. Alice moving around. The creak of the floorboards. The smell of the stew drifting up from the kitchen.

"We need to be careful," Alex said. "About what we tell them."

"I know."

"No talk about the future. No details about what's coming."

"Agreed."

Alice called from downstairs. The food was ready.

They went down together.

The meal was simple. Bread, cheese, stew that had been on the fire most of the day. John ate without speaking. Alice refilled their cups when they were empty and asked no questions. Afterward, John said it was late and they should all rest.

They went back upstairs. The bed was narrow but they managed, and Elias was asleep within minutes.

Alex stayed at the window a while longer. The street below was empty. A single lantern hung at the corner, its light moving in the wind. He watched it for a while without thinking about anything in particular.

Then he thought about Emily.

He closed his eyes. They had shelter. They had help. They had a way to Mercy.

For now that was enough.

12

Strangers In a Strange Land

They left before dawn. The cart was already loaded when Elias and Alex came downstairs. John and Alice had been up before them. Bundles of clothing were stacked and tied down in the cart bed alongside crates of food and a few tools.

"We were already planning to leave Boston. We've been preparing for a month." John paused. "I hate leaving the press. But Freeman agreed to keep an eye on it." He glanced back at them. "You two almost missed us."

"Freeman didn't mention that you were leaving," Elias said.

"Freeman is good at keeping secrets. We all are these days."

They weren't taking furniture since the farmhouse in Cambridge had what they needed. Elias whispered to Alex, "I'm sensing there are a lot of secrets in this city."

Alex nodded. "This is a dangerous time. Be very careful what you say."

John was checking the harness on the horses while Alice packed a basket near the door.

The cart bed was rough wood. Elias and Alex climbed in and

sat with their backs against the side rails. Alice handed them a blanket without comment.

The sky was still dark when John drove the cart out onto the street. The wheels creaked on the cobblestones. The horse moved at an easy walk, its hooves steady on the stones.

Elias watched the buildings pass. Boston was waking up. Candles lit windows, smoke rose from chimneys. A few people moved through the streets on early business, their breath visible in the cold morning air.

They headed west through the city. Elias tracked their direction as best he could, trying to orient himself against a landscape that looked nothing like the city he knew. The streets were wrong. The buildings were wrong. Everything was compressed and close and dark in ways that felt like a different world entirely, which it was.

Alice sat straight-backed beside John on the bench, her hands folded. She hadn't spoken since they left the house.

After a few minutes John said quietly, "The bridge is ahead. Keep still. Let me handle the talking."

Elias looked past John's shoulder and saw it. The Great Bridge, a long wooden structure spanning the Charles River. Torches burned at the Boston end despite the growing gray of early morning. Soldiers stood at the checkpoint, their red coats dark in the torchlight, muskets shouldered.

"Down," John said.

Elias and Alex hunched lower in the cart bed.

The cart slowed as they approached.

A wooden barrier crossed the road before the bridge. Two soldiers stood guard. One stepped forward as the cart came to a stop.

"Papers."

John produced folded documents from inside his coat and handed them over without a word. The soldier looked them over, glanced at Alice, then at the back of the cart where Elias and Alex sat.

"Who are they?"

"Hired hands. Traveling with us."

"Papers."

John handed over two more documents. The soldier examined them and looked at Elias and Alex.

"Out of the cart. Both of you." They climbed down and watched the soldier lift himself into the cart. "Weapons?" he asked.

"I have no need for weapons," John told him.

The soldier stepped back. His eyes moved to Alex and Elias' hair.

"Your hair. Why is it cut so short?"

"Lice," Elias said. John had told him what to say in case they asked. "Had to cut it all off. It's growing back."

The soldier's face twisted. He took half a step back.

"Both of you?"

"We worked on fishing vessels," Alex said. "Close quarters. When one man gets it the whole crew gets it. We all had to cut our hair or lose our jobs."

The soldier handed the papers back to John and stepped aside.

"Move on."

The barrier lifted.

Once they were back in the cart, John snapped the reins and it rolled forward onto the bridge.

The planks rattled under the wheels. Below them the Charles River moved fast, wide and cold with the spring melt. On the far bank, Cambridge spread out ahead of them, dark and quiet, the farms and houses of the mainland emerging from the morning mist.

Elias didn't let himself relax until they were across and the soldiers were well behind them. Alice sighed deeply and placed her hand on John's shoulder.

They rode in silence for a while.

"How did you get papers for us so fast? I assume they grant passage out of the city?" Alex asked, breaking the silence.

John and Alice exchanged hesitant glances.

"We have friends in the city," Alice said. She didn't offer further explanation.

The road widened beyond the bridge. Farmland opened on either side, fields showing the first green of spring. The sky was lightening toward full morning, pale gold at the horizon.

Elias was in Cambridge. The city he knew was two hundred and fifty years away, but this was the same ground. The roads he knew didn't exist, but the path they were on was familiar. Trees stood where he knew buildings to be.

After a while Alice turned in her seat to look at them. "How is your head? From yesterday."

"Dull ache," Elias said. "Behind my eyes."

"John's was worse last night. There's a healer at the farm. A witch. Her name is Sarah. She's been working with Mercy for years. What happened to you and John when the magic touched is a magical injury, and regular healing doesn't do much for those."

Alex looked at Elias. The word witch sat between them.

"A witch?" Elias asked.

Alice frowned at their expressions. "Why do you look like that?"

"Where we're from," Elias said, "that word means something different. Witches haven't been mentioned since the Salem witch trials. We don't have witches with magic like you describe. They're just part of folklore."

Alice stared at him. "Witches aren't folklore. They're human magic users with specific gifts. Communities of them have been part of this world as long as anyone can remember." She turned further in her seat. "You really don't have them where you're from?"

"The word exists," Alex said. "But not the way you mean it."

Alice looked at John. He kept his eyes on the road.

"Ask us if you need to understand how things work here," Alice said. "We'll tell you what we can. Wherever you're from sounds like a very peculiar place."

They rode in silence for a while. The road curved through a stand of oak trees, their leaves new and pale green.

"Witches," Elias said eventually. "They're recognized. People know about them?"

"Of course." Alice seemed genuinely puzzled that this needed explaining. "Most human magic users work alone. Their gifts are individual. But witches are different. Their magic recognizes other witch magic. When they gather together their intent aligns. Their power flows together." She paused. "Like voices in harmony. Each distinct, but together making something none of them could make alone. Sarah will help with the headache."

The road continued through open farmland. John turned onto a narrower track between two fields, the ruts deep from spring rain. Elias gripped the side rail as the cart bounced and lurched.

"Do you have family?" Alice asked after a while. "Back where you're from."

"We have girlfriends," Alex said.

Alice turned to look at them. "Girlfriends?"

"We're courting a couple of ladies," Elias said. "Both of us."

"Good, you boys should be married by now. What are they like?" she asked.

Alex grinned. "Emily is smart and caring. She'd never hurt a fly but she knows how to stand up for herself. She doesn't miss anything." He paused. "She's also very stubborn. She'd have handled that soldier better than any of us."

Alice smiled. "She sounds formidable. Does she have magic?"

"She has a type of memory magic that lets her work with people who have emotional problems."

"And your sweetheart?" Alice looked at Elias.

"Abigail is beautiful and very smart," Elias said. "Funny and kind. Her elemental magic is pretty powerful, but she only ever uses it to translate old documents. She's a historian. And she and Emily are close friends." He looked out at the passing fields. "She makes me feel like I have a future."

Elias felt Alex's hand give his arm a quick squeeze.

Alice nodded.

John turned onto an even narrower track that opened into a wide clearing.

The two-story farmhouse stood at the center with a stone foundation and weathered wooden walls. Two windows sat on either side of a central door on the ground floor. Stone chimneys billowed at each end of the roof. A barn stood to one side with its doors open.

Elias could smell the flowers as his feet hit the ground. He stretched his legs and looked around the clearing while John dealt with the horse.

He walked toward a well with a wooden roof near the center of the yard.

The stones around the opening were worn smooth at the edges from years of hands gripping them. The wooden roof above it was newer, but the well itself had been there a long time. He could see it in the way the ground had settled around the base of it, the stones slightly sunken, the earth shaped around them over generations.

He put his hand on the stone.

Green light flickered at his fingers before he could stop it. A memory trace surfaced immediately, strong and layered. He pulled his hand back and the trace released.

He straightened and looked out across the clearing, taking note of where he was in relation to the direction they had traveled from the bridge.

He had driven from Boston to Cambridge hundreds of times. He knew the way the land sat relative to the river.

He knew exactly where they were.

"Alex," he said.

Alex was beside him. "What."

Elias looked at the well. "This is the only original piece of it in our time. The only thing left." He put his hand on the stone again, not calling his magic this time, just touching it. "Everything else is different. My house is newer and I don't have a barn. But the well is still there." He looked up at Alex. "In exactly this spot."

Alex was very still. "Your house?"

"Yeah."

He looked at John, who had come up beside them. "You said your family has been here for generations."

"The Llewellyn family has been on this land since the founding of the Massachusetts Bay Colony," John said. "Why?"

"No reason," he said. "Just taking it in. It's a beautiful place." He turned away before John could read anything on his face and headed toward the farmhouse without looking back.

"She knows we're here," Alice said as they approached the front door.

"How?" Alex asked.

"Because she always knows."

133

Elias stood at the edge of the porch. Alex moved to stand beside him.

"You okay?"

"This is it," Elias said. "This is where we find out if we can go home. If there's even a way back."

"We'll figure it out."

"Will we?" Elias looked at him. "What if she can't help? What if we're stuck here?"

Alex didn't answer him.

Elias had been trying not to think about it. About what it would mean to be trapped in 1775; to live out the rest of their lives in a time that wasn't theirs.

Alice pushed the door open and revealed a warm interior with low ceilings. "Come inside."

In the farmhouse, a large fireplace burned low, benches lined each side of a long table, shelves sat along the walls holding crockery, tools, and bundles of dried herbs, and a staircase ran along one side, leading to the upper floor.

A woman came through from the back. Mid-thirties, dark-haired, her sleeves rolled up. She stopped when she saw Elias and Alex.

"Sarah," Alice said. "This is Elias and Alexander. Elias needs your help. I believe he and John suffered a magical injury when John tried to use his magic on him. Poor boy has had a bad headache ever since."

Sarah pointed to one of the benches. "Sit down."

"I don't need healing," Elias said.

Sarah didn't argue. "You have a headache still?"

"It's manageable."

"I'm sure it is." She pulled the bench out from the table. "Sit down."

His eyes pleaded with Alex.

"It's a magical injury," Alex said. "Not the same as regular healing I can't help."

"You don't know that."

"Alice said—"

"You know I don't like strangers using healing magic on me."

Sarah hadn't moved from where she stood. He could see her watching their exchange. "Why do you not like healing magic?" she asked.

Elias looked at her. "It's intrusive."

"Mine isn't." Her voice was matter-of-fact. "Witch healing doesn't work by entering a person's mind or consciousness. It uses our magic collaboratively to speed up healing." She looked at him and smiled. "I'm not going to feel anything you don't want me to feel. That's not how this works."

Elias shifted on his feet.

He sat down and looked up at Alex who gave him a knowing nod. Alex would interrupt Sarah if he sensed anything was wrong.

Sarah moved between him and Alex, her hands hovering near his head without touching. Her magic reached out and he braced for the intrusion that didn't come. It was exactly what she had said. Warm and distant, dissolving the pain without touching his thoughts. It simply moved through the surface, and the ache behind his eyes faded and was gone.

He sat with it for a moment after she stepped back.

It was nothing like Alex's healing magic which was something else entirely. His magic was intimate and focused. The kind that only worked because of the trust between them. Sarah's was competent and clean and completely impersonal.

"Better," Sarah said. Not a question.

"Yes," Elias said. "Thank you."

Sarah nodded and stepped back. She looked at Alice. "She's in the garden. She's been there since first light."

"Are you ready?" Alice asked.

They followed her through the back of the house into a kitchen garden larger than the one in front. Beds of herbs and vegetables in neat rows. An old apple tree in the corner, its blossoms fully open.

A woman sat on a wooden bench beside the apple tree.

She was older, sixty or more. Her hair was gray and pulled back simply. She wore a plain dress and apron. Her feet were bare on the grass.

She was looking out across the garden when they came through the door, hands resting open in her lap. When she heard them she raised her head and looked directly at Elias and Alex for a long moment without speaking.

Then she smiled.

"I have been waiting for you," she said. "For a very long time."

13

A Duty To The Future

Mercy didn't ask them to sit down the way Sarah had. She simply turned from the bench and walked back toward the farmhouse and expected them to follow. They did.

She led them through the kitchen and into a small room off the main hall. A table, four chairs, a single window that looked out over the side garden. An open journal sat near an ink bottle, a quill resting across the page. She sat at the head of the table and looked at them both for a long moment before she spoke.

"I've seen you in my visions. Two men who don't belong to this time."

"How long have you known we were coming?" Elias asked.

"Long enough." She folded her hands on the table. "I see what will be and what has been, and sometimes what is happening at a great distance. It isn't a precise gift. The visions come in pieces, and I spend a great deal of time discerning their meaning. What are your names?"

"I'm Elias Sinclair. My mother was a Llewellyn."

"I'm Alexander Sutton. I descend from the Rhys. Also through my mother."

She looked at Elias. "You, I have been seeing for three years. Your face and your magic. Memory work, old and powerful, coming from a time that does not yet exist." She paused. "I didn't understand it until now."

"Three years?" Alex said.

"It takes time for visions to clarify. Your face came later. Combat magic, correct? A shield over everything around you." She tilted her head slightly. "And something else in you that you keep hidden."

Alex said nothing.

"Tell me what year you are from. And tell me how you got here," Mercy said.

Elias told her. He kept it plain and as brief as he could. The journals, Aisling, the earthwork, and the portal. And he told her the year. He watched her face as he spoke and her expression didn't change much.

"2026?" she said.

"Yes."

"Well over two hundred years from now." She said it to herself more than to them. "She sent you back a long way. I hadn't realized that the fae held this kind of magic." She reached for a sheet of paper, dipped the quill, and began to write.

"You know the fae?" Alex asked.

"Of course. I know several Seelie Court members. And I know its queen, Sereliana." She looked at the table. "I know what is coming for them. What is coming for all of us." Her eyes lifted. "Is that why you're here? To prevent it?"

"We don't know anything," Elias said. "Aisling said that we needed to stop what happens to her people."

"Did she tell you what happens?"

"She didn't give details. Just that we needed to find you and stop whatever is going to happen."

Mercy frowned. "It sounds like Aisling acted in haste. It

would have been better if you understood what she expected you to change. Regardless, what has been written cannot be unwritten. Only the Almighty can do that. The fae don't believe in our God, you know. They have their own ways of knowing." She paused. "That does not mean your presence here cannot change things. It means the change may not be the one you came for."

Elias felt his headache trying to return. This was too cryptic for him to wrap his mind around.

Alice appeared in the doorway with a tray of bread, jam, and three cups of cider. She set it down without speaking and left. Mercy waited until her footsteps moved away down the hall.

"Tell me about the woman," she said. "Aisling. What did she seek to gain by sending you here?"

Alex answered, "She said something was happening, and one of the Courts chose wrong and they were all punished for it."

"She told you the fae are victims in what is coming? That they bear no responsibility for it?"

"She said her people were innocent," Elias replied.

"That is not completely untrue," Mercy said. "The Seelie are not responsible for what the Unseelie choose. But the Courts have been interfering in human affairs for millennia, perhaps longer. They value their position and influence among those who rule." She turned her gaze toward the window. "The Seelie more quietly than the Unseelie. But the desire isn't absent from either Court.

"They don't sound very different from us," Alex said.

Elias nodded. "No, but add the fact that their magic is more powerful and we have a dangerous combination."

Though lately it does seem that the Unseelie have been whispering in ears and moving pieces on a board most people cannot see." She looked back at them. "The British and the Unseelie Court have been moving toward each other for some time. What is coming isn't a simple persecution of the innocent. It's the collapse of something long under strain." She reached for the ale. "I don't say this to excuse what may come. Only to make you understand that there are many sides to this war. We aren't just fighting the British for our independence."

"Can it be stopped?" Alex asked.

"I don't know," Mercy said. "I've seen the battle. I've seen what happens after." She turned back toward the window again. "I haven't seen it unfold in any other way."

The room was quiet.

Elias picked up the cider and put it down without drinking. "Can you help us get home? Back to our time."

Mercy sighed as she met his eyes. "I cannot. You will need to meet Queen Sereliana. She isn't difficult to find if you know where to look. For the present, she remains close." Her gaze settled on him. "But finding her and persuading her to aid you are not the same matter. She has no reason to trust men she has never seen before. Not now, with events shifting as they are. The siege of Boston and the war itself are altering the balance quickly."

"Alice and John could take us to her?" Alex asked.

"Possibly. Alice and John have standing with the Seelie, as do all the Llewellyn and Rhys. That will serve you." She paused. "But that conversation comes later. There are things I must understand about you first."

"Your magic," she said to Elias. "The memory magic I know. And I see the bond between you and Alexander. I've worked alongside Llewellyn and Rhys long enough to recognize it." Her eyes narrowed slightly. "Yours is the same... but there is something beneath it I haven't seen in that line."

Elias felt his heart rate increase. "What?"

"It is elemental," she said, tilting her head. "Very strong. You are afraid of it." Elias exhaled deeply. For a moment, he thought she was going to say something horrible. "I can't control it. It comes out when I don't want it to."

"When you are afraid," she said.

"Whenever I've been in danger and not able to defend myself," Elias said. He looked at Alex who placed a hand on his shoulder and squeezed tightly before lowering it again.

Mercy nodded slowly.

"That isn't a Llewellyn gift. And it isn't a Rhys gift either, though the Rhys combat magic is technically a form of elemental magic." She was quiet for a moment, looking at her own hands. "I know every magical lineage that has touched the Llewellyn and Rhys lines. It has been my family's responsibility to record the lines that carry old magic." She raised her eyes. "The magic I see in you, Elias, is witch magic. A very powerful one. No Llewellyn or Rhys has taken a witch into their line. I am certain of this. That was a decision made when the families first made their alliance."

Elias didn't respond right away. A week ago he would have dismissed that outright.

"Then where does it come from?"

"I don't yet know." Her tone didn't change. "But I intend to find out before you leave this place. You must understand what I am telling you." She held his gaze. "The old bloodlines don't mix by accident. The families know each other. They keep records. For witch blood to appear in a Llewellyn means someone made a choice to hide their heritage and join with the line by design."

Elias felt his heart racing so fast it almost hurt.

Alex was very still next to him.

"Why?" Elias asked.

"That is the question." Mercy focused her eyes on him. "What would a witch gain from a Llewellyn bloodline carrying that magic without knowledge or training? What would it produce that could be of use?" She paused and looked off to the side. "I don't have the answer. But you sit before me with elemental power greater than any I have seen outside a trained coven, and you don't know its origin or how to command it." She leaned back slightly. "I didn't expect this."

The morning light had shifted while they talked. Elias could hear Alice moving somewhere in the house, the sound of something being set down on stone. Through the window, the kitchen garden was bright in the late morning sun.

He thought about the DMA watching him in Chicago. The way Deputy Director Rowan had only required him to register the elemental magic he had kept hidden and ensured that no one questioned it. She knew his magic was anchored by Alex and that he wouldn't be disciplined for keeping his elemental magic a secret. She didn't consider him a threat.

Did she know about this witch magic and was protecting what she considered a government asset?

"Can you teach me?" he asked. "What you know about this elemental magic. While we're here."

Mercy looked at him for a long moment. "I can try. Witch elemental magic is meant to be practiced in a coven, not alone. What you have isn't quite the same as what I work with. But the principles are similar." She paused. "It will take time, and it will require you to be honest with yourself about what calls that power forward. That isn't always comfortable."

"I'll be fine."

"Will you?" Her voice had sharpened. "I think you say that often, even when you know it not to be true."

Alex made a sound that was almost a laugh.

"You find that amusing," Mercy said.

"I find it accurate," Alex said.

Mercy's expression softened slightly. "You know him well. Enough for now," Mercy said as she stood. "Come and eat something proper. Sarah has been cooking since you arrived. And I can hear your stomachs from here."

The afternoon passed slowly. Sarah fed them, and John came in from the barn and listened while Mercy asked them more questions, different questions this time, about the world they had come from. What magic looked like. How it was governed. Who held the power over it.

Elias answered carefully, keeping the future vague when he could. But Mercy was precise in what she asked, and hard to deflect.

He and Alex had agreed not to tell anyone they were from the future, but Mercy had other ideas and made it clear that John and Alice needed to know.

"A government body," she said. "That registers and tracks magic users."

"Yes."

"And who runs it?"

"The Department of Magical Affairs. It reports to the federal government."

"When was it created? We're still fighting for our independence from the crown."

Elias glanced at Alex. "I don't know the full history of how it was founded."

Mercy looked at him. "I suspect you know more than you're saying."

"I really don't. We learn that stuff in school and in training, but I don't think most people remember when anything in the government was created. I mean, except for Independence Day."

Alex kicked him under the table.

Elias felt it and didn't look at him.

Alice asked, "Independence day? So we will gain our independence?"

"Yes." What could it hurt to tell them, he thought. They were already aware they were talking to time travelers. What harm could come from knowing they win the war or the government system that follows. It had already happened.

"Thank the Lord," Alice said.

Alex was staring at him, and not in a good way.

Mercy accepted that and moved on. But Elias could see her filing it, placing it somewhere in the larger picture she was building.

In the mid-afternoon, she took him out to the kitchen garden alone. She walked between the herb beds slowly and he walked beside her in the warm sun.

"Tell me about your elemental magic," she said. "Tell me when it comes."

He told her about the crime scene. The wolf attack. Alex going down. The shields shattering. The moment he understood that Alex was in real danger.

"And before you could think, it emerged," she said.

"I didn't call it. I didn't even know I could do that. My elemental magic has surfaced a few times before but just as wind and air."

"That is the problem," she said. "It comes from the part of you that acts before thought. That is where the power lives. But it is also where the least control lives." She stopped beside an old rosemary bush and broke off a small sprig, turning it in her fingers. "What you need to understand is that the magic isn't separate from you. It isn't a force that erupts against your will. It is you. The most honest part of you, the part that does not stop to consider consequence." She looked at him. "That part knows exactly what it values. It isn't confused about what it is protecting."

"Alex," Elias said without hesitation.

"Yes. And now that you understand that, we can start to work with it instead of against it." She turned back toward the house. "Not today. Today you have had enough to absorb. But while you are here I will work with you."

He walked beside her back toward the house. The garden smelled of rosemary and something sweet he couldn't identify.

"How do you know so much about the families?" he asked. "The Llewellyn and Rhys lines specifically."

"Because they matter," she said simply. "The memory keepers and the shield bearers. They have been part of this world's magical architecture for two thousand years. A seer who doesn't understand the oldest lines isn't doing her work." She paused at the garden door. "And because the journals exist. I've read some of them. There are things in those records that most people have forgotten and some that were never widely known to begin with."

"But some of the journals are warded to my bloodline."

"No, they're not." Mercy stopped and met his eyes. "Some are in an old Welsh I don't read and some in Latin. But none are warded. Are you saying the journals in your time are?"

"Yes."

"Interesting. I had never considered that warding them might be a good idea."

"The journals talk about the future," Elias said. "About Alex and me."

"Not precisely. They talk of your ancestors." She opened the door. "The prophecy that appeared in the journal. You have read it."

"Yes."

"Do you remember what it says? Do you know who wrote it?"

He thought about the poem. The revenants unbidden. What was written. "Not really, and no I don't know who wrote it. It's in Alice's journal but the handwriting wasn't hers," he said.

"The part you don't understand yet is the part about defenders," she said. "You will. Before you leave here, you will." She went inside.

He stood in the doorway for a moment looking back at the garden. The apple tree in the corner. The neat rows of herbs.

The light was going amber through the kitchen windows when a knock came at the front door.

Elias heard voices in the hall and John came through with a man behind him.

He was younger than John, mid-twenties, broad across the shoulders. He wore plain work clothes and carried his hat in his hands. He stopped in the doorway when he saw the room.

"Thomas," Alice said. "How is Abigail doing?"

"She is well, thank you for asking." He looked at Elias and Alex. "I see you have guests. My apologies for the intrusion."

"Nonsense, come in," Mercy said.

"Thomas Morgan," John said, looking to Elias and Alex. "A neighbor and good friend."

Morgan pulled out a chair and sat. Alice set cider in front of him without being asked.

"Thomas, these are cousins of ours, Alexander Sutton and Elias Sinclair."

"A pleasure to meet you both," Thomas said with a nod.

Morgan turned the cup in his hands. "My unit is being assigned to the perimeter positions of the city. I was hoping you would check in on Abigail once I deploy there. I don't want her to be alone."

Alice answered without hesitation, "Of course, Thomas. I will go check on her every day and make sure she is well. I promise we will protect her if any trouble comes this way."

"Thank you, Alice. I knew I could count on you and John to help. You are good people."

"Where are you from originally?" Alex asked.

"I was born here in Cambridge. My wife and I have a house not far from here." He looked at Elias. "How are you related to John?"

"I'm related to Alice through my mother," Alex answered.

"And you're a Rhys through your mother as well?" he asked Elias.

"No. My mother was a Llewellyn."

Morgan was quiet a moment. "My wife's family has known the Llewellyns and the Rhys' a long time. Her grandmother used to say they kept the old promises." He looked at the table. "She said that one day they'd be needed again."

Elias didn't know what to say. He was starting to think everyone except him and Alex knew about their family history. And then he realized something.

"Thomas, did you say your wife's name is Abigail? Abigail Morgan?" he said.

"Yes."

Elias remembered Abby telling him about her ancestor. The Abigail she was named after and her husband who had fought in the Revolutionary War. His name had been in the register Abby showed him. Soldiers who fought alongside George Washington in New York.

"Where will you go after Boston? Do you know?"

"Well, assuming we can drive the redcoats from here, I assume I will go south to continue the fight with the Continental Army."

This had to be Abby's ancestor, he thought.

Morgan stood. "I better get home to Abigail. You folks have a good night now."

The door closed.

Elias smiled to himself.

Alex looked at him. "Is he—"

"I think so," Elias said.

Alex kept his eyes on him. Elias knew he wanted to talk about it. But this wasn't the conversation to have now, not with John,Alice, and Mercy in the room.

Mercy sat down in the chair Morgan had left. She folded her hands on the table.

"He will make his own choice," she said. "That is how it has to be."

Elias had no idea what she was referring to, and he was too tired to ask. He picked up his cider and drank.

Mercy looked at him from across the table. "Tomorrow we start on your elemental magic."

He nodded.

"And tomorrow," she added, "you will tell me about the woman in your life."

He raised an eyebrow at her.

"I told you," she said. "Pieces. I've been seeing pieces for three years."

Alex picked up his cider and said nothing. But Elias could hear him trying not to laugh.

14

The Fae

Emily wanted to punch Aisling.

She thought of herself as a rational person not inclined to violence. She was the person who calmed people down when they were spiraling, but in that moment she wanted to cause serious bodily harm to the bitch. Abby must have seen it because she came up behind her and grabbed both her arms.

It was after midnight by the time Emily had demanded to know who the Others were. Aisling had looked at her and said it was a long story. That it wouldn't make sense without context. That if they wanted the truth, she needed to start at the beginning.

"Tomorrow," Abby said. "Eight o'clock."

Aisling had nodded and reached for her jacket.

Neither of them offered to let her stay. There was no chance of that. Emily and Abby stood in the front hall until the door shut behind her and they heard her on the porch calling for a cab.

She read Alice's entries again with the book open on the table in front of her, one hand against her forehead, trying to catch something she had missed the first time. Some detail. A name.

Anything that would tell her where Alex and Elias had gone beyond the impossible fact that they were somewhere in 1775.

She found nothing new.

When she finally went upstairs, she slid into bed and stared at the dark ceiling for a long time.

"Where are you?" she whispered into the room. "Are you okay?"

She prayed before she fell asleep. A plea into the dark for Alex to come home.

The house was too quiet. She made coffee and sat at the kitchen table with her phone in front of her, staring at the screen as if Alex's name might suddenly appear on it.

Abby came downstairs a little after seven, her hair loose around her shoulders. She poured coffee and sat across from her.

"What if she doesn't come back? What if she disappears? We never should have let her out of our sight, Em."

Emily had already gone through that possibility in bed. Aisling had what she wanted for now, but the journals were still here.

"She'll come back," Emily said. "Those journals are the only link she has to whatever she thinks is supposed to happen. She won't stay away"

At 7:50 the doorbell rang.

Emily set down her mug and stood immediately. Abby was already moving toward the front hall. Aisling stood on the porch, her long red hair loose over one shoulder. She looked rested. Emily had no idea how that was possible.

They led her into the library.

Aisling took the same armchair by the window as if nothing

had happened. Abby sat on the couch, while Emily remained standing for another moment.

"The Others," Emily said. "Start there."

Aisling looked at her. "I told you, I need to start from the beginning or it won't make sense."

"Then start from the beginning," Abby said.

Aisling folded her hands in her lap.

"The fae have always existed," she said. "We're not aliens or spirits. And we're not some folklore humans invented to explain strange things in the woods. We're a people. A different race of beings."

Abby frowned. "So you're human."

"Maybe once," Aisling said. "Maybe from the same origin long ago. No fae would call themselves human."

"But you look like us," Abby pressed.

She tilted her head. "Do we? Yes, we're good at that, aren't we."

Emily saw Abby open her mouth to ask more questions and cut in before the conversation could drift.

"Save that for later," Emily said quickly. "Tell your story."

"Thousands of years ago, the fae decided to make themselves known to humans. You had magic of your own and you were spreading quickly across the world. The old stories say the queens of both Courts believed it was better to be seen openly than discovered and feared later."

Emily sat down beside Abby on the couch. She had a sudden, sinking sense that Aisling hadn't been exaggerating when she called this a long story.

"There was one pact that mattered above all others," Aisling said. "The Seelie and the Unseelie both swore that the fae would not interfere in human affairs. That was the foundation of everything. As long as we held to it, we could live alongside humans and be tolerated. Sometimes more than tolerated. In some places we were welcomed."

"And it held?" Abby asked.

"For a long time."

"And then someone broke it," Emily said.

Aisling's expression didn't change. "The Unseelie Court aligned itself with the British once it became clear the colonies were moving toward open conflict with the crown. When that was discovered, humans didn't separate one Court from the other. They didn't stop to ask who had actually acted. They decided the fae had betrayed them. All of us."

"How was it discovered?" Abby asked.

"The Sons of Liberty had been watching for months. They suspected fae involvement with the British long before they could prove it. When the proof came, the story spread faster than anyone could contain it." Aisling glanced toward the window. "It didn't matter that the Seelie had nothing to do with it. We were fae. That was enough."

Emily leaned forward slightly. "What happened?"

"People who had known us for years stopped recognizing us as neighbors." Aisling's voice stayed even. "My mother, Queen Sereliana, and her Court, was in Boston when it started. She had moved some of our people to America a hundred years earlier in the hopes of getting away from the problems in Ireland and England. She wanted more open space, and America seemed like the perfect place. She made friends there. Humans who knew what she and our people were and didn't care. She was friends with farmers and tradesmen. It wasn't like she lived in a palace separate from the population." She paused. "When the accusations started, those same people came looking for us."

Abby was still. "Looking for you, how?"

"To kill us."

Aisling lowered her eyes to her hands.

"They hunted us like animals."

Emily felt Abby shift beside her.

"What did she do?" Abby asked.

"She sent word to John and Alice Llewellyn. Their families, the Rhys' and Llewellyns, had standing with the Seelie that went back generations. We call their lines the defenders, because they came to our aid."

"That's what you call Alex and Elias," Abby said.

Aisling's voice softened. "Yes. My mother told me that the two lines had a special bond of magic and they were defenders. She told me that one day I would hear their magic call to me and that I should go to them. That they would change everything."

Emily wanted to say that sounds convenient, but she held it back. Aisling had already shown she was willing to build an entire plan on what she believed was fate. Emily didn't want to give her an opening to disappear into prophecy again.

"How did you survive?" Abby asked. "After people came after you?"

"There was a cave outside the city. I don't remember where; I was a child. My mother sent some of us out before the worst of it began. Families, children, anyone too young to fight or too important to lose." She paused. "I was ten years old."

Emily turned toward Abby.

"That's what we saw," Emily said. "In Elias' construct. The clearing with the women and the people hiding."

"Yes," Aisling said. "That was the beginning of it."

Abby leaned forward, elbows on her knees.

"What actually triggered it?" Abby said. "The patriots turning on the fae. Something specific had to happen."

Aisling didn't answer immediately. "There was a battle," she said. "The Battle of Bunker Hill."

Abby glanced at Emily. They both knew the battle.

"My mother never told me the details. She said that the

Unseelie were seen. That someone watched them working during the battle and understood what they were doing." She paused. "I only know what I remember and what she told me. She tried to protect me from the worst of it, but a ten-year-old sees more than her mother thinks."

"What do you remember?" Emily asked.

Aisling looked back toward the window.

"Fire," she said. "We were still in Boston then. My mother kept a house near the waterfront. I remember the sky turning orange. You could see the glow from the upper windows. I asked her what was burning and she said it was Charlestown. The town across the river." Her voice dropped a fraction. "I remember asking her why and she said that sometimes fires start and no one can stop them."

Abby stared at her. "The battle of Bunker Hill? That was the start of the persecution of your people?"

"She said the moment the patriots understood fae magic had been used in the battle, there was no going back."

Abby's brow tightened. "Did the fae start the fire that burned Charlestown, or did they do something else to help the British win the battle?" Abby asked.

"She never said, and if she knew, she kept it from me." Aisling looked at her hands. "It didn't matter after a while. It was a story that spread and grew, and by the time it reached most people it had become something larger than what actually happened."

"And the Seelie paid for what the Unseelie did," Emily said.

"Yes."

For a moment nobody spoke. Then the red journal on the table began to glow.

Abby reached for it before Emily registered what was happening. She opened the journal to the page she had book-marked, the blank pages that had followed Alice's last entry.

Light spread slowly across the parchment. Letters began to form, dark ink appearing one by one out of thin air.

Emily leaned in to look at it. Aisling stayed where she was, but leaned forward in the armchair, her attention fixed on the words.

The lines formed slowly enough for Emily to read them as they appeared.

> *Across the fractured tide,*
> *Two bloodlines bound by more than vow.*
> *What time and war divide,*
> *The bond alone will not allow.*

The writing stopped as suddenly as it had started. The glow faded but didn't disappear entirely.

"That's a continuation," Abby said. "And it's not Alice's handwriting."

"No," Aisling said. "It isn't hers."

"Then who's writing in her journal?" Emily said.

"Someone who is with them," Aisling said. "Someone who has access to the journal in 1775." She paused. "It has to be someone from the Llewellyn or Rhys line."

"Someone in Alice's family?" Abby said.

"Possibly."

Abby kept staring at the lines. "The journal connects both sides of the timeline. Whatever is written there appears here."

"It seems that way."

"It's showing us what's happening."

"Not exactly in real time," Aisling said. "Time doesn't move the same through portal magic. What appears here might be happening in that moment in their time, or it may have happened years from now in their perspective."

Emily looked from the page to Aisling. Her voice rose. "So, we could watch this for hours and they could be living through weeks."

Aisling didn't answer.

"They could be dying while we wait for this thing to decide when to tell us about it," Emily said, standing up.

"We don't know that," Abby said.

"No," Emily said sharply. "We don't know anything. We don't know exactly where they are. We don't know if they're safe. We don't know how to get them back."

No one said anything.

Abby looked back at the page. "What does it mean?" she asked Aisling. "The poem. What's it talking about?"

Aisling rose from the chair at last and came toward the table. "I think it's a prophecy, not just a poem. The fractured tide is the break in time. The portal I presume." She paused. "Two bloodlines bound by more than vow obviously refers to the bond between the Llewellyn and Rhys lines. It's older and deeper than any formal agreement between families. It's in the blood itself."

She looked up. "What time and war divide, the bond alone will not allow. That line I don't quite understand."

Abby spoke up. "It means the bond between them holds. That nothing, not time or war, can break what those two lines share. I've seen the phrasing used in other documents."

"It's talking about Alex and Elias," Emily said.

"Yes," Aisling said. "I believe so."

Emily looked at the journal. She thought about Alex somewhere in colonial Boston with no phone and no way to reach her.

"They arrived," she said. "Someone knows they're there and they're writing about it."

"Yes," Aisling said.

Emily reached for Abby's hand.

"They're alive."

15

Elemental

Alex woke to sunlight filling the room and the sound of roosters crowing. For a second he forgot where he was.

He turned his head.

Elias was awake and sitting on the edge of his bed. Elbows on his knees. Looking at the floor.

"You sleep at all?"

Elias shook his head. "You?"

"Some. I was dreaming about our case with the werewolf."

Alex sat up, pushing a hand through his hair. He stayed there a second, watching Elias. "You okay?"

"I'm fine."

"No, you're not. You'd never pass up a chance to tell me werewolves don't exist."

Elias didn't respond.

Alex stood and reached for the clothes folded over the chair. "You've been quiet since last night."

"That's because there's nothing to say."

"You're joking, right?"

Elias finally met his eyes.

"We're in 1775," Alex said.

Elias stared out the window.

"I still can't believe this is happening."

Alex finished dressing, then leaned back against the wall and crossed his arms.

"Are you absolutely sure we're not in someone's memory construct?"

No answer.

"Your father believed what was happening in the one you created last year."

Elias grimaced.

Alex walked over and sat next to Elias. "He couldn't tell the difference, and in his mind weeks had passed."

"We're not in a memory magic construct," Elias said.

"You're sure."

"Yes."

"How?"

Elias sighed. "Because according to the DMA I'm the only one who can do something like that. And because I'd know. I've been extending my magic through this place. Nothing here says it's fake."

Alex nodded once. "Okay."

Elias stood and reached for his clothes.

"The witch thing," Alex said. "You haven't said a word about it since Mercy told you."

Elias stopped. "No."

"Elias."

"It's nothing."

"It's not nothing."

Elias pulled his shirt on. "She's wrong."

"You don't know that."

"I do." Elias stared at the wall. "A week ago I didn't think witches were real. And now she's telling me that's what my elemental magic is." He shook his head once. "If it is," Elias said, "then where did it come from?"

Alex didn't answer.

"Llewellyn doesn't have it. Rhys doesn't have it. I don't know."

Alex already knew where this was going.

Elias spoke again, quieter. "You think he had anything to do with it?"

"Your father?"

Elias let out a breath. "Wouldn't put it past him."

Alex pushed off the wall. "Hey. Look at me."

Elias turned toward him.

"We don't know that," Alex said. "You're filling in the blanks with no evidence. That's not like you. At this point, we have no way to know where that bloodline came from. And it doesn't change what we do next."

Elias nodded.

"We've got one problem to solve," Alex said.

"Getting back to our time."

"Exactly. And that starts with meeting the fae queen and asking her to help us get home. Everything else can wait."

Elias exhaled. "Yeah, of course you're right. This is just a lot to take in at one time."

Alex moved toward the door, then paused. "I would kill for a decent latte."

Elias smiled at that.

"Let's go see what's for breakfast," Alex said. "I want to ask Mercy about the werewolves that Aisling mentioned."

As they walked out the door he heard Elias say, "We've traveled back in time and your pressing question for Mercy is about werewolves?"

The smell scent of toasted bread and coffee drifted up the stairs.

Alex slowed a step in front of Elias. "If that's what I think it is, I'm lowering my expectations now."

Elias moved around him and went ahead into the kitchen.

Alice was already there, setting out plates. John stood near the hearth with a pan. Mercy sat at the table with a cup in front of her.

"You're up," Alice said.

"Yeah," Alex replied.

"Sit, I've just finished."

Alex took the chair across from Mercy. Elias sat beside him.

Alice set down bread, a small crock of butter, and a dish of jam. John brought the pan over and set it in the middle of the table.

There was a bowl of porridge near the end, steam still rising.

Alex picked up the cup in front of him, took a sip, and set it back down.

Elias reached for the bread.

"Was the message sent?" Alex asked.

John nodded. "Just after first light. It will be delivered soon."

No hesitation.

"When will we hear back?" Alex asked.

"If she chooses to answer, we will know today," Mercy said.

Elias kept his focus on his plate as he ate.

Alice glanced between them. "You should both eat more than that."

"We're good," Alex said.

"This is good, thank you," Elias said

John pulled out a chair and sat. "There are more people in

town this morning. Messengers, militia, everyone's moving through Cambridge now."

Alex tilted his head. "That's normal?"

"It is now with the redcoats holding Boston," John said. "No one will look twice if you're with us."

Elias nodded. "That's good. We don't need the attention."

Alex picked up the cup again, hesitated, then took another sip.

A horse galloped toward the yard, hidden by the tree line. He was in the yard with John, helping carry water from the well, when the rider came through the tree line and pulled up hard.

A young man that couldn't be a day over sixteen jumped off the horse and bowed slightly. He looked at John and held out a folded note without speaking.

John read it and looked at Alex.

"She will see you," John said. "This afternoon."

Alex set down the bucket. "All of us?"

"You, Elias, Alice, and Mercy." John folded the note. "She said to come before the light goes. I'm invited as well but I have other matters to tend to."

They started walking toward the house.

"Please don't think I'm abandoning you," he added with a chuckle.

Alex, laughed. "I didn't think that until you said it."

Elias was in the garden with Mercy when Alex found them. He came around the corner and stopped.

Elias was standing with both hands open at his sides, his

eyes closed. A faint yellow light moved at his fingers, not the green of his memory magic. Mercy stood a few feet away watching.

The magic faded when Alex stepped onto the gravel path.

Elias opened his eyes. "I heard the horse. Will she see us?"

"This afternoon."

Mercy looked at Elias. "We continue tomorrow."

Elias nodded. He stared at his hands for a moment and then dropped them.

"Your magic looked different. I don't think I've ever seen it like that," Alex said as they walked back toward the house.

"Actually you have. When my elemental magic flares out of control it emerges with a flash of yellow," Elias said. "It happens fast and merges with my memory magic."

"Hmm. How did I never notice?"

"Because you've always been fighting for your life when I've used it, remember? You're not paying attention to me so you miss it."

"I'm always paying attention to you. It must happen very quickly." He smiled at Elias. "How did it go?"

"Okay, I guess. I didn't set the house on fire." He paused. "Mercy says it runs on emotion. That I have to find a way to use the feeling without being overwhelmed by it."

"Can you do that?"

Elias shot him a skeptical smirk. "Ask me again in a month."

16

Things Long Forgotten

They left at two in the afternoon. Alice walked with them as Mercy led them through Cambridge on paths that ran behind properties and between fields rather than along the main road. The afternoon was warm and the paths were quiet. They passed a woman hanging washing between two posts who looked up and waved. Two men on horseback came toward them from the direction of the river, and Alex stepped off the path to let them through, keeping his eyes down. The riders didn't look twice.

Alex noted what he could as they walked. A farmhouse with a red door. A stone boundary wall that ran east toward the river. A cluster of apple trees spread wide enough to shade the path beneath them. Landmarks he might need in the coming days.

The Charles River came into view through the trees after twenty minutes. Mercy turned south along the bank and they followed.

The house stood set back from the water on a slight rise, hidden from the path by a line of old oaks. When they came through the trees, Alex stopped.

Two stories of dark brick, broad and low, with wide windows

165

and a garden running along the south face that had rose bushes. The river was visible from the front steps, as was Boston across the river. It was strange not seeing the skyscrapers and familiar skyline of the city.

But that wasn't what stopped him.

There was a strangeness in the air around the property that made his combat magic stir without him calling it.

Elias had stopped beside him.

"You feel that?" Alex whispered.

"Yes," Elias said.

"What is it?"

"Something very old," Elias said.

He watched Elias' magic extend out toward the house, and after a few seconds he called it back.

"That was disorienting," Elias said.

"What did you pick up?" he asked.

"I'm not sure. It felt like being in a funhouse where the mirrors keep forcing you in the wrong direction. Does that make sense?"

"Yeah, it does. Stay alert."

Mercy and Alice walked through the gate without pausing.

They followed them across the yard. Two men stood near a low outbuilding to the left. Alex noted their positions relative to the gate and kept them in his peripheral vision as he crossed to the side entrance where a woman was already holding the door open.

She led them through a dim hallway that smelled of roses and into a sitting room off the main hall. Heavy curtains pulled half across the windows kept the heat of the sun from over-heating the room. A fireplace in the far wall that hadn't been used in a while, and four plush chairs and a settee arranged around a low table.

Alex moved to stand near the fireplace where he could see

both the door and the window. Elias stood near him. Mercy and Alice sat in the chairs. Mercy with her hands folded and her eyes on the door.

Somewhere in the house a door opened and closed.

Then the door to the room opened.

The woman who entered had red hair that fell loose past her shoulders, and a face Alex thought he recognized. Then he placed it. She looked like Aisling.

She looked at Alice and Mercy first and smiled.

Alice rose. "Queen Sereliana. These are Alexander Sutton and Elias Sinclair. They are kin to us through the old bloodlines. Mercy has written to you of them."

Sereliana looked at them both. "Sit down," she said.

He sat in the nearest chair and wondered why he had done that. He intended to remain standing. Elias sat as well. She took the chair across from them.

"Tell me how you came to be here," she said.

Alex told her about the family journals, Aisling, and the magic that brought them there. He watched her hands as he spoke rather than her face. When he said Aisling's name, her fingers pressed flat against her knees for a moment and then released.

"She sent you?" Sereliana asked.

"Yes." Alex frowned.

"Without your agreement?"

Elias answered before he could. "She told us she knew how to get the journal to tell us more and used her magic to do whatever that was. We couldn't break free, and next thing we know, we're here, in the past."

"She told you to look for Mercy? Not for me?"

"That's correct," Alex said.

She looked at Elias. "You carry the Llewellyn memory magic." It wasn't a question.

"Yes."

"I sense it is very strong."

"It is."

She looked at Alex. "Combat magic like every other Rhys."

"I know Mercy told you about us."

"The Llewellyn and Rhys lines," she said quietly. "I know those names. I've known them for a very long time. And I can sense the ancient bond between you. It isn't common to see two pairs in the same generation." She looked at Mercy. "You believe them?"

"I do," Mercy said.

Sereliana looked back at Alex. "I have a daughter named Aisling but she is still a child. Let us pretend I believe what you say is true. What did my daughter tell you? About why she sent you here."

"She didn't actually tell us anything about this time. Just that something happened and her people were hunted and scattered." He held her gaze. "She believed that if we were here before it happened, something could be different."

Sereliana was quiet. "Do you believe that?" she said.

"No," Alex said. "I don't think we can stop it."

She looked at him. "Why not?"

"Because in our time it already happened. It's history. Two hundred and fifty years of it."

"Then why are you here?"

"We don't know yet. That's the problem," Elias said.

"At least you are honest," she said. She stood and moved to the window with her back to them looking out at the river. "Before we discuss if I will send you home, I want to understand where you come from. What the world looks like in your time." She turned back. "Tell me about the fae."

Alex looked at Elias. They'd discussed this and agreed not to give out information. "We can't tell you about the future, beyond what we've said."

Sereliana turned and gave him a piercing stare with her blue eyes. "You will tell me what I want to know or you can leave right now and never go home. And don't even consider lying to me. I know when men lie to me."

Alex didn't doubt her. He met Elias' eyes and he could see the doubt.

Elias spoke to Sereliana but kept his eyes on Alex. "You're giving us an impossible choice. If we refuse to tell you what you want to know, we never go home." He turned to look at her. "And if we tell you and you take action, it might change our future. Our families are clearly tied to this. We might end up altering the outcome of the revolution and our country's history, or even our own. We could end up not existing."

Sereliana smiled at that. "I thought you said that you didn't think you could change the future because it's already happened?"

Checkmate. She'd used his own logic against them.

"Alright, what do you want to know about the fae?" Alex said carefully.

Elias turned in his seat and said, "Alex, don't."

"Do they exist in your time? Are they known?" Sereliana ignored Elias.

Alex thought about it. "No. Not the way you mean. There are stories. Folklore. Old myths and legends about fae and witches and creatures that aren't human." He paused. "But no one treats those stories as real. No government recognizes fae as a category of being. No one registers them or tracks them. As far as the world we come from is concerned, none of this exists. You never existed."

"That is not possible."

Sereliana stared at him for a long moment, then slowly moved back to the settee and sat. "None of our history?"

"No."

"No fae?" she said. "And you mentioned the witches."

"The word witch exists. But it means something different. It's not used to describe people with real power," Elias said, leaning back in the chair with a look of disapproval.

Sereliana turned her gaze to the floor. She was quiet for long enough that Alex began to wonder if she was going to continue.

"The fae have been known to humans for two thousand years," she said finally. "Longer, perhaps, but two thousand years that I can account for. We chose to make ourselves known. Both Courts agreed on it." She looked up at them. "The humans had magic of their own and they were expanding quickly across the world. The Seelie and Unseelie Courts at the time decided to get involved in their affairs. They were struggling with disease and war. We thought we could help them become something great. That our influence would be strong enough that they would choose to serve us."

"Clearly it didn't work out that way," Alex said. "How was it at first?"

"Complicated," she said. "Centuries of gradual trust. There were those who feared us and those who wanted to use us, and those who simply couldnt accept that the world was larger than what they had been taught." She pushed her hair back over her shoulders. "But the pact held for a very long time."

"The pact?" Elias said.

"Our history says that some of my people were discovered influencing the outcome of great ancient battles. The humans were going to turn on us. So the Courts swore a pact. The fae do not interfere in the affairs of humans. Both Courts agreed to it as the condition under which we could exist alongside you without conflict." She paused. "We have not always been true to it."

Alex waited.

"There have been times when a plague was moving through a city and the Seelie acted to slow it," she said. "Times when a war was going to consume everything and one side or the other asked for help and it was given. This is how we came to know the Llewellyns." She turned her gaze toward Elias. "Your ancestors were facing the Roman Empire. They wanted the magic your clan held. The gift to see memories and anticipate the feelings of others. The Rhys chose to protect your family and their secrets. That was the start of your alliance. One we aided in creating."

Elias looked down. Alex almost didn't hear him. "Damn it. The Celtic memory discs. Fae magic was used to create them wasn't it? That's how the memory magic was embedded in them. Why they're so powerful."

"You know of them, I see." She let it go when he didn't meet her eyes.

Alex rubbed his eyes. The discs Elias' father had used to hold Chicago hostage last year. The DMA had told them they were created by Druids. Another DMA lie.

Alice broke the moment. "Liana, tell them of the Unseelie and their involvement in the events unfolding now."

"The pact was understood to have limits. Acts of mercy were tolerated if they were small.. What the Unseelie are doing is not that. They were present last month at the battles in Lexington and Concord. They have spies in the colonies pretending to be Patriots. As we speak I'm certain they're sitting in ale houses gathering information for the British. Or in Boston, helping them plan their next attack."

"This violates the pact because it's political interference?" Alex said.

"Yes, and done in the service of the Unseelie's own interests." She looked at him. "They want to continue living among the humans, but don't want to give up their royal status. The world is changing and they don't want to change with it. That is the distinction. They aid an empire that has promised us continued royal status and even countries of our own."

Elias had looked up and was now staring at him. The implications of what Sereliana had said was sinking in.

He said to Elias, "Did something we do or will say affect the outcome of the revolution?"

Elias answered, "Or something we don't do? My memory magic can only see past or present events. If I'd run a trace back in our time, maybe I could see something out of place now."

"I can see events yet to come, albeit in pieces. I've seen a great fire across the river and a battle in the city. But, I haven't seen the outcome. Although many will die," Mercy said.

Alex knew the battle. "You're seeing the battle of Bunker Hill." He thought for a moment. "That happens next month, Elias."

"And?" Elias was rubbing his lower lip as he stared down at the floor.

"The timing can't be a coincidence. What if whatever turns the people against the fae has to do with that battle?"

Mercy made eye contact with him and gave him a smile. She knew something more and she wasn't sharing it here. He glanced back at Sereliana who was staring at the fireplace and lost in her own thoughts.

"Aisling told us something else," Alex said, trying to change the subject.

"About a wolf that's been attacking people in our time. She said it was both man and animal."

Sereliana turned toward him. Then at Mercy.

Mercy said nothing.

"Those are real," Sereliana said. "They're not fae. they're not something we created." She paused. "they're a curse placed on humans. By witches, for transgressions against their families or their communities."

"A curse that persists through generations," Mercy said.

"Yes. The curse is carried in the blood. It passes to children. It is difficult to lift once it takes hold." She frowned. "They're called werewolves. They too do not exist in your time?"

"No," Alex said. "I mean, nobody believes in them."

"Tell me how magic works in your time," she said. "If the fae don't exist, the witches are gone, and the werewolves are folklore, what remains?"

Alex and Elias shared a glance.

"We'll tell you," Alex said. "But I want something in return."

Sereliana raised her chin slightly. "What?"

"Promise you'll help us get home before we tell you more of what our world looks like."

Sereliana looked at him and gave a short laugh. "A promise? I think some of our traditions do still exist in your time. Very well, I will help you get home," she said. "I was going to help you regardless. But I appreciate that you negotiated."

Alex nodded. "Magic users are registered by the governments in our time. The United States has an agency called the Department of Magical Affairs. It registers magic users, classifies their abilities, and tracks significant uses of power. Similar systems exist in almost all countries around the world."

"Registered," Sereliana said. "Like property."

"Like citizens," Alex said. "In theory. In practice it's more like an indentured servitude."

"And the fae are not registered as fae? What of my daughter?"

"The people who choose to break the law are known as fae or just as unregistered people. We were told that the term fae was a play on the word failed. They failed to register because they thought themselves special. Like a fairy or something. Honestly, the term never made sense to me."

"But magic itself exists."

"Yes, of course. Magic users are real, we're born this way. Everyone with power is classified as a magic user and given a specialization. Memory. Combat. Elemental. Healing." He paused. "We're taught that the Registration Act of 1790 came out of a need to regulate uncontrolled magic use."

Sereliana was very still. "What you cannot control, you destroy. Two thousand years of coexisting," she said. "And practically overnight we will cease to exist."

"The witches too," Mercy said quietly. "Not just the fae."

Sereliana looked away. "Yes. Them as well."

"Not gone," Elias said. "Hidden and forgotten. Your people still exist. Your magic is still there in our time. I can sense it and often do. We just don't know who you are. Your daughter knows and is trying to reunite your people. Granted, this wasn't the best way to do that."

"No, she is trying to interfere in the affairs of humans to save the Fae. That is not right either." Sereliana looked at him and Elias for a long time. Then at Mercy.

"I can help you return," she said. "But not yet." She looked at the window. "Portal magic requires a new moon. The alignment of old workings with the natural world. The next new moon is on the twenty-seventh, about three weeks from now."

"Three weeks?" Alex said.

"Yes."

"The journal," she said, looking at Alice. "You have it."

Alice looked at her steadily. "I have several journals at the farmhouse. Which one do you mean?"

"Your personal journal," Elias said. "The red one."

Alice went still for a moment. Then she nodded. "Yes. I have it."

"Good. I will need it. The journal is the anchor between

times. Without it the portal cannot open." She paused. "But the portal magic Aisling used was woven into that journal in the future by me and I haven't done that." She said it without inflection. "In this time the journal holds no portal magic. I will have to place it there."

"Can you do that?" Elias asked.

Sereliana looked at Alice. "The journal belongs to your family. Will you allow it?"

Alice didn't say anything for a long moment. "I didn't know such a thing was possible," she said. "But if it sends them home, yes. Whatever you need from it."

"Good. But it will require more than my magic alone." She tilted her head and spoke to Mercy. "I will need additional magic for this. There are those whose old knowledge runs alongside mine." She paused. "I may need the help of the others."

Mercy held her gaze. "I will speak with them. You can count on the old magic."

"Do not speak of portal magic to anyone," Sereliana said. "Not while you are here. Not when you return home. Not ever. If the wrong people learn of what is in that journal after this day, it will be used for exactly what my daughter is attempting to do. And they likely won't be as honorable as the both of you are."

"Understood," Alex said.

"And don't interfere with what is coming," she said. "Whatever happens in the next few weeks. Do not interfere."

Alex looked at her. "We'll try."

She stood and moved toward the door. She stopped with her hand on the frame but didn't turn back. "Thank you for telling me of my future. It will help us prepare. I believe you have already fulfilled your part of the prophecy."

"What prophecy?" Elias asked, but she was already gone.

The dark-haired woman showed them out through the side door. The two men near the outbuilding watched them cross the yard. The gate closed behind them.

They walked back along the river path in silence. The sun was lower on the horizon, and the air cooler.

"She's going to do it," Elias said. "Put the portal magic in the journal. She knows what it means when she does."

"Yes," Alex said.

"She'll do it anyway."

Alex thought about the way Sereliana had sat across from them after he told her that two thousand years of her world had been reduced to folklore.

"She took that information better than I expected," Alex thought out loud.

"As though she already understood that something like this was likely and just received confirmation?" Elias finished.

"Exactly." Mercy walked ahead of them with Alice. "Mercy?"

"I told you, I get pieces," she turned to face him with a wry smile. Then she frowned. "The future is coming for all of us."

Elias waited a few seconds before he said, "The others she mentioned?"

"Hmm, yes," Mercy turned away.

"Mercy?"

She kept walking.

"The others Sereliana referred to. Who are they?"

Mercy touched Alice on the shoulder and motioned for her to go on without them.

Alex looked at Elias. Elias shrugged.

"You already know who they are. The witches. The fae call us the Others, they always have."

She turned and kept walking.

Alex looked at Elias. Elias stared at Mercy.

"You're a witch?" Elias said.

"I thought you were smart men. Guess I was wrong." She glanced over her shoulder and smiled at them.

17

The Others

The journal was still slightly glowing on the library table when Abby closed it.

She'd read the poem four times already this morning. She knew what it said. She understood what Aisling had told them it meant. What she didn't understand was what they were supposed to do with it.

A faint pulse at the edges of the parchment, like something breathing beneath the paper. She pressed her fingertips against the cover and felt a low vibration move through her palms. Her elemental magic stirred in response and she pulled it back. She wasn't going to do anything to that book without understanding what she was doing first.

Emily stood in the doorway with her arms crossed. She hadn't sat down since the journal had finished writing the latest stanza.

Aisling sat in the armchair near the window.

"You said you wouldn't be the only one who felt the pulse," Abby said. She turned away from the journal and looked at

Aisling directly. "Last night you said the journals had sent something out and that others would feel it."

"Yes."

"You said they would come for it."

"Yes."

Emily came fully into the room and sat on the arm of the couch. "You've been saying that since you walked into this house. You've been dancing around it and telling us pieces and redirecting every time one of us asks a direct question." Her voice was even. "We confirmed tonight that Alex and Elias are actually in 1775. That they're alive, and that someone in that time is writing in this journal." She looked at Aisling steadily. "I am done waiting for context. Tell us who these others are and tell us what kind of danger we're in."

Aisling looked at the journal on the table. Then at Emily and Abby.

"We should move locations first," she said.

Emily's expression didn't change. "Excuse me."

"This house is known," Aisling said. "The pulse the journals sent out when they were first activated crossed the Charles River. Every time the journal has opened since, it sends something out. Others felt it. They may not have understood what it was immediately, but they will have been tracing it."

Emily looked at Abby.

Abby looked at the journal.

"We're not moving the journals," Abby said. "Not without understanding what moving them does to whatever connection we have to Alex and Elias right now."

Aisling pressed her lips together. "I understand the hesitation. But I want you to understand the risk of staying."

"Then tell us who's coming," Abby said. "Stop making us drag it out of you."

Aisling settled back in the chair. Her hands rested open on her knees.

"The fae are not the only beings your governments decided to erase from the history books," she said.

"Witches," Abby said flatly. "In Alice's journal she mentions witches."

Aisling looked at her. "Yes."

"She wrote in her journal about them and where they had gone," Abby said. "Like it was normal to know witches."

"It was normal in 1775," Aisling said. "Witches are humans with a different kind of elemental magic. Their magic works like anyone else's in terms of basic ability, but they developed over time as a separate branch of magic. They formed covens. Alone, they had limited strength. Together, they could level a building." She paused. "They were healers primarily. They worked alongside fae practitioners for centuries and learned from them. They were part of every community that had old magic in it."

"And they were persecuted," Abby said.

"Eventually, yes."

"The Salem trials," Emily said. "The religious persecution in Europe and other countries."

"All of that was real," Aisling said.

"Before the fae persecution started in Boston, the witches somehow received a warning. And they understood what was coming because they had seen it before. They moved so quickly and quietly, nobody even noticed until they went looking for them. Some of the men stayed and fought in the war without anyone ever suspecting them. But the women and children and the elders scattered." She paused. "At first they just moved, but later they moved deliberately. Into cities where they weren't known. Into positions that would allow them to survive whatever was coming."

"So they weren't hunted like the fae?" Emily asked.

Aisling almost smiled. "The witches made sure they survived."

"What kind of positions," Abby said.

"They married strategically into families with standing. They entered professions where they would have access to records and institutions and the machinery of whatever governments were being built around them." Aisling looked at her hands. "Over generations the positioning became natural. The children born into those families didn't know the origin of it. They simply inherited well-placed lives."

Abby looked at Emily.

Emily looked back at her.

"You're describing something deliberate," Abby said. "Across generations."

"Yes."

"And you're telling us this because you think it connects to us somehow," Emily said. Her voice was careful. "You said yesterday that we're connected to what is happening somehow."

"I am telling you because the witches who integrated into those positions didn't forget who they were," Aisling said. "They kept records. They maintained their networks. And some of them have strong reasons to keep the history of what happened in 1775 buried." She looked at the journal. "The Others I spoke of are the witches. That's what we used to call them back in the day. they're the ones who felt the pulse."

Emily set down her mug. "I'm from Spain."

Aisling looked at her.

"You said the witches scattered from Boston. My family has been in Asturias for over a thousand years. Whatever happened here in 1775 has nothing to do with me"

"The bruxas," Aisling said. "They still exist in the north of Spain. They have for centuries. Old magic that runs in certain families in that region. Asturias still holds that tradition in their folklore."

Emily went still.

"I'm a registered memory specialist and elemental magic user," Emily said. "That's what I am."

"Yes," Aisling said. "That is also what the registration system decided you were."

Emily looked at Abby again. Abby could read her face. She wasn't convinced. She wasn't dismissing it either.

Abby turned back to Aisling. "And me?"

"The Morgans," Aisling said. "Your family was here in 1775. You know that. Your father's line carried it. I don't know about your mother's side."

"My family are prosecutors and teachers," Abby said. "We're not witches."

"No," Aisling said. "Not in any practical sense. What remains is the lineage and the magic that came with it, registered now as elemental, because that is the category they created for it." She paused. "And the positioning. Your parents are both prosecuting attorneys are they not? You are a curator at the Athenaeum."

"I know where I work."

"The Athenaeum holds the primary documents of the revolutionary period," Aisling said. "Original letters. Land records. Journals. The sources from which the official history was written after 1775." She looked at Abby. "The witches who survived understood that whoever controlled the record of what happened controlled the history itself. Positions like yours weren't accidental in the first generation. By your generation they're simply what your family does."

Abby kept her voice even. "You're saying my family's been placing itself near historical records for two hundred and fifty years without knowing why."

"Those in power know why, I assure you. Where do you think

that the mandatory service requirement for specialist level magic users originated?"

"What?"

"What better way to control the placement of your witches than under the guise of a mandatory service requirement for all magic users? The registration system started as a way to regulate magic and control the population. The witches infiltrated that system and used it as a way to gain and maintain power."

Abby looked at Emily and saw the same shock on her face. "I've never heard of such a thing. That sounds like crazy conspiracy theory talk."

"Even you two," Aisling said. She was looking at them both with something in her expression that wasn't quite amusement. "You managed to find yourselves right beside the Llewellyn and Rhys lines. The two women who happen to carry distinguished witch ancestry, sitting in the home of the last two living descendants of the oldest magical alliance in the British Isles." She tilted her head. "That is a remarkable coincidence."

Emily stared at her. "Are you saying we infiltrated them?"

"Of course not. That's absurd." Aisling's expression didn't change. "I'm saying that old lines recognize each other. The magic moves toward what is familiar. I am sure you both simply felt an inexplicable pull toward two very specific men and followed it." She paused. "Nothing calculated about it at all."

"That isn't funny," Abby said.

"No," Aisling agreed. "It isn't."

Abby stood. She walked to the window and looked out at the front garden without really seeing it.

"I need a minute," Abby said. She wasn't asking.

She walked out of the library and down the hallway to the kitchen. She stood at the counter and pressed both palms flat against the cool stone.

Emily came and stood beside her at the counter. She was

holding Alex's keys and turning the keychain over in her hand. A small flat gold disc dangled from it. The Celtic symbol catching the light.

"Elias gave this to Alex last Christmas," she said. "So Alex could find him if he was ever lost."

Abby crossed the room and touched the disc. Her elemental magic surfaced without her calling it and she felt it immediately. "It has tracking magic in it. Elias told me that DMA Deputy Director Rowan showed him the magic to make it. How ironic that he actually is lost and that Alex is with him."

"I know," Emily said. She closed her hand around the keys and put them on the counter. "Why would Elias think he needed a way for Alex to find him? Those two are inseparable?"

Abby glanced at the key. "You know, I never asked Elias."

"It's probably his fear of losing Alex. Elias has a lot of trauma over not having a family for so long and then almost losing the closest thing he has to a brother. He probably sees that little piece of gold as always being close to Alex even when they're apart."

Abby looked at Emily. "Did you just psychoanalyze my boyfriend?"

Emily chuckled. "Yeah maybe. Stress makes us say weird things sometimes."

Neither of them spoke for a minute.

"Do you believe her?" Abby asked.

"Yes," Emily said. "Not about the part where we intentionally set ourselves up to be in their lives. But the rest. Yeah. I've heard enough strange stories from abuela to know in my gut that what she is saying about us may be true."

"Me too." Abby exhaled. "I wish I didn't."

"I know."

"My grandmother used to say the Morgans were witches,"

Abby said. "She said it like it was a joke. I never thought she meant it literally."

"My grandmother's protection prayer now takes on a whole different meaning." Emily took in a deep breath. "We need help, Abby. We're completely out of our depth and we have been since the moment they disappeared."

Abby had reached the same conclusion. "We can't trust Aisling," she said.

"No."

"She had reasons for what she did and I don't think she's lying to us. But her interests are not the same as ours."

"No," Emily said again. "They're not."

Abby had been turning a name over in her mind since the previous night. She had pulled it up and set it down three times already. She kept setting it down because she knew what it would mean. She knew that once she made that call, everything would change in ways she couldnt predict.

But Alex and Elias had been in 1775 for two days, maybe more if time did move differently for them. They had no plan, and she had a fae queen in the library who had admitted she didn't know how to bring them home.

She picked up her phone. "I'm calling Catrin Rowan," Abby said.

Emily's went wide.

"I know, Alex will be furious," Abby said.

"Yes," Emily said. "And he can be furious from this century, which is where I want him."

Abby found the number she'd looked up on the Internet.

She pressed call.

It rang four times before a man answered.

"Department of Magical Affairs, Deputy Director's office." His voice was clipped and professional.

"I need to speak with Deputy Director Rowan," Abby said.

"The Deputy Director doesn't take unscheduled calls. I can take a message and—"

"My name is Dr. Abigail Morgan. I am calling about Special Agents Elias Sinclair and Alexander Sutton." She kept her voice steady. "They're missing. A fae is with me who says she transported them to 1775. I need to speak with Deputy Director Rowan."

Silence.

"Hold on," the man said.

Abby looked at Emily, who was watching her with both hands in her pants pockets.

The line opened again.

"Dr. Morgan." Catrin Rowan's voice was precise and unhurried. "Tell me who you are."

"My name is Abigail Morgan and I'm Elias' girlfriend. I'm here with Dr. Emily Cabrera, Alex's girlfriend. She's a psychologist. We're more than just girlfriends, we live with them."

My God, I'm babbling, she thought. The DMA had a way of making the most intelligent of people nervous. "I'm sorry, I'm nervous."

"It's okay, Dr. Morgan. Just tell me what trouble those two got themselves into."

Abby told her. She kept it to the essential facts. The journals activating. Aisling arriving at the house. The earthwork at Middlesex Fells. The portal. The journal writing itself. The second stanza appearing in the present day, written from 1775.

She spoke for less than two minutes.

When she finished, Rowan was quiet for a few seconds.

"You're in Cambridge," she said. It wasn't a question.

"Yes. At Elias' house."

"I'm on the next flight." A pause. "don't let the fae woman leave with any of those journals, Ms. Morgan. Do you understand me."

"Yes."

"And don't tell her I'm coming." Another pause. "Don't trust her. Whatever she's told you, her interests in this are not yours."

The call ended.

Abby set her phone down on the counter.

"Well?" Emily said.

"She's on the next flight. She'll be here tonight," Abby said. "She said not to tell Aisling."

Emily looked toward the hallway. "Good."

"She also said not to trust her."

"I already knew that."

"We don't tell her," Abby said. "We go back in there and we carry on the conversation, and we don't give her anything else until Rowan is here."

Emily was already moving toward the hall. "Come on. She'll start wondering."

They went back into the library. Aisling was still in the armchair. She hadn't touched the journal. She looked up when they returned.

"Better?" she said.

"Fine," Abby said. She sat back down. "That was just a lot to absorb. It's been a tough two days."

"Would you tell us more about the witches? This is all new to us."

They had lunch and spent the afternoon talking.

Aisling was careful in what she offered. She described the older families, the ones whose positioning went back furthest, as being the ones most likely to want the old history buried. The newer lines, the ones who had married in or who had come through different channels, were harder to read. She said that fae could sense witch magic the same way they sensed any old lineage.

She said she had sensed it in Abby the first time she walked into the house.

Emily managed the conversation with precision. She asked exactly enough to keep Aisling talking and gave nothing back. When Aisling moved toward the journals twice with her eyes, Emily redirected each time. It wasn't obvious. It was the lightest possible steering, and Abby watched it happen and felt a distinct gratitude for Emily Cabrera's chosen profession.

Emily asked how Aisling had managed to stay in Boston for as long as she claimed without being identified. Aisling said the DMA enforcement division looked for magic use, not for faces, and that someone who kept their power suppressed and paid their fines when they slipped drew the same level of attention as a speeding ticket. Emily asked if she had ever been brought in for questioning. Aisling said twice, both times before the city had adequate monitoring infrastructure, and that neither time had the interviewing officer understood what she actually was.

"What did they think you were?" Emily asked.

"An unregistered elemental user with a cleaning job," Aisling said. "Which is accurate, as far as it goes."

Emily looked at her. "Did you compel the officers?"

"No," Aisling said. "I answered every question truthfully. There is a significant difference between what is true and what people choose to understand."

Abby half listened to their conversation. Her thoughts had drifted to Elias. She thought about the way he had looked the last time she had seen him, standing on the mound in the dark with the light coming up around his hands, not understanding what was happening. She had been reaching for him when the working sealed them off, and there had been a moment, a very short moment, where their eyes had met across the light and she saw the fear in his eyes.

She hoped he was okay and that Alex was making jokes to make him smile. She hoped Elias was rolling his eyes at him.

The doorbell rang at 6:14 p.m..

All three of them looked toward the hall. Aisling looked at Abby and started to stand. She looked concerned.

Abby stood. "I'll get it. I ordered online. It's the delivery person."

She crossed the hall. She could feel her heart rate speed up. She put her hand on the door and opened it.

Catrin Rowan stood on the porch. Tall, auburn hair, sharp green eyes. A dark coat.

"Ms. Morgan," she said. "I'm Catrin Rowan."

"I know," Abby said. "I'm Abigail. Thank you for coming. Please, come in."

Rowan stepped inside quietly and set her bag on the floor. She walked with Abby to the library.

Emily was on her feet.

Aisling was still seated.

Rowan's eyes moved across the room and met Emily's.

"Dr. Morgan, it's a pleasure to meet you."

Then her gaze shifted to Aisling. She stared at her for several seconds, her expression unreadable.

Aisling stared back and quickly stood up.

Rowan tilted her head to one side, slow and deliberate, and smiled.

"Aisling. Finding you in Elias Sinclair's house was not on my bingo card."

18

Battles Within And Without

The coven was smaller than it had been three weeks ago. Elias noticed it when they gathered in the garden that morning. Two of the women who had come every session for the past three weeks weren't there. The oldest, the one with gray at her temples who had anchored the group's magic with a steadiness he had come to rely on, was absent. In her place stood a younger woman he hadn't seen before.

The older man was still on his bench. That much hadn't changed. A couple of weeks earlier, Mercy had introduced him as Benjamin Hawkins, the man guiding the sessions

Mercy said nothing about the absences. She set up the session the same way she always did, positioning Elias at the center of the garden with the remaining four women arranged around him. She introduced him the same way she always did. A friend of the family. Strong elemental magic, poorly trained.

He was more trained than he had been. That much was true.

"Hands," the older man said.

Elias held them out and called his unruly elemental magic. It came easier now, yellow-green at both palms, without the strain

of the first weeks. The four women reached for it and he felt their presences settle around the edge of his magic. Their familiar steadiness settled around his power.

"Hold it there," the older man said. "Now release the support."

Elias looked at him. They hadn't done this before.

"The women will step back," the man said. "You will hold it alone."

The four women withdrew and Elias felt the difference immediately. The steadiness was his to maintain now with nothing bracing it. For a moment the magic was steady. Then his thoughts began to stray. What if the coming battle prevented Sereliana from helping them? What if they couldn't get home?

And then his magic surged.

Wind started to swirl around him. Not dangerously, but definitely not something he had willed.

He pulled it back quickly.

The older man nodded once. "Better than last week."

"Still not completely under my control, though," Elias said.

"No. But you stopped it." The man shifted on the bench. "The surge isn't the problem. Calling it at will and controlling it. That's what you need to learn."

Mercy was watching from the doorway with her hands folded. She didn't say anything.

When the session ended, the four women left quickly. He heard two of them speaking as they went through the gate, their voices low. Something about the road south. Something about a sister in Philadelphia who had room.

He sat on the bench beside the older man after they had gone.

"How many of your people are leaving?" Elias asked.

The man looked out across the garden. "All of them."

"Why now?"

"Because they see a storm heading our way," the man said. "One that threatens to consume all of us." He looked at Elias. "We must not be here when it arrives."

Elias thought about the sounds from Cambridge Common in the mornings. The columns of men on the road. The way John came inside from the yard with a different expression than he had worn three weeks ago, more closed off and concerned. The dispatches that arrived at the farmhouse were burned after John and Alice read them. He never got to see them.

"There are a lot more soldiers here now," Elias said.

The older man said nothing.

"The new moon is still ten days away." Elias looked at his hands.

"Be patient, son," the man said.

He stood slowly, favoring his left leg, and made his way through the garden gate without looking back.

He found Mercy in the small room off the main hall writing a letter.

"Sereliana mentioned a prophecy," he said. He sat down across from her without being invited. "Before she left the room. She said she believed we had already fulfilled our part of it."

Mercy set down her quill.

"What prophecy?" Elias asked. "The poem that appeared in the journal. Is that what she meant?"

"I don't know," Mercy said.

He studied her face. He had learned to read her silences in the last three weeks, and this one wasn't evasion.

"You truly don't know?," he said.

"I see what I see," she said. "I don't always understand it, but I always share it with the individuals that may be affected. The poem in the journal isn't there now. I don't know who writes it." She shook her head. "What I can tell you is that I've seen you and Alexander in my visions for three years. And in every vision, you are here. In this time. On this path."

"Which is what?"

"Doing what you're doing," Mercy said. "That is all I can say."

She picked up her quill and went back to writing.

Elias sat across from her for a moment longer. He had hoped for more than that.

He went to find Alex.

Alex was at the fence line where he always was in the afternoon. The road through the trees had been busy since morning. A column of militia had passed an hour ago, moving toward Cambridge Common with their gear. Supply carts had followed. Now the road was quiet.

Elias stood beside him.

"I want to ask you something," he said.

Alex looked at his cup.

"You don't have to answer."

"What?"

"Your time in the Army. You never talk about it. In the nine years I've known you, you've told me almost nothing about what it was like."

Alex was quiet.

"I'm asking because I see you standing out here every day, and I can tell that something's bothering you. And I want to help."

Alex set his cup down on the fence post. He looked out across the field for a long moment. "I joined after college," he said. "You know that part."

"Yes."

"I was good at what I did." He paused. "Better than I expected. They put me where they could use me. Forward positions and covert operations. The kind of missions where being able to throw up a shield between your unit and incoming fire made you very valuable very quickly." He looked down at his hands. "I liked it. That's the honest answer. I was twenty-two, and I was good at defending my unit and killing the enemy. People are alive because of me, and I like that feeling."

Elias said nothing.

"The things I did to keep people alive." Alex stopped, picked up the cup again, then set it back down. "You don't need the details. But there were moments where the choice was between protecting my unit and what happened to whoever was on the other side of my shield." He looked at Elias. "I made those choices without hesitating. Every time."

"That's what you were trained to do."

"I know." Alex's jaw tightened briefly. "I don't feel guilty about it."

"Is that why you never told me?"

"I didn't want you to think about it when you looked at me," Alex said. "You've seen enough violence through other people's memories. I didn't need to add mine."

Elias looked at him. Alex was always trying to protect everyone around him.

Elias grabbed him by the shoulder and pulled him in hard. Alex returned the hug. They stayed like that for a moment and then Elias let go.

"You're an idiot," Elias said.

"Yeah." Alex picked up his cup. "Probably."

"Is that what this is?" Elias said. "Standing out here every morning."

"No." Alex was quiet for a beat. "I'm standing out here

because those men on the road are about to walk into something, and they don't know what it's going to cost them. And I know exactly what it costs. And I can't tell them. I can't help."

"You've been helping John every day."

"That's not what I mean."

"We are helping," Elias said. "We're here. We don't know why yet. But we're here."

Alex looked at him.

"Mercy said that," Elias added.

"Mercy says a lot of things."

"She's usually right." Alex almost smiled. It was small and faded fast. "The new moon is June 27."

"The battle is in two days," Alex said. "June 17. Sereliana needs ten days between the battle and the portal. Ten days where Cambridge is going to be—" He stopped. "Where does that leave her? Where does it leave us?"

Elias had been thinking about the same thing. "What if the persecution of the fae starts right away?"

"And Sereliana is living on the Cambridge riverbank in a house full of fae," Alex said. "With soldiers who are going to be looking for them."

"We keep her alive until the 27th," Elias said. "That's what we do."

"And if someone comes after her before then?"

"Then we deal with it."

"Yeah, us against the entire rebel Army? There must be something we can do."

"Alex."

"I know."

"Don't get involved in the battle," Elias said plainly. "I'm telling you now. Whatever you're thinking about, don't. It's a lost cause. The patriots lose Breed's Hill. We know that. Going in there doesn't change it, and it risks everything we still have to do."

Alex looked at him.

"I mean it," Elias said. "Sereliana told us not to get involved."

"I know she did," Alex said. He picked up his cup and walked back toward the house.

Elias watched him go. Alex wasn't impulsive. If he was planning for them to do something, he would tell Elias when he was ready.

Elias and Alex were in the back garden, away from the house, speaking quietly. The coven session had ended two hours ago and the yard had been empty since. Elias had his back to the garden gate and Alex was facing him, and they had been talking about the Unseelie for the better part of an hour without getting anywhere useful.

"They're here," Alex said. "Somewhere. Either on the ships or embedded with the rebel units. That's the most effective placement if you want to influence the outcome without being seen."

"And we can't warn anyone without explaining how we know," Elias said.

Alex looked at the ground. "So we watch it happen."

"Yes."

"Mr. Sutton."

They both turned.

Thomas Morgan was standing at the garden gate. He had a canvas bag over one shoulder and his hat in his hand.

Alex looked at Elias.

"Mr. Morgan," Elias said.

Morgan came through the gate and stopped a few feet from them.

"Is it true?" he said. "The fae are interfering in the fight for independence?"

"Where did you hear that?" Alex said.

"From the two of you, just now." Morgan kicked the dirt with one foot. "I'm not asking you to confirm what I already heard. I'm asking you how certain you are."

Elias looked at Alex. Alex kept his face neutral.

"We have reason to believe it," Elias answered.

Morgan turned his hat over in his hands and glanced at the garden wall.

"I came to tell Alice and John that I'm taking Martha to her cousin's home in North Carolina," he said. "She'll be safe there while things settle." He paused. "I had planned to go with her. See her settled and come back to join the fight."

He looked back at them.

"But if what you're saying is true," Morgan said, "then the militia here in Boston are going to need every advantage they can find." He looked up. "I'll tell Martha we're going to stay and wait a few days. From what you said I believe we may be needed here."

"Mr. Morgan," Alex said. "You don't have to do that."

"I know I don't have to."

"There's a battle coming and you shouldn't be here."

"I'm aware of what is coming," Morgan said. "That is why we were leaving." He looked at Alex. "I also know what I am and what I can do. My coven has already left. Most of them went south last week." He glanced between them. "I know we are all in danger, but I didn't realize it was the fae who were involved. We were just told that trouble was brewing."

Elias stared at him. "Your coven," he said.

Morgan looked at him. "Yes."

"You're a witch."

"Yes, I assumed you knew, given where you've been living

and who you've been working with." He paused. "We don't go around introducing ourselves as witches. Did Mercy not tell you?"

"She doesn't tell us much," Elias said.

"I see," Morgan said. He looked at the gate behind him, then back at them. "My magic is not Mercy's. But it is strong, and I'm well trained on its use."

"Thomas." Alex placed his hand on Morgan's shoulder. "don't stay because of this. Take your wife south and stay with her. You will have your opportunity to join the fight after you get her to safety."

"I appreciate that," Morgan said. "I'm going to do what I think is right regardless."

He picked up his bag. "I'll go find Alice and John," he said.

He walked past them toward the house and Elias watched him go.

Alex stood with his arms at his sides and looked at the garden gate Morgan had come through.

"He heard us," Elias said.

"Yeah, we need to be more careful where we talk."

"He's going to stay and will end up fighting."

"That seems to be his intention."

"Abby told me he didn't fight at Bunker Hill," Elias said. "That he joined after. His name is in a later registry." He looked at Alex. "He's not supposed to be here."

Alex ran a hand through his hair. It had grown longer in the weeks since they arrived.

"If he dies at Bunker Hill, Abby will never exist. He's her direct ancestor. I'm sure of it."

Alex moved closer to him and put one hand on the back of Elias' neck and squeezed firmly.

"Abby will be fine," he said. "Nothing is going to happen to Thomas that changes that. I promise you."

"You can't know that."

"Yes, I can. We're not going to change history, Elias. I promise you," Alex said.

Elias looked at him. He wanted to ask how Alex could possibly know that. But when Alex said it, Elias almost believed him.

"Okay," Elias said.

Alex nodded once and dropped his hand. "Let's get inside."

Later that evening as he came downstairs for more water, he saw the light still burning in the library. He stopped in the hallway short of the doorway when he heard John's voice.

"If the regulars move through Cambridge the way they're talking about, this house will be searched."

"I know." Alice's voice. "They took Reverend Cooper's papers last month. Everything he had."

"The journals cannot fall into British hands." That was Mercy. "Not with all the history they hold."

Elias leaned against the wall and listened.

"We've done this before," John said. "In the old country, every time the lines have had to move, the journals have been protected."

"This is no different," Mercy said. "The knowledge in these books is older than any of these disputes. It will outlast this one too."

A silence. Then the sound of the chest being opened.

"Alice," Mercy said. "Make sure all the books are here, and keep your personal one separate. We will need it for the portal magic. I will ward these older ones first."

Elias stepped to the doorway.

Mercy stood at one end of the chest with her hands resting

on the lid. Alice held her red journal tightly to her chest. None of them noticed him.

He leaned against the doorframe and watched.

Mercy lifted the lid of the chest and reached in, drawing out the older journals one by one and setting them on the table in a row. She placed her hands flat on the first one.

"Use the old Rhys warding. The one that locks them to our bloodlines. That is what Elias and Alexander said their journal had in their time," John said.

Alice smiled. "That's right, they did say the journals were in a language that was unknown and it wasn't until the books recognized them that they unlocked. The old magic, Mercy. Do you know it?"

"What you're describing is blood magic. I will need blood from both of you, just a few drops. I can ward them to create an undecipherable language. Weave in translation magic that will only work when the ward senses both Rhys and Llewellyn bloodlines together."

John pulled the knife from his belt.

"I will also need both of you to join your magic with mine. But I won't be able to ward all of them. This kind of magic draws a lot from the user. We should only ward the most important ones," she said.

Alice was the one who spoke first. "The oldest ones that speak of our alliance, John. Those hold the origin of our lines."

John nodded. "Yes, those are the ones. Here let me pull those out. They already have preservation magic in them."

After they had rearranged the journals and placed them on the chest, Alice and John each made a cut on their thumbs.

Green light moved around John's hand and was joined by the silver from Alice's. Mercy's palms spread across the cover and her golden magic slowly moved across the journals, joining with John and Alice's. The magic spun brighter. A drop of blood from each of them fell onto the cover, and the light sank into the book.

Mercy said something in a language Elias didn't understand. The magic held for a moment and then faded, and the journal looked exactly as it had.

She moved to the next one and they repeated the process.

Elias watched them work through each journal in turn.

He understood what they were doing.

Whatever was coming, whoever came looking, these journals wouldn't open for them. They would open for the bloodline and no one else. He had wondered since the first night he and Alex had touched the cover of the first journal who had thought to protect them that way and why. He was looking at the answer.

Alice looked up and saw him in the doorway. She held his gaze for a moment "They'll be waiting for you and Alexander. The duty to protect them falls on you now."

"I promise we'll protect them." Elias pushed off the door-frame and went back upstairs. He would tell Alex about it tomorrow. He wished Alex had witnessed the beauty of the warding. As he reached their room, he decided that he would make a construct for him and the girls to see. Abby was going to love this.

If she still existed.

Something woke him but he didn't know what.

He lay still for a moment, listening. Through the window the sky was dark, not yet dawn.

He heard it again.

Men on the road. Not a column, not a marching cadence. A large number of people moving quietly past the house.

He got up and went to the window.

Through the trees he could make out shapes on the road in the distance. Hundreds of them, moving south, away from Cambridge. No torches and no drums. Moving quickly and quietly toward Boston.

He watched for a while.

Then he turned and looked at Alex's bed.

It was empty.

On the small table near the window, folded once, was a piece of paper.

He picked it up.

The handwriting was Alex's.

Gone to Breed's Hill. Don't follow me. Morgan is there and I'm not going to let him die on a hill he walked onto because of us. I'll find you at the farmhouse when it's done.
Abby will be waiting for you when we get home. I promise.

–Alex

Elias read it twice. He threw a shirt and pants on and ran down the stairs and through the kitchen.

The back door was already open. John was standing in the yard in the dark with his coat on, which meant John had known, and probably Alice.

"I need a horse," Elias said.

"No," John said.

"John—"

"It is the middle of the night and there are two thousand armed men moving through the area right now." John's voice was stern. "You will ride straight into them. You will not find Alex tonight. You will get yourself killed, or arrested, or both, and then none of you go home."

"He's gone with them." Elias's voice cracked on the last word. "He left without telling me."

"I know."

"You knew he was going."

John said nothing.

"Did Mercy see it?"

Silence.

Elias turned away from him. He pressed both hands flat against the outside wall of the house and stood there with the note crushed in his fist, his jaw tight and his eyes burning and the sound of men on the road moving through the dark.

He had known this was his worst fear. He had known it since Chicago, since the warehouse, since the first time Alex had thrown himself between Elias and something that would have killed him.

Alex was going to walk onto that hill without him.

"At first light," John said behind him. "When the road clears and we can see what we're doing. I will go with you."

Elias said nothing.

"He's good at what he does, yes?" John said. "Whatever he was before he came here, he's very good at keeping people safe. Am I right?"

Elias nodded. He knew Alex could take care of himself, and he was a combat veteran. He wiped his face with the back of his hand and looked at the sky above the tree line. Still dark. Still hours before dawn.

"First light," John said again.

Elias pushed off the wall and went back inside and up to his room. He sat on the edge of his bed and smoothed the note flat across his knees. He read it a third time, and a fourth time. When he was done he folded it and held it. He felt the tears well up in his eyes.

Alex was heading to the Battle of Bunker Hill.

19

The Harbingers of Fate

The sound of cannon fire started before dawn. Elias heard it from the kitchen where he had been sitting since before dawn, his coat on, the note folded in his pocket. John came inside with mud on his boots and said nothing. Alice put bread on the table and neither of them ate it.

The cannon rolled across the water in waves, distant enough that the walls didn't shake, but close enough that Elias felt it in his back teeth. British naval guns. He knew that from the history books. The ships had been firing on the redoubt since first light, trying to break the colonial position before the infantry assault began. It hadn't worked.

He pushed back from the table.

"The road will be clear now," he said. "The militia crossed hours ago. I'm going."

John was already at the door with his coat.

They mounted the horses and John led them south through Cambridge. The cannon fire was louder here, the sound bouncing off the river and coming back doubled. The roads they crossed weren't empty. Men moved in both directions, some toward the Neck with their muskets, some away from it with their families and what they could carry. A woman stood at a gate with two children behind her, watching the smoke rise over the southern tree line. She had a bundle at her feet, and she wasn't going to be at that gate much longer.

The smoke was visible from Cambridge. A dark column rising from the direction of Charlestown, spreading as it rose. It had been rising since first light and it was thicker now, darker at the base.

John stopped at a crossroads south of the Common and looked at it.

"I cannot take you further than the Neck," he said. "I have to get back. Alice and Mercy need to move the journals today. We cannot wait."

"I know," Elias said. "Get me to the Neck."

They went south. The road got busier as they moved toward the peninsula, men on foot and horseback, and two supply carts turned around and heading north. They rode in silence. There was nothing useful to say. Elias kept reaching through the bond, the connection between him and Alex they'd never been able to explain. Each time he reached he found the same thing. Alex was on the other side of the river. He was alive. That was enough to keep Elias moving.

The Charlestown Neck was a hundred yards of low, marshy ground connecting the mainland to the peninsula. The road across it was exposed on both sides, the Charles River to the south and the Mystic to the north, and the British ships had been laying shot across it since morning to cut off colonial reinforcements. He could see the craters in the road from the Cambridge side. He could see men crossing anyway, singly and in pairs, heads down, moving fast.

John stopped at the edge of the open ground.

"There," he said.

Elias closed his eyes for a moment and reached through the bond for Alex. He found him immediately. He was somewhere on the peninsula.

He opened his eyes.

"Go," he said to John. "Take the horses."

John put his hand on Elias' shoulder, a brief hard grip, and let go.

"Come back, son," John said.

Elias walked out onto the Neck.

The ground was waterlogged and soft, the road churned to mud by the thousands of boots that had crossed in the night. Two craters had taken out sections of it completely, and he went around them through the marsh grass, his boots sinking in the water to the ankle. A cannon ball from one of the ships hit the water thirty yards to his left and threw up a column of gray water. He flinched and kept moving. Another hit the road twenty yards ahead of him and sent mud spraying across his coat. The man in front of him didn't break stride. Elias followed his example, kept his eyes on the far side, and crossed onto the peninsula.

He smelled gunpowder, burning wood, and what he thought was charred flesh. The town of Charlestown was to his left as he came off the Neck. It was still standing. Most of it. The British ships had been laying incendiary shots into the buildings since morning, and he could see where it had taken hold— a warehouse near the waterfront with smoke pouring from its upper windows, a house on the south end with flames visible through the roof. Men moved in the streets below, some of them colonials using the buildings for cover, firing from windows and doorways at the British troops landing on the shore. He could hear the crack of their muskets over the cannon. He could see the British return fire hitting the wood frames.

It wasn't yet the fire he knew was coming. That was still ahead of him.

He turned right, away from the town, toward Breed's Hill.

The hill was ahead of him, low and open, the redoubt on its crest a dark line of packed earth against the sky. He could see the rail fences crossing the slope below it, the long uncut hay in the pastureland, and the breastwork extending east from the redoubt toward the water. The British assault was underway. A line of red coats on the slope below the redoubt, moving uphill through the grass, slowed by the fences and the uneven ground. Musket fire cracked from the earthen walls above, steady and controlled.

The first two assaults had already failed. He could see it in the field below the redoubt. Red coats lying in the long grass at intervals down the slope. He had read the history and knew about the deaths. He hadn't understood what they looked like until now.

The third assault was forming at the bottom of the hill.

He reached through the bond again.

The pull was strong enough now that it had a direction. Not just south and east but specific, a point along the breastwork near the left end.

He went toward it.

The ground between him and the base of the hill was open pastureland crossed by wooden rail fences every fifty yards, the hay waist high and full of concealed hollows and stones. He went over the first fence and pushed through toward the earthworks, moving fast, keeping low. His memory magic was pressing in from every direction, the ground here soaked in the residue of the last twelve hours, fear and fury and the imprint of men who had held their position and fired their last shots and braced for what came next. He pushed it down hard. He couldnt afford to lose himself in other people's last hours.

He was halfway across the pasture when the British ships found the range on the Neck again and the cannon fire shifted. A ball came down in the field fifty yards to his right and threw up a column of dirt and grass. Elias dropped flat against the ground, the hay closing over him. His ears were ringing. He stayed down for a count of three. No second shot in the immediate area. He got up and kept moving. He could feel his hands shaking. He'd never been this afraid.

He went over the second fence, pushing through the last stretch of hay to reach the base of the breastwork, and pressed himself against the earthen wall.

Fifteen feet to his right, Alex was there.

Alex saw him coming. His eyes went wide.

Elias dropped down beside him. The men along the breastwork were loading and firing in sequence, the gaps between each volley lengthening as the powder ran low. The noise was deafening. He felt every shot resonate in his chest. Powder smoke lay thick along the breastwork and burned his eyes and the back of his throat. The man beside him was bleeding from a cut above his ear and hadn't stopped loading.

"What the fuck are you doing here, Elias?" Alex said.

"What am I doing here?" Elias said. "What were you thinking walking into a battlefield, and where is Morgan?"

"Left flank." Alex kept his eyes on the field below. "He's been here since before I arrived."

Elias looked down the breastwork to the left. Morgan was twenty feet away, loading his musket. He glanced over and saw Elias and gave him a brief nod.

"You need to leave," Alex said.

"I'm not leaving without you."

"Elias—"

"No." Elias looked at him. "You left me a note? After everything we've been through together and you leave me a note telling me you're going off to get yourself killed? You don't get to tell me to leave."

"You're not a soldier, Elias. You have no idea what you're doing," Alex said.

"Neither do most of them," Elias said, pointing to the men.

"These were different times. You don't even know how to load a musket."

"Yes I do. John taught me, and you forget, I'm an FBI agent. I do know how to fire a weapon," Elias countered.

Alex's jaw tightened. He looked back out over the breastwork at the advancing line below.

"You're impossible. When it breaks we pull back over Bunker Hill to the Neck," Alex said. "Everyone retreats that way. We go with them. We don't stop."

"Morgan too."

Alex looked at him. "Morgan too," Alex said.

Alex turned back to the field. "I'm not sure we can save ourselves, let alone anyone else."

Then something caught Elias' eye on the slope below.

He had been watching the British line advance through the tall grass, and the defenders along the breastwork preparing for the assault. He hadn't been looking at the edges of the field, the spaces between the colonial positions.

Three figures moving along the south side of the slope, below the main British advance, moving parallel to it. Not in any formation or in uniform. They moved without urgency, without watching for cover, and around them the air had a quality he recognized from Sereliana's house, from the earthwork at Middlesex Fells.

They were fae.

His memory magic reached toward them before he stopped it. He got a flash of cold, deliberate intent.

He pulled it back.

One of the Unseelie figures raised a hand. On Moulton's Hill, the British artillery shifted its angle, a small adjustment, the kind of adjustment that couldnt have been communicated through normal channels from that position in that time. The colonial defenders along the rail fence to the north took a volley from the adjusted angle that drove three men back from their positions.

"Alex," Elias said.

"I see them," Alex said. "I've been watching them since the second assault."

"I can sense they're fae. They're adjusting the British fire."

"Yes."

"We have to—"

"No," Alex said. "We can't go near those three. We get Morgan and we go home."

Elias looked at them. At the advancing British line. At the three figures watching everything with no concern for the musket balls in the air around them.

He turned back to the breastwork.

The third assault hit the wall.

The rolling crack of musket fire was closer, the British line no longer at a distance but almost on top of them. Men were shouting. A body came over the wall ten feet to Elias' right and hit the ground inside the redoubt, and one of the defenders was on it immediately. Elias flattened against the wall as two more came over further down. The powder was gone. He could hear it in the silences, he saw men checking their pouches and finding nothing. The man beside him reversed his musket and held it by the barrel. Another picked up a rock from the base of the wall.

Alex was moving.

He had no musket. What he had was his combat magic and Infantry training from his time in the Army. The silver-blue flared at his palms, shields thrown up fast at the places where the British were forcing breaches in the colonial line, deflecting the first men over the wall, redirecting. He wasn't trying to win. He was buying time for the retreat to start. Thirty seconds. Then another thirty. His face was entirely calm.

A British soldier came over the wall directly above Elias.

Elias shoved off the wall to the left. The man landed where he'd been standing. The musket butt came around and caught Elias across the shoulder, hard enough to spin him, and he went down on one knee in the dirt inside the redoubt. The soldier raised the musket and aimed it at him.

Silver light hit him from the side and he went down.

Alex grabbed Elias by the coat and hauled him up.

"Now," Alex said. "We go now."

The line broke.

The British came over the wall at three points simultaneously and the retreat started. Elias was moving, following the flow of men back through the gap in the rear of the redoubt and down the north slope of Breed's Hill. Alex had Morgan by the arm ahead of him, Morgan moving on his own feet but leaning, Alex's hand at his elbow.

Elias stayed three steps behind them.

The retreat was chaotic. Some men ran. Some fell and were helped up, and some fell and weren't. The British pressed through the redoubt behind them, bayonets fixed, and the colonial retreat picked up speed as it hit the open slope of Bunker Hill. Men were shouting, some at each other, some at no one. A man ran past Elias going the wrong direction entirely and was gone before Elias understood what he had seen.

The Neck visible to the north, when Elias looked back over his shoulder and saw the three fae figures again. Still on the south slope of Breed's Hill, watching the retreat. One of them looked directly at Elias across two hundred yards of smoke and chaos.

He turned away and kept moving.

Alex kept Morgan upright who was breathing hard, both hands tight on Alex's arm, and his feet steady. They were going to make it. Elias kept his eyes on the back of Alex's coat and kept moving.

"Stay close to me," Alex shouted.

They were halfway up Bunker Hill when he heard the shot.

A single crack, close, from the British line thirty yards below them.

Morgan went down.

Alex caught him before he hit the ground. Elias knelt beside him.

Morgan was conscious. His eyes were open, looking at the sky above Bunker Hill. The shot had taken him in the side, below the ribs on the right, and the blood was coming through his coat dark and fast. Alex had his hand pressed flat to it. He was trying to use his healing magic but it wasn't working. At the same time, maintain a shield around them. It was impossible, even for Alex. Healing magic needed concentration.

"Help me get him up," Alex said.

Elias got Morgan's arm across his shoulders. Alex took the other side. Morgan was heavy and the slope was steep, and men ran past them on both sides without stopping.

"Thomas," Elias said. "Stay with us. We've got you."

Morgan turned his head and looked at him. His face had lost color and his eyes were unfocused.

"Give my love to Abigail," he said.

His weight shifted all at once and they fell to the ground.

They held him together while the battle continued around them. Morgan's eyes closed and he stopped breathing.

Thomas Morgan was dead.

Elias couldn't move. He was still kneeling on the slope with his hands on Morgan's coat and he couldn't make himself stand up. Morgan's eyes were closed.

"Elias." Alex's hand closed around his arm. "We have to go."

"He's not—"

"He's gone." Alex pulled him up. "We have to go. Now."

Elias let himself be pulled to his feet. The British line was twenty yards below them and closing. Alex kept both his hands on Elias' arm and moved them up the slope.

Then the air changed.

Elias felt the fae magic and turned.

One of the three figures from the south slope was closer now. His hand was raised, and the air between them bent and compressed and hit Alex straight on. Alex staggered and went down hard on both knees, his combat magic flaring and then sputtering, the silver-blue struggling against the exhaustion from fighting all morning and then the healing attempt.

A British soldier on the slope below them raised his musket.

The shot cracked past Alex's ear close enough that Elias heard it.

He wouldn't lose Alex today.

He called on his elemental magic and it answered.

The wind came first.

It rose from behind him and went south hard and fast, strong enough to stagger the fae figure and break his concentration. The compressed air released. Alex gasped and got one knee under him.

Elias didn't stop.

The wind hit the slope and rolled down toward the town, and he felt the moment it reached the fires already burning in the buildings below. He couldn't pull it back. The wind above Charlestown changed direction and the fires moved with it, faster and spreading across the southern end of the town, cutting across the ground between the fae figure and the British line. The heat surged up the hill.

The fae figure looked at the flames and back at Elias. Then he turned and walked back into the smoke and was gone.

Elias grabbed Alex by the arm and got him upright.

"Go," Elias said.

Alex was bleeding from his ear. He looked at Elias for one second and then they were moving, up the slope and over the crest of Bunker Hill, into the retreat, away from the smoke rising behind them.

"Elias, pull your magic back. It's getting out of control."

He tried to call it back and it wouldn't obey. Alex grabbed his arm.

"Elias, concentrate, pull it back."

It was too late by the time he got it under control. The fire in Charlestown was fully established now with the direction he had given it. The column of smoke above the town was no longer a column. It was a wall. The heat pushed back up the slope toward them and the air tasted of ash and charred wood.

The fire had moved across the route the British were using between their landing point on the south shore and the hill. The advance slowed. The regulars pressed around the edge of the new fire line.

Alex had him by the arm and was pulling him along.

"Nobody was in those buildings," Alex said. His voice was

low and direct. "They evacuated this morning. There's nobody in that town."

They crossed back over Bunker Hill with the retreat and down the north road to the Neck with several hundred other men. The Neck was still under fire but lighter now, the ships repositioning, and they crossed at a run. On the Cambridge side, the road turned north, and the retreat stopped being a retreat and became men standing in the road not knowing what to do next.

Alex stopped and looked back at the peninsula.

Charlestown was burning completely. The south end was gone. The fire had moved north and the last buildings still standing were going. Above the smoke the sky was yellow-gray, ash falling in flakes over Cambridge, settling on the grass and the road and the backs of the men around them. The cannon from the ships had stopped. The battle was over. The British had the peninsula, and the dead lay on the slopes of Breed's Hill in the afternoon heat, while Thomas Morgan lay on the ground where they had set him.

Elias stood beside Alex and said nothing for a long moment. "She won't exist," he finally said.

Alex turned to look at him.

"Abby." Elias' voice was flat. "He's dead. He died on that hill and he didn't have children yet and she won't exist. I won't go home to her." He lowered his head. He stood there with the ash falling around them and his eyes red and wet.

"She's gone, Alex."

"Elias—"

"Don't." Elias turned away from him. He walked three steps toward the road and stopped with his back to Alex and his hands at his sides. The men around them were drifting north, sitting down in the road and the grass. A man sat twenty feet away with both hands flat on the ground and his head down. Two men carried a third between them going toward Cambridge.

Alex came to stand beside him.

"She's gone," Elias said again.

Alex furrowed his brows before he said, "How do you know what she looks like?"

Elias turned to look at him.

"Her laugh," Alex said. "The way she sounds when she's annoyed at you. The thing she does with her hands when she's explaining something." He looked at Elias. "You remember all of it."

Elias stared at him.

"If she never existed," Alex said, "You wouldn't have those memories. They wouldn't be there to lose." He paused. "We both remember her. Somehow we do. I don't think she's gone."

"Or it means memories work differently and once we get back we'll forget," Elias said. "Or it means—"

"I don't know what it means," Alex said. "I'm telling you what I know. We remember her. She's not gone." He looked at the smoke. "We'll find out when we get home."

Elias looked at him.

"We have ten days," Alex said. "Before we can open the portal. We just need to stay alive until then. Both of us."

Elias looked at him for a long moment. "You saved my life back there," he said.

"Yeah, well, you burned down a town saving mine, so I think the win goes to you," Alex said.

They turned north and walked back toward Cambridge.

20

The Fae That Were Hidden

They made it back to the farmhouse before dark. John was in the yard when they came through the tree line. He looked at them both for a moment without speaking, taking in the mud and the blood and whatever was on their faces, and then he said, "Come inside."

Alice had water heating over the fire, bread and sausage on the table. She didn't ask questions. Elias sat down and put both hands flat on the surface and stared at them. Alex pulled off his coat and sat across from him.

"Eat something," Alex said.

Elias picked up the bread and put it down.

"Elias."

"I know." He picked it up again and ate.

Alice filled their cups without being asked. John came in from outside and washed his hands at the basin and sat with them. Nobody talked about what had happened. The fire in the hearth and the sound of the house settling around them was enough for now.

Later, after they'd washed and eaten properly, Alex lay on his

219

bed in the dark and listened to Elias pacing on the other side of the room. He'd been pacing for an hour before finally lying down.

"Elias."

Nothing.

"I can hear you thinking from here."

Elias turned over. "Sorry."

"Don't apologize. Talk to me."

"I'm fine."

Alex got up and pulled the chair from the corner and sat. "Talk to me."

"I'm fine."

"You're not fine. You watched men die in battle today and then you burned down a town. You're allowed to not be fine."

Elias looked up at him. His eyes were red. "I keep hearing the shot. The one that took Morgan." He shook his head. "I've read about battles. I've seen worse things in crime scenes through memory magic." He stopped. "This was different."

"Yes," Alex said.

"How did you do it for three years?" Elias said.

"You find what's in front of you and you deal with that. You don't think past it."

"That's it?"

"That's it."

Elias looked at his hands. "I couldn't pull my magic back. You told me to and I couldn't."

"You did eventually."

"Not soon enough."

"The town was already burning," Alex said. "The British set those fires. You accidentally helped them along. That's different from starting them."

Elias didn't answer.

"Nobody died in Charlestown," Alex said. "The residents were gone. The snipers had cleared out. I'm telling you that because it's true, not because I'm trying to make you feel better."

Elias nodded slowly. He didn't look convinced, but he didn't argue either.

"The fae," he said after a moment. "The one that hit you. I've never felt magic like that before."

"No," Alex said. "Neither have I."

"It went right through your shields."

"They're old magic," Alex said. "I wasn't prepared for it. And I was tired." He paused. "Luckily for us, you weren't."

Elias looked at him.

"You drove him off," Alex said. "Your elemental magic saved us. Again. Don't lose sight of that."

Elias was quiet for a long time. Alex stayed in the chair. Outside, the night had turned dark and the road through the trees was empty. He could hear someone moving around downstairs.

Eventually Elias lay back on the bed and closed his eyes.

Alex waited until his breathing evened out. Then he went back to his bed.

In the morning the town was different.

Alex was at the well with John when two men came up the road from the direction of Cambridge Common, moving fast, and stopped nearby to speak with a man that was walking by. He didn't catch everything they said, but he caught enough. Fae. British. Battle. Seen with their own eyes.

John listened without expression. When the men moved on, he looked at Alex.

"It's starting," John said.

"How fast does news spread here?"

"Fast." John picked up the bucket. "By tonight, everyone in Cambridge will have heard. By the end of the week it'll be in every colony."

They went inside.

Elias was at the table with Alice. He looked better than he had the night before, which wasn't saying much, but he'd eaten and his hands were steady.

Alice set down her cup.

"They're not going to distinguish," Alice said quietly. She had her hands wrapped around her cup. "Seelie or Unseelie, it won't matter to them. Fae is fae."

"I wonder if this is how it started, or if us being here has changed anything," Elias said.

Nobody answered him.

Mercy came in from the back of the house and sat. She'd been in the garden. She looked at John.

"I heard," she said.

John sat down. "I received word from Sereliana this morning. She's asking for sanctuary for her and Aisling. I told her to come tonight."

Alice nodded.

Mercy folded her hands on the table. "Sarah has gone. She left two days ago. Three of the others from the coven went with her."

"How many are left?" Elias asked.

"Enough," Mercy said. "Enough for what we still need to do. The rest have gone south or west. They'll be safer there." She looked at Alex. "The troubles will reach them eventually."

"And us?" Alex said.

"You have nine days," Mercy said. "The new moon is nine days from today. Between now and then Sereliana needs to weave her magic into Alice's journal, and we need to keep her alive long enough to get the portal open for you."

"Simple," Elias said.

Mercy looked at him. "No. But possible."

More men came past on the road through the morning. Alex split wood in the yard and watched Elias sit on the fence with a cup going cold in his hands, not drinking it and not moving, just watching the road. He'd been like that for an hour. Alex left him to it.

He was still in the yard when Alice came to the door.

"Alex," she said. "There's someone here you should both see."

She was younger than Alex had expected. Not much more than twenty, with dark hair and blue eyes. She was sitting in the front room with her hands in her lap when Alex and Elias came inside.

"Mrs. Morgan," Alice said. "These are the men Thomas spoke of."

Abigail Morgan looked at them both. Her eyes were dry. She'd been crying before she got here, Alex could see that, but she'd stopped.

"He spoke of you," she said. "He said you were honest men."

"He was a good man," Alex said. "He died fighting for something he believed in. He wasn't alone."

Elias stepped forward. "He asked us to give you his love." His voice was steady. "Those were his last words. He wanted you to know."

She smiled and briefly looked down. "Thank you," she said.

They sat with her for a while.

Then Abigail Morgan set down her cup and looked at her hands. "My child will never know his father, but I hope to tell him or her everything about Thomas. She placed one hand flat against her stomach. "He knew before he left. He was very pleased about it."

Alex looked at Elias.

Elias was looking at Abigail Morgan's hand across her stomach.

He looked up at Alex.

Alex felt the relief. He hadn't let himself believe it until this moment. He had told Elias she'd be there when they got home but he hadn't been certain, and now he was.

"That's very good news," Alex said. His voice came out rougher than he intended.

"Yes," Elias said. He let out a breath. "That's very good news."

Abigail Morgan looked between them with faint puzzlement. She probably didn't understand why two men she'd only just met were so affected by her news.

John appeared in the doorway. He looked at Alex over her head.

"I'll be taking Mrs. Morgan to her cousin's house this afternoon," he said. "She'll be safer out of Cambridge for now."

Abigail stood. She took each of their hands in hers and said, "Be safe. And thank you for being with him in the end."

She went with John.

Alex stood in the front room after they'd gone. He heard Elias exhale behind him, long and slow, the breath of someone who'd been holding something for a very long time.

"She's pregnant," Elias said.

"Yes," Alex said.

"Abby isn't gone."

"No."

Elias sat down heavily on the chair nearest to him, put both hands over his face and stayed there for a moment. Alex didn't say anything. He just stood and gave him a minute.

"She's alive," Elias repeated.

Sereliana and Aisling arrived just after dark.

Alice brought them through the back and into the library without lighting extra candles. Sereliana moved through the house without hurrying, taking in the room before she sat. Aisling stayed close behind her and kept quiet.

Elias and Alex stood when they came in. Alex couldn't take his eyes off Aisling. She looked younger than he expected.

Sereliana looked at them both. "You survived," she said.

"Just barely," Elias said.

"And the fae you encountered on the hill?"

"One of the Unseelie, I think."

Sereliana's jaw tightened. She sat, and Aisling took the chair beside her.

"They'll deny it," Sereliana said. "The Unseelie Court will deny any involvement, and there'll be no one left to contradict them. That's how it works." She looked at the table. "And it won't matter. The damage is done."

"The Sons of Liberty already know," Alex said. "We heard it this morning. Word is spreading fast."

"I know. I've been sending word to those of my court still in the area. Telling them to stay inside, stay quiet, do not use magic." She looked at Mercy. "It won't be enough."

"No," Mercy said. "It won't."

Alice came in from the kitchen and sat beside John. She had her hands folded in her lap.

"You can't stay here," she said to Sereliana. "This house will be searched. It's already known that John and I have connections to the old families, and there are people in Cambridge who know what that means."

Sereliana looked at her. "Where, then?"

The front door opened. John came in moving faster than his usual pace. He looked at Sereliana and then at Alex.

"I stopped at the tavern on my way back," he said. "There was a group of men talking and they weren't being quiet about it." He pulled off his coat. "They're going out tonight. They've got a list of addresses. Houses where they think fae have been sheltering."

"Is this house on the list?" Alex said.

"I don't know. But it might be." He looked at Sereliana. "We need to move now. Not tomorrow. Now."

"Where?" Elias asked.

"North," John said. "There's rough country north of Medford. Rocky hills, dense wood, almost no settlement. It's been that way since before we arrived here." He looked at Mercy. "You know the place?"

"Yes," Mercy said. "I know it."

"Your people would be harder to find there," John said to Sereliana. "And there are places in those rocks where twenty people could shelter without being seen from ten feet away."

Sereliana sat in silence. Alex watched her think through it. She didn't take long.

"I'll send word tonight," she said. "Those who can move will go before dawn."

Sereliana stood. She looked at Aisling, who was already on her feet. "I'll get word to the rest of my people," she said. "They'll meet us on the road north of Medford."

"How many?" Alex said.

"Twenty. Maybe twenty-five depending on who has been able to leave town already." She looked at him. "Not all of them will make it in time."

Nobody said anything to that.

"We'll go with you," Elias said.

Alex looked at him.

"We will," Elias said again, looking at Alex.

Alex didn't argue. "We'll go with you," he said.

Mercy was already moving. She came back with a canvas bag. John went for his musket. Alice went upstairs and came back down with her red journal under her arm.

"I'm taking my journal with us. We don't have much time left and you need this one," she said.

"What about the rest of them?" Elias said.

"They're safe. We shipped them out this morning with one of John's brothers who's headed to Maryland. They'll be in Rhys hands for now."

Alex wondered who this brother was. As everyone was getting ready to leave, he pulled Elias to a corner of the living room.

"My parents live in Maryland, and their house is my mother's childhood home," he said.

"Colleen mentioned that to me once. She said the Rhys have been in Maryland for several generations but were originally from New England. I totally forgot that she ever told me that," Elias whispered.

"Do you think this is how the journals came into my family?"

"Maybe. I've been wondering how they made their way into your line and not mine."

They were out of the house in twenty minutes.

The road north was dark and quiet as they moved fast.

John took the lead since he knew the area well. They went single file, no lanterns, the waning crescent moon giving just enough light to see the ground ahead.

Alex stayed near the back to provide a defense. Elias rode

beside him. Sereliana and Aisling rode ahead with Mercy, in a cart driven by Alice. John had taken point on his horse. A good place for someone with combat magic.

They picked up the others in a field north of Medford, eleven people who came out of the shadows of the tree line and fell in without a word.

"I'm sensing the same magic that I always associate with the fae, but it's stronger here. In our time it isn't this strong," Elias spoke in a low voice.

"It's probably what happens when magic is suppressed and diluted over generations," Alex said.

The hills came into view after an hour. Even in the dark Alex could see the change in the landscape, the ground rising and roughening, the trees thickening, the shapes of the rock formations visible against the sky.

Sereliana stopped at the base of the first real climb and looked up.

"This will do," she said.

Mercy moved past her and led them up through the boulders on a line of slightly easier ground that she navigated with some difficulty. They climbed for ten minutes and came out on a flat shelf of rock beneath a massive overhang, the ceiling of old volcanic stone above them cutting off the sky, the space underneath wide enough to shelter all of them but not much room to spare.

It was cool but dry. The overhang blocked sight lines from below on three sides.

Alice moved to the front and turned to face Sereliana.

"Liana," she said. "Alex and Elias will help protect you here."

She gestured toward them.

"Yes," Sereliana said. "We're fortunate to have you here to help defend us."

"Defenders," Aisling spoke for the first time.

"What, my dear?" Sereliana caressed Aisling's hair.

"The defenders."

Sereliana looked at him and Elias. "Yes, you can call them that if you like."

Alex heard Elias draw a breath beside him.

He felt it too. The recognition hitting him. He had stood in this moment before. Not in person, but in Elias' construct, built from Alice's journal. The forest clearing and the lantern light and the woman leading the fae into the old places.

He looked at Elias. Elias looked back at him.

"It's not exactly the place you showed us," Alex whispered to Elias.

"Our presence here has changed where they brought them. Or maybe my constructs aren't precise." Elias rubbed at his lower lip.

Alex suspected Elias was going to be thinking about this for a long time to come.

But they were the men in Alice's journal. They had always been the men in Alice's journal.

Elias turned back to the rock face and pressed his hand flat against it. His memory magic moved at his fingers, green and quiet, reading what the stone held. He stood there for a moment and then let it go.

"This place is old," he said to Mercy. "It's been used before."

"Yes," Mercy said. "Long before us, by the first peoples of this land."

Elias dropped his hand and turned to look at Alex.

"Nine days," Alex said.

Elias nodded. "Nine days."

Behind them, in the shelter of the rock, Sereliana was already speaking quietly to her court.

21

What Mercy Always Knew

They stayed at the Fells protecting the fae for the next week. Elias and Alex made the decision the morning after they arrived. The first stragglers reached the overhang before dawn with nothing but the clothes they'd fled in. More came over the next two days, moving through the rocks in the dark, finding each other in ways Elias couldn't sense and Sereliana didn't explain. By the third day there were thirty-one. By the fourth, thirty-eight.

John set the watch rotation and took the first shift. Elias tracked the pattern he used along the perimeter, how he moved between the rock formations without exposing himself. At dawn, John reported to Alex, and Alex took the next shift. The fae who were strong enough rotated along the southern approach. Two of the older men kept a fire buried deep in the overhang where the smoke thinned into the rock and didn't carry down to the road.

It wasn't comfortable, but they were safe.

Mercy took Elias into the woods on the second morning.

She found a clearing no bigger than a farmhouse kitchen and stood in the center of it and looked at him.

"Again," she said.

He called the wind. It came up gently, he held it and directed it and let it go.

"Good. Now I want you to direct it at me."

He looked at her.

"I'm not going to move," she said. "I want you to call the wind and push it directly at a person instead of across open ground. Try it."

He called it and pushed it at her. The wind hit her cloak and her hair but she didn't flinch.

"Harder," she said.

He pushed harder. She took a step back.

"Good. Now hold it there."

He held it. The wind ran from his hands to her chest, steady and directed, and he felt the difference from pushing it across empty air.

"Now stop it."

He called it back to him and it answered.

"Good," she said. "Do you feel the difference?"

"Yes."

"That's what control feels like. Calling, directing, holding, and stopping. All four are separate skills and you need control of all four." She straightened her cloak. "Again. This time with fire."

They worked through the morning. By midday he could call fire to his palm, direct it at a target, hold it steady, and release it on a specific target. Mercy made him do it standing still, then walking, then at a run. She made him hold two elements at once. Wind in one hand and fire in the other, directing them at different targets simultaneously. He managed not to burn the forest down by keeping the fires small and easy to extinguish.

On the fourth day she changed the exercise.

"There's a patrol," she said. "Alex said there are two men who come up from the south road every morning around this time. They haven't found the overhang yet but they're getting closer." She looked at him. "I want you to stop them. Not hurt them. Stop them and make them want to go somewhere else."

"How?"

"Think about it."

Elias thought about it. Two men on a wooded hillside. He didn't want them hurt. He wanted them discouraged, wet, cold, convinced that this slope had nothing worth searching for.

He waited. When he heard them on the rocks below he called the wind from the east, cold and sharp, and behind it he pulled water from the marshy ground and pushed it up into the air as mist and then as rain, a hard driving curtain of it that came sideways off the rocks and soaked through a coat in thirty seconds. He held it steady and directed it down the slope, into the patrol's faces, into the gaps between their collars and their hats, into their boots where they stood in the wet ground.

He heard them swearing below. Then the sound of them moving back down the slope.

He let the rain go.

Mercy looked at him. "You chose water over fire."

"Fire would have hurt them."

"Yes. And you made that choice in the moment, under pressure, without thinking about it." She held his gaze. "That's what I've been trying to teach you. Not just control over the magic. Control over the decision to use it." She paused. "You can aim and fire now. Like a musket. You choose the target, you choose the force, you choose when to stop. That's what it means to have command of this magic." She looked toward the path the men had taken. "Just remember that what you carry is more powerful than any musket. The responsibility that comes with your magic is a great one."

Elias looked at his hands. The rain had stopped. The hillside below was empty and dripping.

"I understand," he said.

"Hey." He heard Alex behind him. He was soaking wet and had his hands on his hips.

"Next time you decide to cause a rainstorm, warn me, will ya?" He turned and walked back the way he came.

Elias looked at Mercy and they both broke out in laughter.

The portal working happened on the sixth night.

Sereliana chose the flat rock near the edge of the overhang. She had Alice's journal open on the stone and she stood over it for a long time before she spoke. "I need another witch," she said to Mercy. "The fae magic alone isn't enough to anchor this across time. I need witch elemental magic to help me bind it into the book."

"I know," Mercy said. "I've been thinking about that." She looked at Elias.

Sereliana followed her gaze.

"His witch lineage," Mercy said. "It's there, and it's strong enough."

"He's not trained as a witch," Sereliana said.

"He doesn't need to be. He just needs to hold the channel open. I'll direct it." Mercy looked at Elias. "You don't do anything. You hold my hand and you let me work through you. Your magic stays passive. Understood?"

"Understood," Elias said.

Alex stayed back with Alice and John at the edge of the overhang. This wasn't their working.

Mercy took Elias' hand. Her grip was firm, and the moment their palms connected, he felt her magic move through them, drawing on the hidden lineage in his blood.

Sereliana raised her hands.

Four of the older fae came forward and positioned themselves around the stone, one at each compass point. Their magic came up together, a deep sustained pressure that Elias felt pass through him. It was the old magic he had become accustomed to sensing now when around the fae.

The pressure built.

His vision narrowed. The edges of the overhang blurred. The journal on the stone stayed sharp, the pages lifting slightly as if something beneath them was trying to surface.

Mercy said something under her breath. He didn't catch the words.

The pull through him increased, steady and relentless. His hands started to shake. He focused on keeping his grip on hers.

Then it stopped.

Elias staggered a half step and caught himself.

"The portal magic is now part of this book," Sereliana said. "It will be there when you need it."

She turned and walked back into the overhang.

Alex was already moving toward him.

"Are you okay?" Alex asked him.

"Yeah, that was intense. I'm not sure I can describe what it felt like, though."

"You look like you're about to pass out."

"You know, I am capable of feeding myself."

Alex glanced at him with a grin. "Sure you are," he said.

Elias didn't argue. He let Alex steer him toward the fire and sat where he was told. The exhaustion hit all at once.

The next morning, Elias found Alice sitting with her journal. She looked up as he approached.

"I can't find Mercy. I've looked everywhere for her. Do you know where she is?"

"No, I was looking for her as well," Elias said.

Alice wrote something in her journal and closed it.

"I'm supposed to protect her. She's the only seer we have, Elias. She knows everything that's to come," she said. He heard the worry in her voice.

"And where have all the witches gone? None came here with her, and she wouldn't tell me where her coven went." She stood, the journal clutched to her chest as she looked around.

"She told me they were leaving to other places. That they'd be safe," Elias told her.

Alice stared at him and tilted her head. Then she turned and continued her search.

Aisling was awake when he and Alice went into the overhang and asked if anyone had seen Mercy.

She looked at them both and said simply, "She went back to the house."

"Why?" Alice said.

Aisling was chewing on some dry meat as she spoke. "She told me she had something she needed to collect."

"Did she say what?" Elias asked her.

"I don't know. But she went back to Cambridge."

Alex had walked over to them. "What's going on?"

"We need to go back to the Cambridge. Mercy's gone, and it sounds like she's headed back to the house," Elias said.

"She went alone?" Alex asked as he put on his waistcoat.

"It appears that way. Alice doesn't know where she is."

Alex looked over at him and stared.

"What is it?" Elias asked.

"She can't find Mercy. And the fae are in hiding. This is what Alice wrote in her journal, remember? We read it the first time we looked at the journals."

Elias had forgotten. That felt like so long ago now.

"We need to get John and go find her."

John led the way south. Cambridge looked different as he approached it. Elias saw a house with its door hanging open and its contents scattered across the road—furniture broken, papers blown against the fence. There was a group of men moving quickly on horseback two blocks ahead of them, and a woman watching from an upstairs window who pulled back when she saw them looking.

John kept moving without stopping and they followed his lead.

When they reached the farmhouse, the door was locked. John used his key and they went inside.

The house was quiet and undisturbed.

"Mercy," John called up the stairs.

Nothing.

"She's here, in the attic," Elias said. His memory magic was reaching out, searching for any presence in the house before they'd crossed the threshold.

Elias walked up the stairs toward the attic, Alex close on his heels.

John knocked and said her name, and after a moment the door opened.

Mercy looked at them. She was sitting on a trunk with a small cloth bag in her lap and she didn't look surprised to see them.

"You came for me," she said.

"Of course we came for you," Elias said. "What are you doing up here?"

She opened the bag. Inside, on a piece of cloth, was a simple gold wedding ring. She lifted it out and held it for a moment and then looked at Elias.

"My husband's name was William," she said. "He died ten years ago. I buried him in the garden." She turned the ring over in her fingers. "I came back for this. I want you to take it home with you." She held it out to him. "Give it to your Abigail. Tell her it belonged to a woman who loved her husband very much."

Elias took the ring. It was warm from her hands.

"You're going to ask her properly when you get home and she's going to say yes, and I want her to have this." She stood and put the bag away.

"Shouldn't this go to your children? You told me you have two sons," Elias asked.

Mercy smiled. "My boys are already married with their own families, my dear. They went to Illinois last year. They don't need that ring. You do. And this way you will always have a part of me in your life."

"We need to go now," John moved away from the window he'd been looking through.

They reached the bottom of the stairs and started for the back door when the front door opened and two men Elias didn't recognize walked in.

John was already moving toward them, his hand on his pistol.

"Gentlemen. Can I help you?"

"We're looking for the old woman," the stocky one said. "The witch who lives in this house."

"This is my home and the people in it are my family. Whatever your quarrel is with the fae, it has nothing to do with the people under this roof."

"This isn't just about the fae," the younger one said. "We know what she is."

"Witches are human beings," John said. "Same as you and me. This isn't the Salem Witch Trials and we are not going to act like it is."

"They meddle in our business," the stocky man said. "Same as the fae are doing in our fight against the British. They think themselves above us, and they should be dealt with the same way." His eyes found Mercy.

"And him." He pointed at Elias. "I've seen her training him. He's a witch too. I'm sure of it."

Alex spoke and his voice was very calm, but Elias could see his combat magic sparking at his fingers. Alex was ready to take them all out if he had to.

"We're human magic users. Same as the man standing next to you whose magic I can sense," Alex said. "So before you start talking about who's using magic and who isn't, you might want to think about who you brought with you."

"That's different," the stocky man said. "He's human. That's different from fae and witches who—"

"How?" Alex said. "Tell me how it's different."

A silence.

The younger man's hand moved toward his pistol.

Elias felt his elemental magic starting to rise.

Mercy's hand closed on his arm from beside him. "Don't," she said quietly. "This isn't your fate."

The younger man drew his pistol and quickly fired at Elias.

But Mercy had already moved in front of him.

The sound of it in the hallway was enormous. Mercy jerked back and Elias caught her before she hit the floor and went down with her.

His ears were ringing when he looked up at Alex.

Alex's magic exploded in a bright flash. The younger man was thrown back against the door and collapsed.

John threw the stocky man toward the stairs, but he didn't go down. He reached for his pistol. John was faster. One bullet to the head ended it.

Mercy looked at Elias as she lay in his arms, lifting her hand to grip his arm.

"Alex," Elias shouted. His voice didn't sound like his voice. "Alex."

Alex was beside him on the floor. His hands were already moving, silver-blue healing magic spreading from his palms, and Elias knew from the look on Alex's face what it meant before he said anything.

"Elias—"

"Don't say it," Elias said.

"I can't..." Alex's jaw was tight. "She's bleeding out—"

"Don't." Mercy's breaths were coming in short measures, her hand still on his arm. "Mercy. Stay with me."

"My boy," she said. Her voice was clear. "Don't be afraid."

"You're going to be fine," he said.

"I've always known how this ends," she said. "Don't grieve it. I had a good life and I made it count." Her fingers pressed into his arm. "Go home to your Abigail. Take care of Alex. He needs you more than he'll ever admit." Her breath was shorter now. "Name one of your daughters after me. I would very much like to be remembered."

"Mercy," he said. He felt the tears rolling down his cheek.

"I'll be here." She smiled. "I'll be right here when you need me. Keep a candle lit for me."

Her hand went still on his arm and then dropped to the floor.

The hallway was quiet.

Elias sat on the floor of the farmhouse with Mercy in his arms. He pressed his face against her gray hair and cried.

He heard John sobbing.

Alex's arms came down around his shoulder and stayed there. He was crying too. He'd never seen Alex cry.

After a while Elias looked up.

The two intruders were dead on the floor.

He didn't care about them.

22

The Future is No Longer Clear

They buried Mercy in the garden. Her husband, William's marker was a flat stone near the back of the property. His name was carved in it along with the year he died. Elias set Mercy beside him and they dug in silence.

When it was done, John went to the shed and came back with a piece of wood and a chisel. He sat down in the dirt and began to carve. Elias watched him work. The letters came slowly. Mercy Rowan Bishop.

"Rowan?" Elias asked.

Alex turned toward him.

"That was her family name before she married," John said without looking up from the wood. "The Rowans have been in Cambridge since the first families came. It's an old line." He kept carving.

Elias stared back at Alex.

"I know," Alex said quietly.

John set the marker at the head of the grave and pressed it into the earth. "I'll have a proper stone made when things settle," he said. "She deserves better than this."

Nobody argued with him.

Elias stood at the grave for a moment. There was no cemetery on his property. He knew that. No markers, no stones, no record of anyone buried there. Two hundred and fifty years of weather and city growth had taken whatever had been here.

Alex and John went inside to wash their hands.

Elias stood there a moment longer. "I promise I will make a proper headstone for you when I get back. And for your William," he whispered.

They left Cambridge under cover of dark. John led them north without speaking. The city was quiet around them and they kept to the back lanes and moved fast. Nobody talked. There was nothing they could say.

The fae watch saw them coming and let them through without challenge. Sereliana was awake. She looked at the three of them when they came into the overhang.

"Where is Mercy?" she asked.

"Mercy's gone," Elias said.

Sereliana closed her eyes briefly. When she opened them she looked at Aisling, who had woken and was watching from across the shelter.

"She saw her death coming," Sereliana said. "She told me once, years ago, that she knew it would find her in Cambridge. She never said when or how." She paused. "She must have known it was her time."

"That doesn't make it better," Elias said.

"No," Sereliana said. "It does not."

The rest of the group had woken, and word passed through them quickly without Elias having to say it again. He was grateful for that. Some of the fae who had known Mercy in better years sat together and spoke quietly. Aisling went to her mother and Sereliana put her arm around her.

Alex pulled Elias to the edge of the overhang and they stood looking out into the distance.

"She knew," Alex said.

"I'm not surprised. She knew a lot of things."

"And she went back anyway. For a ring to give to me."

"This isn't your fault."

Elias thought about that. "No, it wasn't. The only ones to blame are the fae who started this whole thing in the first place."

Alex turned to him. "I'd say the man who shot her had some blame in this too."

"Yeah, of course he does. I'm sorry, I'm just angry at this whole situation."

"This situation is a lot more complicated than we realize," Alex replied.

They sat in silence for a while.

"Are you going to be okay?" Alex asked him.

Elias thought about that. He wanted to get away from the fae. He didn't feel any hatred toward them. Not really. Just toward Aisling. But in this time, she was a child and there was nothing he could say to her. He and Alex avoided having any real conversation with her. He'd learned his lesson about trying to change history.

"I want to go home," he said.

After Mercy's death, the days at the Fells changed. No one spoke unless they had to. The watch rotations tightened. No one wandered far from the overhang.

The fae wanted to leave. Elias understood it. They had been in the hills for over a week, sleeping on rock, eating what could be foraged or hunted. The rotating watches had everyone exhausted. The persecution in the town below showed no sign of slowing. Every morning the watch came back with the same report—more houses searched, more names on lists, more people taken. The Fells offered the safety of being invisible, and that only held as long as nobody came looking on the right hillside on the right night.

Two of the older fae men came to Sereliana on the third day after the burial and spoke to her in low voices for a long time. Elias couldn't hear what they said, but he understood the tone and felt their impatience through this magic. Sereliana listened without interrupting. When they finished, she spoke briefly and they looked at each other, nodded once and walked away.

"What was that?" Alex asked from beside him.

"They want to go," Elias said.

"She's holding them here for us."

"Yes."

Alex sighed. "We need to get home."

"Tomorrow night," Elias said. "New moon is tomorrow."

Across the shelter Aisling was with two of the younger fae, close to the fire. She was perhaps ten years old and was nothing like her mother. Where Sereliana was quiet and reserved, Aisling moved constantly and asked questions of everyone around her in a steady stream that the older fae answered with varying degrees of patience. She had tried twice to talk to Elias, and both times he had found reasons to be somewhere else.

He watched her now from across the shelter.

"Stop," Alex said.

"I'm not doing anything."

"You're staring at her like you're trying to think of a way to influence her decisions."

Elias looked away from Aisling. "She's going to spend two hundred and fifty years trying to fix something that can't be fixed," he said. "And she's going to send two people she doesn't know through time to do it." He paused. "She's ten years old and she has no idea what she's going to become."

"No," Alex said. "She doesn't."

"I keep thinking I should say something to her. Something that might change it."

"I knew it."

"I know. I know we can't." Elias looked at his hands. "That doesn't make it easier to watch."

"Nothing about any of this is easy," Alex said. "That's not the same as it being wrong." He glanced across at Aisling, who had made one of the younger fae laugh at something she'd said. "She gets to be a child today."

Elias looked at her again. She was laughing now too. Sereliana looked up from across the shelter at the sound of it and smiled. But the smile quickly faded.

"Her mother knows," Elias said quietly. "Sereliana knows what's coming and I think she's accepted that it's fate."

"I think she already knew," Alex said. "Mercy told her something before we arrived. She didn't do anything to stop the Unseelie at Bunker Hill."

They sat in silence after that.

It was later that morning that Sereliana asked Alice for the journal.

Alice handed it over. Sereliana took it to the flat rock and sat down with it in her lap. She opened it to a blank page, held her hand flat over them, and picked up the quill and ink that Alice had left with it.

She wrote slowly. She stopped several times and looked up at nothing in particular, and then came back to the page. Her lips moved once without sound.

Elias watched from where he sat with Alex.

After a long time, Sereliana raised her other hand over the page. The violet shimmer of her fae magic moved across what she'd written, and the words disappeared beneath it. She lifted her hand. The page looked blank. She closed the journal.

Elias and Alex walked over.

"What did you write?" he asked.

"Mercy told me something before you arrived," Sereliana said. "I've been keeping her words since then. They belong in here."

"What were they about?"

"About this." She motioned to their surroundings. "About you and Alexander, and choices you make." She ran her thumb along the spine.

"All that was written, cannot be unwritten."

"What does that mean?" Alex asked.

"Do you believe in fate?" She looked between them.

Alex spoke first. "I don't know what I believe anymore."

She looked at Elias. "And you?"

"I believe that there is something in this universe greater than ourselves. Something that explains how we can travel back in time, why some have magic and others don't. Why the witches are able to curse a person into becoming a werewolf with no way to break it."

He looked around and then said, "I don't know what any of this means. But if fate is real, it is a cruel thing. And I'd rather believe that we have free will."

"Mercy said that you were a smart one." She stood. "The curse on the werewolves can be broken. The witches don't know how but there is a way. I don't know if the knowledge will be lost in your time. Perhaps you will find out when you return. And speaking of your return, don't forget it is tomorrow night."

She handed him the journal.

"Sereliana, with respect, I swear, if you say one more cryptic thing I'm going to lose what's left of my mind."

Sereliana laughed and shook her head. "My apologies. It is the way of my people." She motioned for them to walk with her.

"The new moon is tomorrow, and we have several details to discuss."

She led them into the overhang and they sat near the entrance. Alice brought them cups with ale. Her eyes were red from crying, and she turned away without saying anything. Elias saw her go to John and they stood alone, whispering.

"The portal needs to open from both sides," Sereliana said. "Your people in your time need to open it from there while we open it from here."

"How do they know when?" Alex said.

Sereliana looked at the journal in Elias' hands and then back to Alex.

"Oh," Alex said.

"Write them a message. Tell them exactly where to be and when. Tomorrow night, at the same location from where you were sent. The old mound site near here I presume."

Alex nodded. "Yes, it was near here I believe."

She looked at Elias. "But there is still the question of how the portal finds the right moment in time. Opening a portal is one thing. Opening it to the correct year, the correct night, is another."

"How do we do that?" Elias asked.

"Your bloodline and the book brought you to this time." She paused. "Going back is different. I need you to reach through the portal with your memory magic and find something in your time that you grab onto. This may not work."

Alex said, "My keychain."

Elias looked at him.

"The keychain charm you made me last Christmas," Alex said. "The Celtic knotwork disc that you and Rowan put magic in so I could find you if we got separated."

"Yes," Elias said. "About that key charm. I may have made it so it works both ways. I wanted to be able to find you if you were ever lost. I can find you with it the same way it finds me." He paused. "It wasn't designed for crossing time."

"Can you reach it from here?" Sereliana asked.

"I don't know. I can try."

"When the portal opens, reach for it," she said. "The portal will give you a channel. Your memory magic already crosses time. That's how you can see past events."

Elias thought about that. "I never thought of memory magic as crossing time. But it is one way to think about it, I suppose."

Sereliana sighed. "So much knowledge has been lost in your time. This disc you speak of carries your magic. You're already connected to it." She looked between them. "Let it pull you home."

She stood and walked further into the enclosure calling out Aisling's name.

Elias turned and found Alex looking at him with furrowed brows. "You put a tracker on my keychain?"

"I mean, yeah, kind of," Elias said as he took a step away from Alex.

"And you didn't think to mention that when you gave it to me?"

"I'm sorry, I wasn't trying to be weird. I just wanted a way to find you if something ever happened," Elias said.

Alex started to laugh. "You really think you could give me a magical charm that lets me find you, and that I wouldn't know you made it a two-way tracker? And here I thought you could read me better than that."

"You knew?"

"Of course I knew. It was a great idea. And no, I'm not mad, Elias. I don't think there is anything you could ever do to make me truly angry with you," Alex replied.

That made Elias smile.

"Thanks, Alex. After everything that's happened, I don't think I could've handled you being angry with me."

"You're an idiot," Alex told him.

Elias looked at the journal in his hands.

"We should write the message now," he said. "While we still have light. We need to give Abby and Emily enough notice, and we have no way to know when they will see this."

Alex sat down and held out his hand for the journal. Elias gave it to him and Alex opened it, turning past Alice's entries to the page where Sereliana had written and hidden Mercy's words.

"If they're trying to figure out what happened to us, they'll probably start with the poem. So if we write the message here, they should see it," he said.

He pulled out a ballpoint pen from his coat.

"Where did you get that?" Elias asked.

"This?" He looked at the pen. "I had it in my pocket when we arrived. I made sure not to lose it. I can't write with those quill things," he replied.

"Tell me what you want to say," Alex said.

Elias thought about it. "Tell them we're okay," he said. "We're in 1775 Boston and we're coming home. Be at the Fells tomorrow night at midnight, at the mound where this started. We had to wait for the new moon. Bring the journal and bring

Aisling. Not sure if it's going to work." Alex wrote it and added that he loved Emily.

"Anything else?"

Elias looked at the page. "Tell Abby..."

Alex started to write.

"Wait, give it to me," he said. "This part should be in my handwriting."

Alex turned the journal toward him without asking what he was going to write. Elias sat down on the ground beside Alex and looked at the blank space for a moment. Then he wrote. It didn't take long. He closed the journal when he was done and set it on the rock.

Alex had been watching him. He put his arm around Elias' shoulders, a firm, solid grip, and pulled him in briefly.

"Abby is going to love that," Alex said.

"You think so?"

"I know so." Alex didn't let go, and he didn't stop grinning.

23

The Secrets of Their Families

Aisling was on her feet before Rowan cleared the doorway.

Abby stepped back. Emily stood and moved away from the table. Aisling's magic rose at her hands in a violet shimmer, her jaw set, her eyes fixed on Rowan.

"What the hell did you do?"

Aisling held her gaze and didn't answer.

"Did you actually send them back in time?" Rowan said. "Are you insane?"

"It was necessary," Aisling said.

"Necessary?" Rowan said flatly. "You used portal magic on two federal agents without their consent, and you're calling it necessary?" She looked at Abby. "How long ago did you say this happened?"

"Last night," Abby said.

Rowan looked at the journal on the table. Then back at Aisling. "I'm placing you under arrest. You're coming with me."

Aisling's magic flared.

Rowan's combat magic answered it immediately. Gold and blue magic sparked from her palms, and the force between them

253

hit the room all at once. The books on the shelves rattled. The chairs scraped backward across the floor. Abby grabbed the doorframe and Emily moved toward her as the overhead light swung hard on its fixture.

The floor shook under their feet.

Not the power of the magic between Rowan and Aisling—something else. The windows rattled hard in their frames. Wind moved through the room and Abby had no idea where it came from, cold and sharp against her face. It lifted the pages of the journal on the table. A book fell from the shelf and hit the floor.

The magic between Rowan and Aisling suddenly disappeared. Both women stood with their hands raised and nothing coming from them.

Near the bookshelf on the far side of the room, something appeared.

Abby saw it, and she could tell from the way Emily went rigid beside her that Emily saw it too. A shape, pale and loosely defined, the height and width of a person but with no features, no face, nothing she could hold onto long enough to describe. It stood near the bookshelf for two seconds, maybe three, and then it moved through the wall and was gone. The cold went with it and the wind stopped.

Nobody moved at first. Then Rowan lowered her hands slowly and flexed her fingers, but Abby saw no magic come forward. Rowan hurried toward the front door. The handle turned but the door didn't open. Aisling moved to a nearby window and tried to raise it but it wouldn't budge.

Rowan came back into the library.

"What the fuck is going on here?" she shouted.

Abby moved toward the journal. "Elias thought the house was haunted," she said. "From the first week he moved in. We never took him seriously."

Rowan's eyes narrowed. She looked around the room.

"Of course," she said, taking a deep breath. "Of course Elias Sinclair would have a haunted house."

"None of us are leaving," Aisling said.

"I can see that," Rowan said.

"I think the house wants Elias back," Emily said. "You can't take Aisling. She's the only one who understands portal magic."

Rowan side eyed her. Then she came further into the library and stood at the far end of the table from Aisling.

"Tell me exactly what you told them," she said. "About why you sent them back."

Aisling told her about the persecution that followed the battle at Bunker Hill, and the fast and indiscriminate killing and imprisonment of her people.

Rowan moved to sit in a chair as she listened without interrupting.

When Aisling finished talking Rowan crossed her legs and spoke. "So you left out the fact that the fae interference in human affairs wasn't just during the Revolution? But centuries of involvement before it. Both Courts making choices that pushed the boundaries of the pact they'd sworn. Both Courts, not just the Unseelie.

"The Seelie did nothing but try to help you. My people helped the witches learn how to use healing magic and even stop plagues," Aisling said

Abby heard Aisling's voice rise in anger.

Rowan spoke. "I'm not going to sit here and tell you the fae didn't help us or that everything they did was wrong. But their involvement in the Revolution was a tipping point." She paused. "One that threatened every magic user that was even slightly different from mundane humans. The fae didn't belong in our world, and their presence was a danger to us all."

"They hunted us into near extinction. Then the witches disappeared and positioned people inside every institution that mattered," Aisling said. "You erased us from history. Not just the fae but yourselves." Aisling was shouting.

"We made a plan to survive the hysteria," Rowan said.

"The Registration Act of 1790," Abby said. "Did the witches have a part in that?"

"The witches didn't create that act," Rowan said. "We weren't embedded in government at that level in 1790. But it was a good idea that we ran with later."

Abby thought about that. The Registration Act of 1790. She had read about it at the Athenaeum. Primary sources, the original congressional record. She had held the documents. She knew who had introduced the bill.

"It was introduced by a representative from Boston," she said. "Samuel Llewellyn."

She paused. "Wait, was that Elias' ancestor? Or a relative?"

"Or Alex's," Emily said. "Remember the lines were still intertwined then. It could have been someone from his line."

Rowan shifted in her seat. "Yes, it was a Llewellyn. Why did I just remember that?" she said.

Abby sat on the couch. "How didn't I know this? I work at the Athenaeum. I've held those documents."

Aisling sat down. She put her hand over her mouth.

Emily turned to her. "What is it?"

"This can't be right," Aisling said. She was looking at the journal. "They're the defenders of the fae. The Llewellyn and Rhys protected me during the persecution." She looked up. "Why would they create a registration system that intentionally targeted us?"

Nobody had an answer.

Emily sat beside Abby. "There's no point in dwelling on that," she said. "We need to focus on what we can actually do now." She shifted her gaze to Rowan. "You confirmed Aisling's account. What I want to know is what you weren't going to tell us."

Rowan tilted her head to the side and gave her a questioning look.

"We're witches," Abby said. "Aisling told us. Is it true?"

"Ah, I see. Yes," Rowan said.

"Our parents know," Abby said.

"Yes."

"And you were going to tell us when?" Emily said.

"The practice is to inform witch bloodlines on their thirtieth birthday," Rowan said. "You would have been told next year."

"How do you know our ages?" Emily leaned forward.

"Elias is—" Rowan clasped her hands together. "His mother was a close friend of mine. I keep tabs on him and Alex. I ran a background check on both of you once I received word that they were in serious relationships. The DMA needs to make sure that—"

"You did what?" Emily shouted and started to stand. Abby grabbed her wrist and forced her to sit down.

Rowan held her gaze and didn't answer.

"Emily, think about it. Elias is probably the most powerful memory magic specialist in the country—"

"The Western hemisphere. We think," Rowan interrupted.

"Right. Okay." Abby stared at Rowan for a moment. "So it makes sense that the DMA wants to make sure some foreign spy or criminal element isn't trying to influence him." She looked back to Rowan. "Please, tell me that's the reason. That you were just trying to protect him."

Rowan looked at her and then at Emily before she answered. "Yes, of course."

Abby realized she didn't believe Rowan.

"How many witches are keeping this secret?" Emily said.

"Exact numbers and locations are classified."

"Hundreds of thousands?" Emily guessed.

Rowan didn't answer.

"How do you keep that many people silent?"

"Once they know the truth, they choose to keep the secret. It's mutually beneficial," Rowan said.

"And if someone decides not to stay silent?"

Rowan crossed her legs and then sniffed. "Divulging the secret of our history is a major threat to national security, and treated as treason. It would start a civil war in most countries around the world."

Aisling turned toward Emily. "Treason is punishable by death," she said. "In case you weren't aware."

Emily's gaze snapped to Rowan and she balled her fists. "*Joder*," she said. Emily was angry. She only cussed in Spanish when she was fuming.

Abby's own chest tightened. Two hundred and fifty years of keeping secrets under threat of death for anyone who broke it.

"Don't forget about the werewolves," Aisling said. She was smiling.

Rowan glanced at Aisling, her expression unreadable.

"Your witches created them," Aisling said. "Curses placed on human bloodlines." She paused. "Tell them what your system does for them."

"The curse can't be lifted," Rowan said.

"I didn't ask if it could be lifted."

"They're classified as unregistered threats," Rowan said. "When identified, they're dealt with."

"Killed," Aisling said.

"When necessary."

"Your system created them," Aisling said. "And now it hunts them. People whose bloodlines were changed without their knowledge or consent and your answer is—"

"My answer is to protect the public," Rowan said. "A werewolf in a city means people are going to die. It's more humane than locking them away forever."

"Your system is broken," Aisling said.

"Every system is imperfect," Rowan said. "This one has func-tioned for two centuries and it isn't—"

"Stop."

Emily's voice cut across both of them. She was done. "Stop," she said again. "Both of you." She looked at Rowan. "You kept things from us that we had a right to know. We will deal with that later." She looked at Aisling. "You aren't going to fix a government system in this room. That's not the problem right now." She put both hands flat on the table near the journal. "None of this gets them home. You two can duel to the death later if you want. Right now, I want to know how we bring them back."

Rowan uncrossed her legs. "That may not be so easy. And the longer they remain in the past, the higher the chances that they might alter history. They might have already and we don't even realize it. Maybe that's why we forgot a Llewelyn was involved in the Registration Act."

Then the journal began to glow.

New lines began to form, continuing the poem.

Abby read aloud as the ink appeared.

> But even fate can fail, and every path can start to
> veer.
> For those who pierce the veil
> Can change the end they used to fear.
> If choices can prevail, the future is no longer clear.

The glow faded.

"What the—Is that what it's been doing?" Rowan asked. She

stood and knelt beside the table staring at the journal. "Read it to me. The whole thing."

Abby read the full poem from the beginning, her finger tracing each line on the page.

From the years yet to flow,
Came the strangers unbidden.
To rewrite what was written,
And unmake what we know.

Across the fractured tide,
Two bloodlines bound by more than vow.
What time and war divide,
The bond alone will not allow.

But even fate can fail, and every path can start to
veer.
For those who pierce the veil
Can change the end they used to fear.
If choices can prevail, the future is no longer clear.

Nobody spoke for a moment.

"They can change the end they feared," Aisling said. She had moved to kneel at the table as well. "That is what it means. They can change the future." She paused. "The fate of the fae can still be changed."

"But the last line," Emily said. "If choices can prevail. That's conditional."

"Yes," Aisling said. "Whoever wrote this isn't certain they succeeded." She stared at the poem for a long moment. "That last stanza. The phrasing of it feels familiar to me." She shook her head. "I can't place it."

"I wonder who wrote it?" Abby said. "It isn't Alice's handwriting. We still don't have any idea who wrote it."

Aisling crossed her arms. "Whose journal is this?"

"It's Alice Rhys' journal. She was married to John Llewellyn. So it's possible that he, or maybe one of their children wrote this."

"How did portal magic get into this journal? That's powerful fae magic. The Llewellyn and Rhys bloodlines don't carry fae blood," Rowan said.

"How are you so sure?" Emily asked.

Rowan hesitated then glanced at them. "It has been my family's responsibility to record the lines that carry old magic."

Abby felt the cold return before the lights flickered and everything in the room shook. Everyone looked around.

The journal glowed again and Abby made out the single letter that appeared below the poem.

"It's the letter S," she said.

Aisling reached for the journal. "It's my mother," she whispered.

"Sereliana, Queen of the Seelie Court. It's my mother who wrote this poem."

"Was it your mother who put the portal magic into this journal?" Rowan asked her.

"It must have been her," Aisling said. "She was the most powerful fae in that time, and that is her initial."

Emily returned from the kitchen with the bottle of aguardiente that she had brought back from Spain that summer. A gift for

Elias they hadn't opened yet. Abby needed a drink, and aguardiente was as strong as it gets.

She was also holding Alex's keys.

"The disc," Emily said. The small gold disc and its Celtic knot work caught the light as she set it on the table. "Elias made this for Alex."

Rowan touched the disc. "I know, I taught Elias the magic in this disc," she said. "It was designed to find Elias if Alex ever needed it. Like a magical tracker if a case went wrong and they were separated." She paused. "It was intended to work across a city or the country."

She picked it up and turned it over in her hand. "But we might be able to use it as a compass needle. To locate Elias wherever he is." She set it down. "Maybe."

"And the portal," Abby said. "You said you can open it."

"I had Elias and Alex's magic to draw on when I opened the portal. I can't do it on my own. My mother, Sereliana, taught me that opening one requires either an object with portal magic or someone who can wield it. And a new moon."

"That's fae superstition. The magic is already embedded in the journal. And belief that magic is dependent on lunar cycles is nonsense." She looked around the table. "We have a fae, three witches, and the tracking disc. We don't need to wait for anything celestial." She paused. "This is exactly why magic needs to be regulated. So we aren't at the mercy of folklore every time something needs to be done."

"Even if we can open the portal," Aisling said. "We still don't know when they will be on the other side. The portal needs to open from both sides."

"We could open it too early," Abby said. "Or too late."

"Yes," Rowan said. "We don't know if they've even found a way to come back. We don't know what's happening on their end."

"Time moves differently with fae portal magic," Aisling said. "A day here isn't necessarily a day there."

Rowan shook her head. "And all of this is one of many reasons why time travel is illegal."

Abby stared at her. "You knew this was possible? You knew fae portal magic could cross time?"

"That's classified," Rowan said.

"You knew," Abby said.

"We're aware of accounts in the distant past," Rowan said. "We have been for some time. There's only a few people with access to that information."

"And it's illegal? Even though nobody knows it even exists?" Emily said.

"Obviously, some people do." Rowan gave Aisling a side glance.

"Alright, so we don't know when to open it," Abby said.

"No," Rowan said. "That's the problem."

"Then what do we do?" Emily said.

Rowan opened her mouth to answer.

The journal started to glow again. But this time, the glowing was different. Instead of golden, it was blue.

The pages turned, past Alice's entries, past the poem, to a blank page just past it. A faint glow spread across the parchment.

All four of them looked at it.

Letters began to form.

Emily and Abby, hopefully you see this. Elias and me are okay. We're in 1775 Boston. We're going to try to come home. Be at Middlesex Fells tomorrow at midnight. At the place where this started. We had to wait until the new moon. I'm sorry we've been gone so long. Bring the journal and bring Aisling. You need her to open it from your side. Not sure if it's going to work. I love you Em. Elias says...

Abby saw the change in handwriting.

> *Abby, will you marry me? I promise I'll learn to cook. I*
> *love you.*
> *-Elias*

Abby stared at the page, tears running down her cheeks. Emily held her hand tightly.

24

Out of Time

They left the overhang an hour before midnight. Sereliana led them to the mound. Alex and Elias behind her, then two of the older fae who would return to the shelter once the portal was open. John and Alice came last. The path down through the boulders was darker than it had been on the way up. It was thick cloud cover and the moon provided no illumination.

They were halfway down the hill when they heard the dogs.

They sounded close. Coming from the south in fragments through the trees, a distant baying that stopped and started. Then distant male voices shouting at one another.

Sereliana stopped.

She stood with her head slightly turned, listening. The baying came again, closer than the first time, and with it the flicker of torchlight below the tree line, orange and moving.

Alex moved up beside Sereliana. "How far to the mound?"

"Ten minutes," she said.

"And them?"

"About fifteen minutes, if they have the dogs tracking."

A silence. Then Sereliana started walking again.

"We keep going," she said quietly. "Stay low and stay close." She spoke to one of the fae men. "Arvin, try to hide our scent, send them in the opposite direction if you can."

He nodded and turned toward the sound, his magic moving like fog through the trees.

They went faster now, single file, Sereliana taking a line through the boulders that kept the rock between them and the torchlight below. Elias kept his elemental magic close to the surface, not calling it yet, but ready if he needed it. He felt Alex's combat magic doing the same thing, a low silver-blue warmth at the edge of his senses.

The voices below moved parallel to them for a stretch and then fell back. The baying faded. Elias didn't stop watching the tree line until they reached the flat ground near the hill and the mound came into view.

It sat in the clearing the way it did in his time, a low rise in the earth with the old volcanic rock breaking through the grass around it. Elias could feel the magic coming from it, old and powerful. The same thing he'd felt on the night Aisling had brought him and Alex here.

John touched his arm, making Elias turn.

John and Alice had stopped at the edge of the clearing. Alice was holding the journal against her chest with both arms. She looked at Elias and then at Alex and took a breath.

"I wasn't going to say anything until we were sure. But I want you to know," she said, glancing at John, "we're expecting. It's early yet and I don't know when I'm due."

John's hand found her shoulder.

"If it's a girl," Alice said, "her name will be Mercy."

Elias looked at her. He couldn't find words for a moment.

Alex put his hand briefly on Alice's arm. "She would have liked that very much," he said.

Alice nodded and held the journal out to Elias. He took it.

John shook Alex's hand and held it. "You're good men," he said. "Both of you. Whatever this country becomes, you were part of making it." He looked at Elias. "Go home."

Elias shook his hand and held it for a moment longer than necessary. There was nothing else to say that was adequate, so he didn't try.

They turned and walked to the mound.

Sereliana was already there, standing at the center of it with both hands at her sides. The two older fae positioned themselves at the edges of the clearing, watching the tree line. From the south, the baying started again, closer now.

"We need to hurry," Sereliana said.

Elias and Alex stepped onto the mound on either side of her. Elias held the journal in front of him and Alex put his hand over it. Sereliana had her hands resting on top.

Her fae magic came up and pulled from within the book. The mound lit from below, a bright shimmering blue light, rising up through the grass and the rock, and into their feet and up through their hands. The ground hummed under Elias' boots. He saw his green memory magic reach for Alex's silver and blend together with the magic from the mound. Sereliana's violet magic swirled around them.

A vortex of light and wind opened a few steps away from them.

It grew wider. The wind pulled at their coats and their hair. The journal lifted against their palms wanting to go with it. Alex reached for his wrist with one hand, gripped hard.

Elias pushed his memory magic into the vortex and reached forward through time the way he'd reached through a hundred crime scenes, except this time he wasn't reaching backward. He was reaching forward. Two hundred and fifty years forward, toward something small and gold with Celtic knot work and his own magic threaded through every groove of it.

He found it.

A faint thread, but it was there, and it was pulling.

The vortex widened further and the blue light spread across the mound. The wind was loud now, loud enough that he heard one of the older fae shout something behind them, and from the south the dogs were very close.

Sereliana pressed her hands harder over theirs and her magic surged.

The vortex opened fully.

"Go," Sereliana shouted.

Alex turned and met his eyes.

The blue light closed in around him and he felt cold air hit him. All he could see was the blinding light, but he felt the thread of the disc pulling harder. He felt Alex's hand gripping his tightly. The sound of the forest and the dogs in the distance cut off all at once.

Suddenly, the pull of the disc started to fade. He could sense that he was losing the connection. Something was going wrong on the other side. He focused on Abby and her face. He poured all his intent into that thought and tried to will himself toward her.

25

The Witches' Circle

Rowan had been on the phone until nearly two in the morning.

Abby sat in the library with Emily and listened as Rowan worked through it, her voice low, the calls short and clipped. When she finally put the phone down, she looked at them and said they would go the following night and would need the full day to prepare.

Abby got a blanket and pillow from the linen closet and left them on the couch without comment. Rowan nodded once. She wanted to stay where she could watch the door in case Aisling tried to leave.

Aisling was upstairs in one of the guest rooms. Rowan had placed a containment ward on the door, gold light pressed into the frame, and Aisling had gone inside without argument.

Emily sat beside Abby in her room for a long time after that.

Abby spoke quietly. "He proposed to me from two hundred and fifty years away through a magical journal." She let out a breath. "He added another love story to them."

Emily laughed. "I can only imagine the look on Alex's face

when he saw what Elias wrote." They both cried and laughed a little longer. Then they went to bed.

In the morning, during breakfast, Aisling looked at Rowan.

"If I help you open the portal," she said, "will you let me go?"

Rowan was quiet for a moment. "Under restrictions," she said. "But yes."

"Define restrictions."

"You register. You check in monthly. You don't leave the country without notifying me." Rowan met her eyes. "And you stay alive. I'm not interested in you disappearing."

Aisling held her gaze for a long moment. Abby watched from the other side of the kitchen and thought she didn't believe Rowan, but she said nothing.

"Fine," Aisling said.

The day was long. Rowan and Aisling stayed in the library, working through the mechanics, arguing. Abby and Emily asked questions, listened, and asked more. By evening, they understood what their roles were.

What neither Rowan nor Aisling said out loud was that Abby and Emily's magic might not be strong enough for this. Abby saw it in the way Rowan assigned their roles. They wouldn't be the ones holding the journal.

They took two cars. Emily drove Alex's car. Abby sat in the passenger seat with the journal in her lap, one hand braced over the cover. The tracking disc had been removed earlier from Alex's keychain and sat in Emily's pocket.

Rowan followed behind them. Abby checked the mirror more than once. The headlights stayed with them the entire drive.

They pulled off near the trailhead. Doors opened. Cold air hit immediately.

Rowan came around the front of her car and opened the passenger door. Aisling stepped out. The detention ward settled around her again, a low gold pressure that tightened as Rowan moved closer.

"Stay with me," Rowan said.

Aisling didn't answer.

They started into the woods.

Emily took the lead with her flashlight. Abby followed, holding the journal against her chest. Rowan stayed close to Aisling, never more than a step away.

The trail narrowed as they moved deeper in. The trees closed in overhead.

Abby saw the break in the trail first. "There."

They stepped off the path and climbed the rise. The mound sat in the center of the clearing.

Rowan stepped onto the mound and turned back to them.

"Let me have the journal and give us some space," she said.

Abby moved forward and held out the journal.

Rowan took it and opened to the page where Alex and Elias had written their message the night before.

Abby stepped back, stopping a few feet to Rowan's left.

Rowan spoke to Emily. "Stand on the other side of Aisling. Don't come closer unless I tell you. Direct your magic toward the book. It should amplify ours. I hope."

"Got it."

Aisling stepped onto the mound across from Rowan, close to the center.

"Not that close," Rowan said.

Aisling didn't move.

Rowan held her gaze for a second, then shifted her attention back to the journal.

"The disc."

Emily pulled it from her pocket and stepped forward. She placed it in the center of the open page, then stepped back.

Aisling's magic came forward immediately, violet light rising faster and trying to merge with Rowan's magic.

Rowan's magic followed with a controlled gold and blue.

"You're moving too fast," Rowan said.

"I know what I'm doing," Aisling said.

"You're going to destabilize—"

"This is how it works." Aisling's voice was flat. "I've done this before. You haven't."

Rowan's jaw tightened, but she didn't pull her magic back.

The disc began to spin on the journal page, following the grooves of the Celtic knotwork as the magic touched it. The knotwork lit from inside, bronze and deep green, and the disc rose slowly off the page and hung in the air above the mound.

Abby saw Emily move closer to Rowan. They had made a contingency plan on the drive up. Just in case something started to go wrong.

Abby moved closer to Aisling.

The disc spun faster. The air above the journal began to distort, a faint shimmer that bent the tree line behind it out of shape, the first sign that something was trying to open.

"More," Aisling said. She pushed her violet magic harder and the disc swung sideways. Rowan's gold snapped around it and dragged it back to center.

"You're going to lose it," Rowan said.

"It's not enough," Aisling said. "The two of us aren't enough."

"Abby, Emily, direct more of your magic toward the book if you can."

"It's not enough magic." Aisling's voice cracked.

Rowan pulled back slightly. The disc dropped half an inch. Aisling grunted as she pushed harder and the disc lurched again, the working going unstable, the light in the knotwork flickering.

"That's it," Rowan said. "We're pulling back. This is getting dangerous. We can regroup and—"

Abby stepped forward and pulled the journal out from between them.

Rowan turned. "What are you doing?"

Emily stepped in on the other side and pushed Aisling back a step. She put her hands on the journal with Abby. Their elemental magic came up together, instinctively. The power they both held but never needed.

Rowan's eyes went wide as she was pushed away by the wind.

"What are you doing?" Aisling shouted over the noise.

"We didn't know about witches," Emily said.

"But we never said our parents didn't teach us their magic," Abby finished.

Emily's memory magic joined their elemental and reached for the disc.

It was searching for Elias.

The mound lit up from the ground and up through their feet just as it had the night it had taken Alex and Elias. A blinding white light rose up to meet their joined hands where they held the journal. It came from the old earthwork beneath them. From the fae working that had been sleeping here for hundreds of years.

Abby could feel Aisling's strange fae magic joining theirs. Their combined magic hit all at once.

A vortex of light and wind appeared next to them.

Aisling moved away and tried to leave. "It's opening, you don't need me here now."

Rowan's hand closed around her arm.

"You promised," Aisling said. Abby could barely hear her.

"The second this is over," Rowan said, "You're coming with me. You have knowledge of dangerous portal magic and you're out of control. I can't trust you not to try to use it again."

"You lied. You're going to lock me away somewhere," she said.

"Yes, in the darkest hole I can find," Rowan said.

Aisling raised her free hand and her violet magic came up hard and fast and Rowan's grip broke. She stumbled back two steps, now behind Abby and Emily.

Abby could feel the pull of the portal trying to suck them in.

She held the journal tightly and felt Emily's fingers squeeze above hers. She knew they couldn't let go of the working. If they did, the portal would close, and Alex and Elias would be trapped. Abby knew that Rowan wouldn't let Aisling try again.

Abby looked at Emily. "It's trying to take us."

"Not gonna happen. Rowan, shield us. Now," Emily shouted.

Abby turned her hand in time to see Rowan raise a ward around Aisling. It wouldn't hold her for long.

Then Rowan's blue combat magic flared around them and her elemental witch magic surfaced for the first time. Abby recognized it as she saw the earth-toned light reach for the journal, grounding them in this time.

The portal held.

Nobody moved.

Something was coming through.

26

At Fae's End

Elias hit the ground on his hands and knees at the edge of the mound, the impact ringing through his palms. The bright light was gone.

The whistling cut off all at once.

Cold night air pressed in around him, carrying the scent of damp earth and crushed oak leaves.

He lifted his head.

Rowan was there.

She stood at the edge of the clearing with her combat magic already at her hands, her jaw set, looking past him.

Emily was on the ground nearby, one hand pressed to her face above her eyebrow, blood running down into her eye as she pushed herself upright.

Abby was on her feet at the edge of the mound.

Then she wasn't.

Aisling had her from behind, one arm locked hard across Abby's throat and pulling her backward. Abby's hands came up immediately, locking onto Aisling's arm and trying to break it.

Elias moved toward Abby.

275

"Don't." Aisling's voice was high and shaking. "Nobody move. I mean it."

He stopped.

Alex was beside him, and Elias felt the surge of his magic—silver-blue and steady

Rowan took one step forward. "Aisling. You need to let her go."

"You lied to me." Aisling's arm tightened and Abby's chin came up, her hands tightening on Aisling's arm. "You promised me safe passage. You were going to lock me away."

"I'm telling you one more time to release her," Rowan said. "You are surrounded. You didn't think I came here alone."

"Then tell them to stand down," Aisling said. "Tell them to stand down and let me walk out of here or I will kill her. I will kill all of them."

"You're not going to do that," Rowan said.

"You don't know what I'll do." Aisling looked at Elias and then at Alex. Her expression changed and she started to cry. "You didn't change anything. Nothing changed. I sent you back and my people are still gone. Everything is exactly as it was."

"The fuck is going on?" Alex stood, swaying as he rubbed his eyes. He squinted, his gaze wandering before it finally landed on Elias.

"Aisling has Abby. Rowan is here."

Alex looked at the scene for one more second and then he started moving, his combat magic fully up, going wide around the mound instead of straight at Aisling, cutting off her angle of retreat, coming at her from the side so she couldn't focus on both him and Rowan at the same time.

Rowan raised her hand and sent a gold and blue blast toward Aisling. Aisling deflected it with her free hand, the violet flaring bright, and the blast scattered sideways and hit the ground ten feet away.

Emily got to her feet and sent her elemental magic forward to join Rowan's. The two streams combined and pushed toward Aisling with real force, but she diverted that too, throwing it into the rock face at the clearing's edge where it cracked the stone.

Alex reached the angle he wanted and his combat magic targeted the specific point of Aisling's hold, the joint and the leverage of it, and pushed hard against it.

Aisling's grip broke.

Abby dropped to one knee with both hands on the ground and pulled air in hard, coughing, her head down.

Elias moved toward her.

Aisling stepped back toward the far edge of the mound. "Let me go. I will kill every person on this mound if you don't let me go right now." She looked at Elias and Alex and her voice cracked. "You were supposed to fix it. You were supposed to change it, and you didn't. My people are still gone. Everything I did, and nothing changed."

"Aisling," Elias said.

Alex moved toward her.

She raised both hands. The violet magic came up in both palms at full force, and she hit Alex with everything she had. The blast took him square in the chest and lifted him off the ground, throwing him back six feet. He hit the grass and rolled. He got one knee under him and his combat shields came up, silver-blue—

She hit him again before they were fully formed.

The shields buckled and flared, trying to hold.

She hit him a third time.

They failed completely.

Alex went down and stayed down.

Abby reached him and dropped beside him with both hands on his chest.

Aisling swung toward Emily and Rowan and hit them with a

wide sweeping blast that caught both of them and threw them backward off their feet. They hit the ground hard and their combined magic scattered and went out.

The clearing went quiet except for the wind.

Alex turned his head slowly and found Elias across the mound. His voice came out rough and even and certain.

"Elias. I can't fight her."

Elias looked at him for one second.

Then he looked at Aisling.

He called his elemental magic.

It rose at his hands as Mercy had taught, deliberate and controlled. Yellow-green built at his palms, and with it came the wind, pulling hard from the north and running across the mound, bending the grass flat and pushing against Aisling so that she had to widen her stance to hold her ground.

He let the fire build behind the wind, not releasing it yet, holding it steady.

The combined light of it lit the clearing around him.

Aisling focused on him.

He walked toward her.

"You're under arrest," he said. "Stand down or I will put you down. Permanently."

Her hands were shaking with the effort of holding her magic against the force of the wind. She looked at him and he could see her hesitation.

"My mother was wrong," she said. Her voice broke on it. "You were never the defenders of the fae. You never were."

"You were the only one who called us that," Elias said.

He kept walking toward her through the wind he was making.

She made her decision and threw everything she had left at him in one concentrated violet blast aimed directly at his chest.

He pushed his wind forward, hard.

It hit the blast and tore through it and scattered it into nothing before it reached him.

He kept walking.

When he was close enough, he pulled the fire from both palms into his right hand and shaped it into something small and focused and controlled and precise, just as Mercy had shown him.

He looked at Aisling one last time.

"It's over."

He released it.

The fireball hit her in the chest. She left the ground and landed hard three feet back. Her violet magic went out completely and she didn't get up.

A thin curl of smoke rose from where the blast had hit her and drifted upward in the still air above the mound.

From the tree line, Rowan's agents moved in fast, combat shields raised, toward where Aisling lay. Rowan called something to them as they passed, but Elias didn't catch the words.

He called his magic back to him. It came fast and smoothly as he let it go. The wind stopped and the clearing went quiet.

He ran toward Abby.

She was kneeling beside Alex with both hands on his chest and Alex had one hand over hers. Elias dropped to his knees beside them both.

"I'm okay," Alex said. The words came out steady, but his face was pale and his breathing was careful.

"You're not okay," Elias said.

"I will be." Alex looked at him and then let go.

Elias turned to Abby. She was already moving. He pulled her against him. Her arms locked around him and they held each other without speaking. He pressed his face into her hair and felt her hands grip the back of his coat.

Emily ran to Alex. She dropped beside him, both hands on his face, speaking to him in a low voice. Alex turned toward her and said something back. She laughed once, sharp and short, and pressed her forehead against his.

Rowan came to stand beside Elias and Abby. She looked at him over Abby's shoulder.

"Elias," she said. She nodded toward where Aisling lay. "Something you want to tell me about your magic? Because it looks like I'm going to have to create a new classification just for you."

Elias held her gaze and didn't answer.

"Let's get you two to a hospital," she said. "Then home."

She walked back across the mound.

Elias held Abby and didn't move for a long time.

27

All That Was Written

Elias woke up at noon. The mattress gave under him the way it was supposed to. The sheets felt soft against his skin after a month of straw and rough linen.

The room smelled of old wood.

He lay still and let it settle.

Abby was asleep beside him, her hand loose near his arm on the pillow. He got up without waking her.

The shower ran hot and stayed hot. He stood under it, palms flat against the tile, eyes closed. The pressure. The smell of his shampoo. He thought about the basin and pitcher at the farmhouse. Cold water every morning.

He turned the water off, dried off, pulled on a clean soft cotton T-shirt. He paused in the doorway. Then he went downstairs.

Alex was already at the kitchen table, both hands around a mug, eyes closed. Elias poured a coffee and leaned against the counter.

"The coffee," Alex said, without opening his eyes.

Elias smiled. "I know."

"I spent a month drinking whatever that was they called coffee."

"It wasn't that bad."

"It wasn't coffee." Alex opened his eyes and squinted at Elias. "We made it back," he said.

"Yes we did."

"I can't believe we really traveled to the past. It feels like a dream."

Elias sat in the chair across from Alex. "More like a nightmare."

Alex met his eyes. "How are you doing?"

"I'm fine," Elias said.

"I know you're not." Alex set his mug down. "You didn't have any choice. Aisling was going to kill me and Abby. You did what had to be done."

Elias knew Alex was right. "I just wish it hadn't come to that."

Emily came into the kitchen without a word. She sat beside Alex. He put his arm around her.

Abby came down a few minutes later. She went straight to Elias. He poured a cup of coffee and handed her the mug. She looked up at him, and he pulled her against him with one arm.

"Okay?" she said.

"Getting there." It would take time, but he had Abby, Alex, and Emily. They were his family.

Rowan arrived at one. She came into the library, sat, and looked at all four of them.

"I'll need a full written report from both of you," she said to

Alex and Elias. "What you saw, who you spoke to, what happened at Bunker Hill. All of it."

"I'm not sure we should," Elias said.

Rowan looked at him.

"We'll consider what we're willing to put in a formal report and what we're not." He held her gaze. "Some of what we saw in 1775 isn't going into a DMA file."

"That's not how this works," Rowan said.

"I know how it's worked until now," Elias said. "I'm telling you how it's going to work going forward."

A silence.

"Aisling's death," Rowan said. "Will be deemed a necessary use of deadly force. There won't be an inquiry." She paused. "My statement is enough to confirm the threat she posed." She looked at Elias. "I'm not going to change your classification. You're already ranked as a specialist level elemental user."

"You know I have witch lineage. You want to hide that?" Elias said.

"I suspected it last year. You proved it last night," she replied.

"We were told that witches never married into the Llewellyn and Rhys lines. Yet here I am. The DMA must know who married into my family and when. I want you to tell me who, when, and why."

Her expression gave nothing away.

"I'm not sure, but I will look into the records and tell you."

Elias didn't believe her, but he let it go for now.

"I want you both to consider coming to work directly for the DMA. Given what you now know about the real history, and the display I saw last night, it makes sense to have you inside the department rather than—"

"No." Elias stood and walked to the bookshelves on the far wall and stood there with his back to the room.

"No," he said. He didn't turn around. "I don't think so."

"Excuse me?"

"I said no, we're not joining the DMA."

He turned then. He looked at her across the library, his hands loose at his sides.

"Here's what's going to happen. You're going to let Alex and I resign from the FBI. You'll make sure that we get glowing evaluations and no questions asked. You're going to give us your unconditional support to leave government service entirely. In exchange, we don't say a word about the real history of the fae, the witches, or everything that happened in the past that your people erased."

Rowan's hands were folded on her lap. "And if I decline?"

"Then I will make sure the world finds out the truth," Elias said. "About the witches, and this system you built. All of it." He held her gaze.

"You'd be signing your own arrest warrant," Rowan said. "Treason." She glanced at Alex, Abby, and Elias. "All four of you."

"You don't ever interfere with Abby and Emily." He paused. "And you don't threaten us. Ever," Elias said. He took a step toward her and placed his hand on a bookshelf.

"I learned a lot during the time I spent in the past." He tilted his head and looked up. "Did you know a witch can curse another witch?"

Alex turned around and looked at him.

Emily went still beside him. Abby smiled.

Rowan didn't move.

"Have you ever wondered what being a werewolf might feel like?" Elias said.

"You can't do that," Rowan said. "That's not possible. You don't have that kind of—"

"Can't I?"

The house answered before she could form a reply.

The bookshelves rattled. The door to the library slammed shut. A cold wind moved through the library and the journal on the table opened. The overhead light flickered.

Near the bookshelf where Elias was standing, he watched a shape appear. Gray-haired and translucent. She stood between Elias and Rowan and smiled at Elias. He smiled back at her.

When she turned toward Rowan she frowned.

Rowan uncrossed her legs and grabbed the arms of the chair she was sitting in.

The shape held for a few seconds. Then it dissolved into a mist and disappeared. The wind stopped. The cold eased. The room settled back into silence.

Rowan's mouth was open and she stared at the space where the shape had been.

"She lives here. She has since before 1775." He sat back down closer to Rowan. "That was Mercy Rowan Bishop, she was my teacher, and my friend."

He smiled at Rowan. "I believe you know who she is. Seeing as she's your ancestor, and all," Elias said quietly.

Rowan was quiet for a long time. When she looked at him again, something had changed in her.

"What will you do?" she asked. "If you leave."

"We've been talking about it," Alex said. "Private investigative work, maybe. Security consulting. Cases where our abilities are actually useful instead of wasted on whatever the Bureau decides to point us at." He looked at Elias. "Cases we choose."

"Would you be willing to help us if we needed your... services?" Rowan said.

"Depends," Elias said. "As long as it's to help people."

Rowan looked at the journal on the table and then at the space near the bookshelf where the shape had been. She stood.

"I'll have the paperwork drawn up," she said. "You'll have clean resignations within the week. The references will say whatever you need them to."

"And the other conditions," Elias said.

"No threats and no action will be taken against any of you," she said.

She walked out of the library without looking back. They heard the front door close.

Nobody spoke for a moment.

Then Emily said in Spanish, "*Que te siga siempre.*" And Abby laughed.

"What does that mean?" Alex asked.

"May it follow you always," she replied.

Alex smiled and shook his head. Then turned to Elias.

"We're doing it?" Alex asked.

"We're doing it," Elias said.

"No FBI."

"No," Elias said. "Just us and whatever we decide to do."

Alex crossed the room, grabbed him by the back of the neck and pulled him in. Elias held on. They stood there for a moment, and when Alex stepped back his eyes were bright and he looked away.

"Don't," Elias warned.

"I'm not," Alex said.

"You are."

"I'm not." Alex cleared his throat.

"We're going to need an office," Abby said.

"We're going to need a business name," Elias said.

Emily leaned forward. "I have some ideas."

"We have time to figure everything out," Elias said.

Emily stood. "I'm going to go grab a bottle of wine to celebrate."

"It's two in the afternoon, Em," Abby said.

"Yeah, and I'm a Spaniard. It's never too early for wine. Come and help me."

That evening, Elias found Abby in the kitchen.

He'd gone into Boston while Alex and the girls enjoyed their wine. He had the ring in his jacket pocket, in a small box. He also had Mercy's wedding band in his other pocket. Still in the pouch it was in when she had given it to him.

Abby was at the counter cutting vegetables, and she looked up when he came in and read his face immediately.

"What is it?" she said.

He took the box out of his pocket and set it on the counter, pulling the diamond ring out.

She looked at it. Then she looked at him.

"I had something more planned, a restaurant, and probably a speech." He looked at her.

"Instead, you asked me from two hundred and fifty years in the past, through a magical book," she said with tears in her eyes.

"Sorry about that," he said.

"You added to the love stories in the journals, that's the most romantic thing any man could do," she said, smiling.

Elias got down on one knee. "Abigail Morgan, will you marry me?"

Her eyes were bright with tears.

"Yes," she said before he'd finished asking. He put the ring on her finger. She pulled him up and hugged him tightly.

After a moment he reached into his other pocket.

"There's something else," he said. He held out the plain gold band. "This belonged to Mercy Bishop. She was a witch. She died protecting me." He turned the ring over in his fingers. "Her husband's name was William. He died twelve years before she did and she kept his ring until the end." He looked at Abby. "She asked me to bring it home. She wanted you to have it."

Abby took the ring carefully from his hand. She held it and looked at it for a moment.

"She's here," Abby said. "She was your ghost."

"Yes," Elias said.

Abby closed her hand around the ring. "We'll put it somewhere she can see it," she said. "Until we get married."

"There's one more thing," Elias said. "Her grave is on this property. Hers and her husband. The markers were lost a long time ago." He looked at her. "I'm going to use my memory magic to locate them. I want to have proper headstones made and plant something there. Something that lasts."

Abby looked at him for a long moment.

"Yes," she said. "We'll do that together."

From the hallway, Alex's voice carried through into the kitchen. "Are you two done in there? Emily and I have been standing here very patiently."

Emily said something pointed in Spanish.

Abby laughed and held her left hand out to look at the ring.

"Come on," she said to Elias. "Let's go show them."

He followed her out of the kitchen.

He located the graves the next day. Elias stood in the back garden with his hands flat on the ground and let his memory magic move down through the soil. It took nearly an hour. Alex stood nearby and grounded him through the decades of memories that were held by the property.

The markers were in the southeast corner of the garden near the old stone wall, buried deeper than they should have been, the ground built up over them across two centuries. John's carved wood had long since dissolved to nothing, but the stones beneath where they'd stood were still there, two flat rocks set deliberately apart.

Elias stood over them for a long time.

He would order the headstones tomorrow. White granite. Mercy Rowan Bishop on one. William Bishop on the other.

"I'm going to plant lavender beside them," he said.

Because Mercy had grown it in her garden in 1775 and he remembered the smell of it from the mornings he'd worked there with her during his training sessions.

He'd kept his promise to Mercy. She and her William would always be remembered.

Later that day, they were in the library. Abby had been rereading Alice's entries and showed him and Alex the completed poem.

"We never saw what Sereliana wrote in the journal," Elias said. "These words are Mercy's. They were a vision that she must have had long before we arrived."

"A prophecy," Emily added.

"What do you think happened to Alice and John? After we left," Alex asked him.

"I don't know," Elias said. "The land is still here. This house is newer, but it's been Llewellyn land for a long time." He paused. "They survived it or I wouldn't exist. The persecution must have moved through Cambridge fast. John said they would move away. He knew how to keep his head down."

"The Registration Act," Alex said. He was looking at the ceiling. "Samuel Llewellyn introduced it in 1790. We told John and Alice about the registration system. About how magic works in our time."

"And maybe he told his family," Elias said.

"Or his brother. Or his son." Alex lowered his eyes. "Someone who eventually sat in the Massachusetts congress and introduced a bill that became the foundation of the DMA." He looked at Elias. "We built it. We went back and we told them about it and they built it."

"And the witches took it over," Abby said quietly.

"Yes," Elias said. "And the witches took it over."

"So the system that's been controlling magic users for two hundred and fifty years," Emily said slowly, "exists because you two went back in time to stop it from ever happening?"

Alex glanced at him.

"It's not a good outcome," Elias said. "I'm not going to pretend it is. Fae in hiding, werewolves being hunted, every magic user classified, the mandatory service requirement for specialists. We didn't mean for that to happen." He looked at the journal.

"What came first? The chicken or the egg?" Alex said.

"Yes," Elias said. "Exactly that."

He heard a faint whistle.

Then the journal began to glow.

All four of them looked at it.

The pages turned on their own, to a blank page at the back just after the prophecy and Elias and Alex's note. A warm blue light spread across the parchment and letters formed in a handwriting they all recognized.

Abby read it as it appeared.

This journal has served its purpose and will be warded and sealed. The portal magic within it must be preserved and protected. We will not continue the tradition of recording. What happens next belongs to you. We want to preserve your future.

Take care of one another. We did.

—Alice Rhys and John Llewellyn
April 10, 1776 Annapolis, Maryland.

P.S.
We had twins. We named them Mercy and Elias.

The glow faded.

No one spoke for several seconds.

"They went to Maryland," Emily said. Not a question.

"My mother's home?" Alex said. "That's how the journals ended up with her. We need to ward Alice's journal again. I don't trust that the DMA won't try to take it and the portal magic it holds."

"I know the warding process. I saw them doing it to the other journals. We'll do it tomorrow," Elias said.

Then he reached under the table and brought up the journal Alex had given him at Christmas last year, leather-bound, with the first page inscribed in Alex's handwriting. He set it on the table beside Alice's journal.

"I'm going to write all of it down," he said. "What happened to Mercy. Who Sereliana was. Alice and John's magical bond. What helping to protect us cost them." He looked around the table. "It should be recorded somewhere."

Alex looked at the two journals on the table. "You know, that's how we ended up in the past," he said. "Someone wrote stories."

"Love stories," Abby corrected.

"Yes," Elias said. "So I will too."

Abby looked at the journals side by side. The old red leather and the new. The one that had started everything, and the one that would carry it forward.

"Write it well," she said.

Elias smiled at her. "I'll try."

Later that night, after the others had gone to bed, Elias moved through the house turning off the lights.

He paused in the library doorway.

The room was dark except for the streetlight through the curtains. The two journals where they had left them.

He lifted a hand. A small thread of yellow magic moved toward the candle on the mantel where he had placed it the day after they returned.

The wick caught.

He watched it for a second.

"Goodnight, Mercy," he said, and walked up the stairs to his Abigail.

In the pages of a book that holds all that was written,
Lie the secrets of their families,
And the fae that were hidden.

The End

Thank You for Reading

Thank you for reading *All That Was Written*. If you enjoyed it, please consider leaving a review on Amazon or Goodreads. Reviews help other readers discover my story and supports future releases.

Visit my website to sign up for the newsletter and be the first to know about new releases. https://www.Irene-Lee.com/

ABOUT THE AUTHOR

Irene has been immersed in fantasy since childhood. She writes stories where the supernatural weaves through everyday life. Her travels around the world and her experience as a pilgrim on the Camino de Santiago convinced her that magic lingers in every city. She continues to explore new places with her husband and believes that airports are just poorly operated portals to new worlds.

instagram.com/ireneleeauthor

facebook.com/authorirenelee

tiktok.com/@authorirenelee

Acknowledgments

A special thank you to my street team without whom I would never have been able to market my book—or keep my sanity. They supported me through some tough days prior to publication. My team was small but mighty and spanned the USA, Canada, and Australia.

Allanah Hockam

Caitlin Cabanas

Gail Guilliams

Liz Feidler

Ashley Jurczak

Heather Fowler Mylek

Crista Sedlacek

Rose Dinsmore

Debbie Hill

Mikayla Harshman

Candace Cross

Thank you to editor Keeley Patton at The Authors Archive for her work on this book.

Read the story that started the Duology.

Elias Sinclair's memory magic has never lied to him. Until the night it did, and seven agents died in an explosion he should have seen coming. His partner Alex Sutton nearly died protecting him from the blast. Convinced his magic can't be trusted, Elias requested reassignment before Alex could ask the questions he couldn't answer.

Alex Sutton doesn't take partners anymore. His combat magic and six-year partnership with Elias made them one of the most effective teams in the Bureau, until Elias walked away without explanation. He's moved on. Or so he tells himself.

When infrastructure attacks begin tearing through Chicago, the Bureau forces them back together. The attackers aren't terrorists. They're ordinary people whose perceptions have been manipulated into seeing threats that don't exist, turned into weapons who die the moment they're used. Someone wants magic users to believe they're under attack. Someone wants them to fight back and seize control.

As the body count rises and the city fractures along magical lines, Elias and Alex are hunting an enemy with access to magic that shouldn't exist. The kind that can rewrite what people believe is real. As the city edges toward panic and buried secrets resurface, survival may depend on whether they can trust each other and their magic again.

Available for sale at Amazon on E-book and worldwide in paperback.

www.ingramcontent.com/pod-product-compliance
Lightning Source LLC
Chambersburg PA
CBHW060520160726
47991CB00001B/114